GW00362217

Richard Conrad

A DREAM TOO FAR

A DREAM TOO FAR

by

RICHARD COWARD

LONDON

Richard and Erika Coward

WRITING AND PUBLISHING PARTNERSHIP

1992

First published in 1992 by
Richard and Erika Coward
Writing and Publishing Partnership
16 Sturgess Avenue
London
NW4 3TS

Photoset by B P Integraphics
Printed in Great Britain by The Bath Press, Avon

British Library Cataloguing in Publication Data
Coward, Richard 1955
A Dream Too Far
I. Title
823.914 (F)

ISBN 0-9515019-1-7

To my sons
Alexander and Oliver

SURREY, ENGLAND, FEBRUARY 2005

Tom often played Bach for her at night before they went to bed. And now he smiled at her gently as his fingers slid gracefully over the strings of the cello, attempting to coax an ever greater intensity from the music he loved so very much. She returned her husband's smile and then let her eyelids begin to drop. It was the first time that day she had allowed herself to relax.

Rachel Mary McNie had never found relaxation an easy art to master. She was consumed with a restless energy which had served her well in her chosen professional career, as she had moved smoothly through university, journalism and television news to her present exalted position as director of the London wing of the European Broadcasting Corporation. But she knew it was also an energy she used as a kind of mask, a technique for pushing aside secret fears that from childhood had lain hidden, ready at any moment to emerge and assault her senses.

The Bach sonata rose to a new crescendo, its powerful rhythmic harmony strangely soothing. When he played music, Tom was like a man transformed, the reserved manner with which he generally confronted life's vicissitudes replaced by an inner intensity which even she did not fully understand. He was in so many ways a remarkable person, yet she knew full well that other men laughed about her husband behind his back. For the suave libertarian veneer of European cultural life in the first years of the twenty-first century was only paper thin, and Tom's quiet and purposeful decision some seventeen years earlier to opt for a supporting role seemed for some quite irrational reason to threaten and disturb other men.

The sonata drew to a close and Rachel opened her eyes. Tom rose from his chair and placed the cello carefully against the wall.

"Would you like some coffee, darling?" he asked quietly.

Rachel shook herself out of her reverie and looked at him fondly.

"I'll make it," she said, rising to her feet.

Tom followed her into the kitchen and sat down on a high stool.

"Did you have a good day?" she asked, watching as he picked up a tin from the side and carefully selected his favourite biscuit.

"Not bad," he replied, making little attempt to conceal the fact that he was lying.

"Soon he'll be at playgroup," she offered, hoping the mere thought

1

of imminent relief from the endless daily round of childcare would cheer him up. It didn't.

"It's not Sam's fault," he muttered through a mouthful of chocolate biscuit. "I think it's me. I think I'm past it."

She remained silent.

"I know what you're thinking," he said at last. "I know full well I've only got myself to blame."

Rachel had often wondered why he had pressed her so hard for another baby. When Sam had been conceived nearly three years earlier, Rupert had been nine and Jane seven. The terrible thought crossed her mind yet again that it was fear which had driven him to start the endless dreary round of childcare all over again, a fear that his critical role in her life would evaporate as soon as the children became independent. She shuddered at the thought that two-year-old Sam, now sound asleep in his cot upstairs, was the result of a carefully-concealed belief in her husband's mind that his place in her affections was under some kind of threat.

"I love you, Tom," she said quietly, taking his head in her hands and kissing the little bald patch which had recently become impossible to ignore.

Tom sipped the coffee and grunted.

"Bloody water!" he said gruffly, picking up the cup and chucking the contents down the sink. "Can't you put on some programme that will galvanise them into doing something about it? This stuff is undrinkable."

Rachel looked at her cup of coffee with disdain, rapidly deciding not to risk a sip.

"We did a two-hour programme about it last week, darling. Simultaneously screened in twenty-two languages. Doesn't seem to make a scrap of difference to the Eurocrats in Vienna. Maybe they like their water this way."

Tom snorted.

"More likely the Commissioners are getting some fat back-handers from the water companies," he said.

"We tried that angle, darling. Trouble is, there's no proof."

Tom gestured at the sink. "What d'you mean there's no proof, Rachel. The proof is coming out of that bloody tap."

She smiled wryly, trying to imagine how the European Broadcasting Corporation would stand up in court if it started accusing the Commissioner for Utilities of taking bribes on the basis of Tom's preferred form of evidence.

"It's always the same story," she observed drily. "Nobody's ever

2

culpable in that kind of dramatic way. It's just a long slow slide towards environmental disaster. I'm afraid nobody's yet thought of making inertia into a criminal offence."

Tom wandered disconsolately over to the cupboard and helped himself to a glass of orange juice, as if despairing of ever getting a decent cup of coffee again. He wasn't alone in being angry. In the previous year's elections to the European Parliament, even experienced political commentators had been shocked by the dramatic rise in support for the Green Party.

Tom downed the orange juice in one gulp and picked up a recycled news-sheet that had been delivered a few days before by the local branch of the Greens.

"They've been a bit of a wash-out, haven't they?" he said, his question largely rhetorical.

Rachel smiled. Tom was so very sweet, but when it came to politics he was pathetically naive.

"What do expect them to do?" she asked. "They keep getting frozen out by the chaotic assortment of quasi-nationalistic parties and special interest groups that prop up the Commission. Just about the only thing they can agree upon is the need to prevent the Greens from gaining any influence within the Community institutions."

Rachel was in the good company of almost every other professional news commentator in Europe in sensing that the Greens' dramatic emergence as a major political force in the 2004 elections heralded a sea-change in European political development. The euphoria engendered in the early 1990s by the headlong rush towards full European unity had long since faded, and most observers now agreed that change had come too fast. For the democratic institutions of Greater Europe had fallen prey to an increasingly petty factionalism that was all too often linked to age-old linguistic and nationalist feuds. That political fragmentation had not brought complete chaos in its wake was in large part thanks to the skill with which the vast army of Eurocrats – first in Brussels and then in the new capital city of Vienna – had maintained a firm grip on the levers of power behind the shifting and unstable political coalitions of the previous ten years.

The arrival of the Greens had changed everything. For here at last was a political party that transcended the old national outlooks in more than just name. But if the Greens were the first genuinely European party, they were also by far and away the strangest. Tracing their political roots back to the myriad ecology parties and green parties of the 1970s and 1980s, Green activists were committed to their beloved planet with an almost messianic zeal. Refusing to conduct their internal affairs in the fashion of the conventional "grey" parties, their assemblies bore a greater resemblance to gatherings of religious revivalists than serious contenders for political office. So odd were their ways that prior to 2004 nobody had taken them particularly seriously.

Yet the commentators, including Rachel, had all been proved wrong. The voters – or at least thirty percent of them – despaired at the increasing signs of environmental degradation all about them. The traditional parties, with all their mindless muddle and pointless infighting, had got the political blame. And the Greens had stepped in to reap the reward.

Tom had stopped talking. He was reading an article in the Greens' newsletter with great attention.

"What's it say, Tom?" Rachel enquired, puzzled by the look of concentration on his face.

"It's about the White Death," he mumbled, continuing to read.

Rachel said nothing. The White Death was a topic of conversation most people in early 2005 preferred to avoid.

Tom stopped reading.

"They're blaming it fair and square on an animal testing programme in Denmark," he said bluntly. "They say it was an accidental by-product of industrial research aimed at developing a new range of pesticides."

Rachel picked up the newsletter and scanned the article. It was presented in the rambling, unstructured way that characterised so much of Green rhetoric. Doubt, scientific restraint, caution – these were concepts regarded by Green Party members as pernicious heresies cultivated by non-believers.

"I'd already heard about that rumour, Tom," Rachel said quietly, pausing for a moment before continuing. "I've put André onto it."

As well as being a close personal friend, André Rostropov was an investigative documentary producer of some considerable distinction.

Tom looked at her with a coy sideways glance.

"He'll have more clout with the masses than a Green newsletter," he grunted. "Has he confirmed any of this yet?"

Rachel shook her head. "No. It's not his style. First he probes quietly, on his own. Only when he's sure of the facts does he deliver the hammer-blow."

"And what do you think?" Tom asked.

Rachel sighed, helping herself to some orange juice.

"Too early to say, really. It's a pretty big coup for the Greens if it's true, bearing in mind how much they've said over the years about that kind of research, but then I'm somewhat sceptical of their claims precisely because it's so convenient for them. My guess is they're kicking themselves for missing a trick during last year's elections."

She remembered being surprised at the time how little any of the political parties had made of the emerging problem of the White Death. Perhaps none of the politicians had sensed votes in taking up a position on a disease that was so little understood. Only in the last few weeks had the Greens decided to break cover and try to establish a link with one of their favourite hobbyhorses.

Tom yawned.

"I'm off, darling. Can't keep me bloody eyes open any longer," he mumbled, rising from his stool and heading wearily for the stairs.

Rachel downed the orange juice in one gulp and rose to her feet. Often she sat up longer than Tom, reading some report or other she had brought home from the office. But tonight she felt she could not let him go alone.

"I'll come too," she called after him, resolving to overcome her husband's exhaustion before he fell asleep, but no sooner had she spoken than the videophone in the corner of the kitchen began to bleep impatiently.

Rachel glanced in surprise at her watch. It was gone midnight, a strange time for anyone to be phoning.

She flicked a switch.

"François!" she exclaimed, surprised to see the face of François Dupont, Managing Editor of the European Broadcasting Corporation and her immediate superior in New Vienna, beaming out at her from the tiny telescreen above the kettle.

Dupont's smile broadened.

"Good evening, Rachel," he began, making no attempt to hide his heavy Parisian accent. "I am sorry to bother you so late at night. And I am glad to see I have not roused you from your slumbers."

Rachel eyed him carefully. She knew perfectly well that François Dupont was not the sort of man to ring someone at midnight without a very good reason.

"Has something cropped up?" she asked.

"'Cropped up'?" he murmured, speaking slowly and placing a strong emphasis on the words of the idiom as if savouring a new and interesting variety of fine chocolate. "No, Rachel, nothing yet has 'cropped up'. But I suspect something might possibly be about to 'crop up'. We need to talk."

"O.K." she replied hesitantly, still wondering why he had chosen to ring her in the middle of the night. "When?"

The smile vanished instantly from Dupont's face. In its place there was an unmistakable tension.

"Tonight, Rachel. I need to see you tonight and I need to see you in my office here in Vienna. I have arranged a special flight to pick you up from Heathrow. And at this moment you will find a car outside your front door to convey you to the airport."

Rachel stared at him incredulously.

"Are you serious?" she asked.

"I think that you have known me well enough over the last ten years to know the answer to that last question," he replied. "It goes without saying that I would not be taking this step if I was not certain it was absolutely necessary."

Rachel leant over to the window and pulled the curtain aside. A small saloon car was sitting in the street outside, its driver smoking a cigarette and carefully eyeing her house.

She turned back to face the hidden camera inserted into the telescreen.

"I can see the car," she said quietly.

"And you will come?"

"Yes. Since you say it is important, I will do as you have asked."

Dupont's smile returned to his face as suddenly as it had vanished. But hidden beneath the smile she could not help but glimpse a quiet look of triumph flash across his face as he slowly nodded his head and faded from the screen.

* * * * * *

The aeroplane was a small one, some kind of executive jet, and Rachel was the only passenger. It was a clear winter night, and as she gazed through the window she could see the lacework pattern of countless lights in the towns and villages of Europe's ancient heartland laid out beneath her. She lay back in her seat and listened to the quiet hum of the plane's engine, trying to work out a plausible explanation for Dupont's bizarre midnight summons.

Rachel had never been certain whether to be flattered or insulted when people said she bore a great similarity to François Dupont. Like her, he was a man of tremendous personal drive, subjugating pretty well everything in his life to his burning desire to climb to the top. He also shared with her the capacity to work long and arduous hours in order to ensure that he was always one step ahead of the competition. But secretly she dreaded the comparison, since she knew that many seemingly decent people had been hurt during the course of Dupont's relentless climb towards his present exalted position.

François Dupont had emerged in France in his early twenties as an investigative journalist specialising in the destruction of hitherto respectable politicians and other leading public figures. In his search for newsworthy material he had employed the services of a small army of private detectives to probe into the innermost reaches of his victims' public and private lives, refusing to relent until the figure in question had been forced from office. As a publicist he had chosen the way to the top with consummate skill, for the average citizen finds nothing so entertaining as watching the mighty fall from grace, while the victims generally obliged by providing a rich fund of material from which scandal could be drawn. It did not take long before he had won his own prime time series on the French networks, a series in which he had negotiated for himself both a huge budget and absolute editorial control.

During those early years Dupont would frequently appear in court, as one wealthy magnate or another would attempt a fight-back against the flood of accusations flowing out of several million tiny screens across the land. But the evidence presented at the trial was inevitably impeccable and the attempted fight-back would only serve to hasten the victim's demise and reinforce Dupont's growing reputation as a protector and champion of ordinary citizens against the evil machinations of their rulers.

In such a climate it was simply a matter of time before the fear engendered amongst the rich and famous brought matters to a head. A new French Justice Minister, a man regarded even by his political enemies as being completely beyond reproach, began proceedings to bring Dupont under some kind of check. A special subcommittee of the French Assembly was charged with looking into the legality of the methods he used to compile the programmes, with a clear implication that new legislation would be brought forward if necessary. And with so many politicians from across the political spectrum nervous about Dupont's investigative activities, it really began to look as if his days were numbered. Until, that is, a special edition of Dupont's series revealed that the Minister of Justice had himself been involved in financial dealings of highly dubious legality.

From there on out Dupont's power remained unchallenged. The establishment quivered at the mere mention of his name, hoping like the wilderbeest when confronted by a pride of lions that he would choose someone else. Rumours began to circulate that deals were being struck behind closed doors, as this politician or that businessman agreed to Dupont's demands in exchange for immunity from further media investigation.

As Dupont's sense of security within the French political system grew he began to broaden his horizons, mirroring the wider trend towards European unity. Two European Commissioners were forced from office by his revelations, and several others were believed to have 'revised' their political positions at his suggestion. It was one of the latter – the Commissioner for Media Affairs – who had been responsible for pressing through his appointment as Managing Editor of the newly-formed European Broadcasting Corporation.

A scantily-clad air hostess glided down the narrow aisle from the cockpit and asked Rachel to put on her seat belt prior to landing. The time for speculation would no doubt soon be over, and in less than an hour she would know the reason for Dupont's strange request and, perhaps, the reason for that disturbing look which had passed across his face at the end of their brief videophone conversation.

* * * * * *

Vienna lay in silence under a cloudless black sky as she sped round the Ring towards the Danube bridges. Through the car window she could see the imposing silhouette of the Hofburg, home of the Hapsburg Imperial House during the final years of the Austro-Hungarian Empire a century before. Franz Josef would perhaps have found it fitting that the capital of the new united Europe should have come to the city which had lain at the heart of his own multi-ethnic empire. For Brussels had been abandoned in favour of Vienna in order to reflect the greater Slav influence in a European Community that had grown beyond its exclusively Western European roots to include the polyglot of peoples and nations left isolated by the final traumatic collapse of the Soviet giant.

The car swung out over the Danube canal and on towards the heart of the new Europe. Buildings that had once housed agencies of the United Nations had become the core of a vast and growing European capital that had left native Austrians as an ethnic minority within their own city. And now, through the windows of the car, Rachel could see the towering skyscrapers of what had come to be called New Vienna rise like jagged teeth into the night sky, a European Manhattan to mock the waning power of the American version, a symbol of Europe's new potency as awesome as Versailles had ever been in the time of Louis XIV.

The car drew silently to a halt outside the second tallest of the skyscrapers and Rachel stepped out onto the deserted pavement. She glanced about her, watching as the solitary car disappeared around a corner, and pulled her coat up around her shoulders. And for the first time since she had left home in London some three hours earlier she became aware of a slight tingling at the back of her neck, a tingling she knew spelt fear.

She approached the main entrance of the building and waited as the huge glass doors swung open before her. To either side she could see tiny red lights glimmering in the dark as video cameras silently tracked her movements. And then, as she stepped over the threshold, the vast deserted foyer before her was suddenly bathed in brilliant light.

Rachel flinched. Countless times she had been inside this building, both during the day and for evening meetings, but always there had been people present. Never before had she seen it deserted in this manner. She approached the array of lifts that provided the only access to the offices and transmission studios that lay above the car parks on the lower stories of the building. A lift door opened and she entered, but before she had time to press any of the buttons the door closed automatically and the lift began to glide effortlessly upwards.

The lift stopped abruptly but the door did not open. For several seconds she waited, uncertain what to do, and as she waited the slight tingling of fear she had felt since her arrival began to grow stronger within her. She pressed the button for the thirty-fifth floor several times but the lift remained motionless. Then she pressed the red emergency button, but no voice appeared to reassure her.

The seconds began to stretch out into minutes. And as she waited, she knew it would not be long before the fear within her would begin to turn into a blind uncontrollable panic.

* * * * * *

Her father had always made a joke about it when she was a child. It was the silent ghost of Bonnie Prince Charlie seeking the freedom of his birthright that made her afraid of confined spaces. But despite her father's words Rachel suspected that a more likely explanation of her claustrophobia was that it was a bizarre reaction to the wild and empty Scottish moors in which she had spent the long lonely years of her early life.

Angus McNie had been over forty years old when his only child was born. At the time of his dramatic move from Knightsbridge to the Highlands he had probably been running away from something, although whether it was his wife's sudden death or something else

9

about which he had chosen to remain silent, Rachel had never been sure. Whatever the reason, the forty-year-old had taken his infant daughter to a remote lochside croft in the wild hill country of Knoydart. The nearest road was a two mile walk away, the nearest village some five miles further, but unperturbed by these tedious practicalities he had bought himself enough land and enough sheep to survive and settled down to raise his only child.

During her early years Rachel had known of nothing else. The croft had no television and the ancient radio in the kitchen held little interest for a tiny pre-school child. Her first memories were not surprisingly of sheep, their comical and innocent black faces her playmates in times of joy and her comforters in times of sorrow. Her memories of those early years were of a kind of idyll, a wild empty idyll in which, unlike other children, her home had no walls.

Her discontent had started at the age of six or seven, pre-dating by several years the growing open conflict with her father. She could remember becoming obsessed by the road, that twisting snake of grey tarmac winding its way over the familiar moors towards ... towards what? She knew of the village, of course, but the road continued far beyond the village and vanished around a steep hill at the far end of the loch. At night she used to lie in bed and dream about travelling along the road to all the strange and colourful places that lay beyond. And slowly, inexorably, she began to tire of the sheep.

In view of the virtually impossible journey to the nearest school her father had decided to exercise his legal right to educate his daughter at home. At first, while the education was concerned primarily with the basic skills of reading, writing and arithmetic, this had presented no great difficulties. But before long the need for a broader curriculum began to assert itself, and with it the need to provide Rachel with more information about the world beyond the moors.

The simmering conflict between father and daughter had finally erupted over the question of a television set. Nearly every other family in the remote Highlands possessed one and Rachel had occasionally encountered a set at one of the other houses in the village. Now she demanded one for herself. At first her father had resisted so, in an early display of the kind of gentle manipulation that had served her well in later life, Rachel had secured the support of no less a person than the Local Education Advisor. This gentleman was a God-like figure who descended wearily across the moors from the road in order to check upon her educational progress whilst in her father's charge. On his annual visit, and largely as a result of Rachel's subtle prompting as she accompanied him on the last leg of his tedious trek to her home, he had suggested fairly forcibly to her father that he invest in a television set in order to broaden his daughter's education.

And so, with the arrival in their cottage of a small portable black-and-white television, her enduring love affair with the media had begun. Strangely enough, it was the sheep who appeared to benefit most from the arrangement. Of late Rachel had found their continual bleating tiresome, but now she formed a kind of secret triumvirate with the television and the sheep. The television would provide her with information about the outside world and she would then explain whatever she had learnt to the ever patient sheep. They became her audience, and Rachel had always craved an audience.

* * * * * *

She could feel the claustrophobia beginning to overwhelm her. Gripping her skirt hard with her hands, she knelt down on the floor to steady herself. Then, with slow deliberation, she lowered her head down onto her knees and closed her eyes tightly shut.

"But Rachel, what on earth are you doing down there?"

She opened her eyes with a start and looked up into Dupont's astonished face. Taking his outstretched hand, she raised herself slowly to her feet.

"The door must have jammed," she said apologetically, straightening out her skirt.

"I know," he said. "We will have to tell the engineer. But why were you kneeling on the floor?"

"Claustrophobia."

Dupont looked shocked.

"Oh my goodness," he said quietly. "How terrible."

Rachel remembered the circumstances of her visit.

"Now I'm here, shall we talk?" she said, her self-control fully restored.

"Of course. Are you able to walk?"

She looked at him with annoyance.

"Yes," she said, stepping firmly out of the lift into the corridor, but before she could explain to Dupont that the effects of the claustrophobia passed off as soon as the confinement was over she stopped dead in her tracks and stared about her at the corridor in which she found herself.

"Who the hell are they?" she mumbled at last, staring at the group of some twenty heavily-armed men who were lolling about in the corridor.

11

Dupont smiled.

"Security," he offered non-committally, taking her arm and steering her gently past the guards.

By the time Rachel had arrived in his office she could feel an anger growing within her, elbowing aside the fear that had shadowed her since her arrival.

"What the bloody hell is going on in here?" she demanded, rounding on Dupont as soon as he had closed the door.

He glided gracefully over to his desk.

"Three-thirty in the morning is perhaps a little late for a drink. But you would like some coffee, I expect?"

"Like I said, François, I'd like an explanation. At your request, I've just travelled half way across Europe in the dead of night to talk to you. I'm dog tired and I want to know what it's all about."

Dupont said nothing. Instead, he beckoned her over to a sofa opposite which was a large picture window covered by drawn velvet curtains.

"I am sorry for the circumstances of my call," he said, speaking slowly and deliberately. "But I did not judge that I could put you fully in the picture until the last minute. I have asked you to come here tonight in order to ask you for your help."

Rachel looked at him hard. She was used to Dupont telling her what to do. Now his tone caught her off guard.

"My help?"

"Yes. Your help."

For a few moments silence descended, but then Dupont moved over to the window opposite the sofa and drew back the curtains. Outside and far below, the old city of Vienna lay still and silent, spread out like a carpet around the floodlit spires of St Stephan's.

"There is to be a change tonight, Rachel," he said at last, gazing out at the city beneath him. "Nothing will ever be the same again."

Rachel remained silent. The anger had vanished, but the fear had not returned. And that, she knew, was not entirely rational.

"Do you have any conception how many of those people sleeping down there in that city before you are going to die of the White Death?" he asked suddenly, swinging round to face her.

Rachel shuddered, remembering the Green newsletter and her earlier conversation with Tom.

"Nobody knows for sure, do they? In Vienna, at a guess, maybe fifty thousand."

"I didn't ask you how many have already contracted the disease. I asked you how many will die."

He didn't wait for an answer. The words flowed fluently, French and German expressions freely mingled with his English in the weird kind of Eurospeak that was the logical corollary of the Greater European dream. And as he spoke, Rachel could not quite tell whether he was addressing her or himself.

"The White Death has been amongst us for only two years but already it has become like an overclose relative. It lives with us and we try to ignore it, but it clings on tenaciously. We know so much about it, but hitherto we have been unable to take the steps which are required to bring it to heal. I am sure you know all this. I am sure you know that each infected person is allowed at least six months of healthy living before showing any symptoms. I am sure you know that an estimated one quarter of those who become infected do not develop any symptoms at all and seem destined to live out their natural lives as carriers. I am sure you know that the disease is easily transmitted by any kind of close body fluid contact. You know these things just as everyone else knows these things. But despite knowing them we have chosen to look the other way, to ignore the terrible plague in our midst."

He paused for a moment, turning away from her to face the vast expanse beyond the window. And as Rachel watched him, she became certain that it was neither her nor himself he was addressing, it was the entire world beyond the glass.

"History will call it the Great Paralysis. One day historians will write about the last two years in the same way as they wrote about the years before the First World War, speculating about how the leaders of Mankind could have allowed such a terrible situation to arise. But in truth the explanation is simple. People will not face this crisis because they do not see how they can overcome it. Like an animal in danger, they have been frozen into inactivity."

The flow stopped and he turned to face her.

"Are my words crazy?" he asked.

Rachel looked at him and thought of her own reactions and the reactions of people she knew. Many people were more careful now, many more ignored it completely, but nearly everyone hoped and believed that the essentials of life could simply go on as before. Perhaps it was because they knew that as yet most people were free of the illness or perhaps it was because they inwardly believed that it would be cured as Aids before it had been cured. Perhaps it was because they thought it was always somebody else's problem. But whatever the reason, they point blank refused to address in an honest and straightforward manner the simple question of what to do next.

13

"No," she replied. "Your words are not crazy. But what has this to do with my presence here in Vienna tonight?"

"Like I said, there is to be a change. At long last the Commission has summoned up the political willpower to address the problem and take the necessary measures to deal with it firmly. They are to seek special powers from the Parliament to rule by decree. At seven o'clock this morning the Commission is to announce that Parliament is to be recalled from its winter recess to approve the special powers."

Rachel stared at him in amazement, as the faces of the various European Commissioners flashed across her mind. They were a motley bunch of politicians from around the continent whose incessant infighting was scarcely concealed by the doctrine of collective responsibility they had inherited from the British political tradition. In her lengthy political experience, they were a group who would be hard-pressed to agree about the precise borders of the different European time zones, let alone a coherent strategy for dealing with the White Death. Then she remembered the armed guards in the corridor.

"A coup," she murmured quietly. "There's been a coup, hasn't there. And you're involved in it."

Dupont shook his head emphatically.

"No, Rachel. There has been no coup in that sense. The Commission has voted with only one abstention to grant temporary powers to Nicklaas Vintner to act in its name. You probably know they are able to do so under Article 45 of the Treaty of Brussels."

Rachel looked up at him sharply. She had always thought of Nicklaas Vintner was a rather comical figure with little real influence. He had been appointed to the Commission shortly after the last elections and within months had become its Vice-President, but everyone knew that his elevation was due more to the Green Party's success at the polls than his own exceedingly limited talents.

Born the son of an unmarried actress in occupied Holland during the Second World War, Vintner had developed a reputation in his youth as something of a hothead in the Dutch environmental movement. He had even spent some time in jail as a young man for refusing to unchain himself from the front door of the Dutch Prime Minister's residence after gaining access on the pretext of presenting a petition. But by the early 1990s the fiery Vintner had begun to mellow, revising his earlier opinions and entering the Dutch National Assembly as a representative of one of the mainstream parties. Although his voice was still frequently heard on environmental matters, his tone became more measured and his arguments more carefully qualified. And so he had ended up in the European Parliament as a kind of environmental poodle for one of the main ruling parties, the man they would wheel out in front of the television cameras whenever they needed to allay public fears that the party was insufficiently committed to the latest environmental causes. In recent years he had become a rather popular figure, even amongst supporters of the Greens, and it seemed only sensible to draw him into a position of prominence within the Commission after the latter's success at the polls in order to head off the far more radical Green Party leaders.

"Vintner? Why Vintner? Why not the President of the Commission?"

Dupont scowled.

"The President was the abstention. He did not have the stomach for the necessary measures. He has resigned. Vintner is the Acting President. I expect he will be confirmed in office by the Parliament as soon as it reassembles."

Rachel looked thoughtfully at Dupont and remained silent for a long time. Then she rose from her chair and moved to stand beside him by the window. She had always felt an affinity for this man, an affinity which she had never fully tried to understand.

"You have not called me half way across Europe in the middle of the night to lie to me, François. You could have told me a lie in the morning."

Dupont turned and met her gaze.

"Vintner knew the Commission would take no action. So he coordinated a small group of people with the determination to fight the White Death in the only way it can be fought. No more endless talk of education campaigns; no more promises of extra cash to care for the afflicted; no more carefully stage-managed suggestions of a cure just around the corner. Just the blunt, straightforward measures that are needed to protect public safety."

He walked over to his desk and picked up a single sheet of paper which he handed to Rachel. It was classified 'Top Secret' and had printed on it a single graph.

"According to the latest Commission estimates, this is the likely course of the death rate in Europe over the next three years on the most probable assumptions about behaviour modification and disease containment."

Rachel glanced at the thin red line as it snaked ominously upwards across the page. Dupont fetched another graph from his desk and handed it to her.

"And this is a projected European population forecast over a similar period."

Rachel stared in horror at the graph. She had seen other forecasts, of course, but this was by far the worst.

"Why so bad?" she asked quietly. "I thought most projections just petered out as the most risk-prone populations become saturated."

Suddenly, without warning, Dupont turned on Rachel and grabbed her arm, pulling her roughly round to face the city that lay beneath them.

"And what chance do you think they have?" he said angrily, pointing towards the sleeping city. "What chance do they have when even you with all your experience of such things have fallen prey to their deliberate disinformation campaign?"

Rachel stared down at the graphs. Suddenly she remembered the endless stream of circulars issued by the Bureau of Health about the infectivity of the illness.

"Are you sure?" she said at last, reluctant to believe Dupont's accusations for the simple reason she did not like the conclusions which flowed logically from them.

"Not me. Vintner. He was there when the package was agreed. They didn't call it disinformation, of course: they called it 'allaying public disquiet'. But it amounts to the same thing, doesn't it?"

"And you're trying to tell me this thing's far more infectious than everyone out there thinks?" she asked.

"No, not yet. But the evidence coming in suggests very strongly that the infective agent is becoming more robust. Soon it will be passed on as easily as the common cold."

Rachel looked again at the graph.

"But if they knew all this, why didn't they do something?"

Dupont rolled his eyes as if to heaven.

"Like I said, they'd rather stick their heads in the sand and hope the problem will go away by itself."

Rachel put the graphs down on the desk and returned to the window.

"So the Commission has been coerced into passing power to Vintner, and Parliament will soon be coerced into ratifying his dictatorship."

Dupont turned and stared at her. His dark Gallic eyes seemed to be pleading with an intensity she had never before seen, begging her to give him her support.

"I don't like it any more than you do, Rachel. But you must see it has to be like this. There really is no other way."

LONDON, ENGLAND, MARCH 2005

The videophone on her desk buzzed and with a grimace she pressed a button.

"André Rostropov on the line, Mrs McNie. Will you speak to him now?"

Rachel winced. She had been dreading this call for over a week.

"Yes, Miss Drummond. Put him on."

André's face appeared on the tiny screen built discreetly into her desk, his normally jovial features drawn and strained.

"I want to see you, Rachel," he said bluntly.

Sometimes she dearly wished the videophone had never been invented. It had been far easier to hide your true feelings back in the days of the humble telephone.

"Social or business?" she asked, trying to look as well as sound casual.

André's scowl deepened.

"Is there a difference these days?" he grunted.

Rachel pretended to look offended.

"André. Don't be so unpleasant. If you want to see me that's fine. I was just wondering whether it should be at the office or over dinner with Tom at my place."

"I'd rather it was just the two of us. Preferably in confidence, if you could manage it."

There was an unmistakable sarcasm in his voice.

Rachel glanced at her watch.

"I've no lunch dates today, André. I'll come and see you wherever you like."

A thin smile spread slowly across André's lips.

"O.K. Rachel, let's make it by the bridge over the lake in St James's Park."

An hour later she spotted André standing on the bridge just as he had promised. A sparrow had landed on his hand, and he was feeding it with tiny morsels of bread. As Rachel approached, the sparrow flapped its wings and flew away to perch on the branch of a nearby tree.

"Tame, aren't they?" André remarked quietly.

Rachel leant against the side of the bridge beside him.

"I'm sorry you're so angry with me, André."

17

He remained silent, carefully keeping his gaze on the little bird.

"You should have resigned, you know," he said at last, turning to face her.

Rachel rounded on him angrily. Normally she controlled her emotions with an iron fist, but the tension of the last few weeks must have been beginning to tell.

"I'll talk if you like, but if you've just come here to insult me then I'm going to leave."

She turned and started to walk away. For a moment André remained motionless, but then he quickly followed her.

"I'm sorry, Rachel. But you know that with my background I can't help but think this whole situation stinks."

Rachel stopped and sat down on a wooden bench by the water's edge.

"What kind of sandwiches did you get?" she asked with a smile.

André sat down and pulled a paper bag out of his coat pocket.

"Prawn, but I'm afraid I gave some of the bread to the bird."

Rachel took the remains of the prawn sandwich and held it on her lap.

"You're one of only a handful who've resigned, André. Did you know that?"

"Of course. Ninety percent of those who've gone were given the push on your orders."

André certainly knew how to punch where it hurt. She took a bite of sandwich.

"In the last two weeks I've sacked more people than in the previous fifteen years," she said eventually. "And if you think I've enjoyed doing it, you're wrong."

"Orders?" André muttered sarcastically.

"If you like. Some staff wouldn't accept the new situation in Vienna. They obviously had to go."

André threw a piece of his sandwich into the lake, prompting a considerable commotion amongst the assembled wildfowl.

"I always thought you were like Dupont," he muttered, "but I never thought you were his poodle."

Suddenly Rachel could feel the anger welling up inside her. She didn't have many friends, and she had always counted André as one of the closest, but he had no right to speak like that about François Dupont.

"I think you've got to get a few facts straight, André, if you can escape for fifteen seconds the blinkered vision foisted on you by a childhood in Brezhnev's Russia."

André turned to face her and for a fraction of a second his pleading eyes reminded her of Dupont's two weeks before in New Vienna.

"Has it occurred to you that you're the one with the blinkered vision, Rachel? Don't you understand that the road you've embarked upon is leading us straight back into Brezhnev's Russia. That's why it scares all hell out of me."

"O.K. So what would you do, André? I agree that Vintner's accession is only barely constitutional and was only achieved under considerable duress. I also agree that many people are going to find their liberties seriously curtailed over the coming months and perhaps longer. But surely that's better than watching your skin turn white while you wait to drop dead?"

André scowled. They both knew the logic of the argument perfectly well.

"My neighbour's boy went this morning, Rachel. Only sixteen years old. A perfectly healthy boy. They came in the morning and told him the results of the test. He had ten minutes to pack his bag before they took him away in the car."

Rachel took another bite of prawn sandwich and remained silent. She didn't need to tell André that an infected sixteen-year-old boy in perfect health was a far more serious health hazard than Jack the Ripper had ever been.

"And that's the trouble with democracy, isn't it, André? We've all become too nice. You're nice. The sixteen-year-old is nice. His Mum and Dad are nice. The only thing that isn't nice is this damned disease. And that's why François is right and you're wrong."

André fingered his sandwich nervously.

"Maybe you're right," he said quietly. "Maybe you're right about democracy. Perhaps nobody would have faced up to it until it was too late. Perhaps they would never have faced up to it at all. But what frightens me is how will it ever end. Once we've torn up all our cherished and in some cases hard-won liberties, how will we ever get them back again?"

Rachel looked at André's anguished expression and knew that she was right to respect him more than virtually anyone else she knew. And as usual, he had identified the central question that disturbed her most about recent developments.

"Just now you asked me why I didn't resign, André. And you've just put your finger on why. You know me well enough to know that I share every one of your fears about the current situation, every single one of them, just like I treasure the liberties we have so carefully cultivated in our European life during the last half century.

But it is precisely because I value those liberties that I am staying put and not resigning. Only if I retain my position of influence will I be able to help ensure that the measures are revoked as soon as possible. If decent people like you and I hide away in order to retain our precious purity, there are plenty of totalitarian snakes queuing up behind us to take our places. They're your real danger, André, not people like me."

André didn't reply. Quietly, he stood up and put the remains of his sandwich back in his pocket.

"You remind me of my social studies teacher back in Smolensk," he said. "He was a nice guy too. But every time one of us had a go at him about the system he used to use exactly the same line of argument as you used just now. So goodbye, Rachel, there's nothing more to say since we both know exactly where we stand. All I can say is that I hope you're right and I'm wrong."

He started walking slowly, almost hesitantly, away towards the imposing classical buildings which had once housed the British Foreign Office. But after a few yard he stopped and walked swiftly back towards her.

"I nearly forgot. I also bought you this."

He handed her a small bar of chocolate with a wry smile before walking briskly away. Moments later he was out of sight, lost among the London crowds.

Rachel watched him depart with a leaden feeling in her heart. Disconsolately, she started to unwrap the chocolate bar, for although she didn't normally eat chocolate, the prawn sandwich she had shared with the little sparrow had left her feeling hungry. But then she froze, and again that strange tingling sensation of fear surged through her body. For scrawled on the back of the wrapper was a brief handwritten note.

'I have sadly concluded I cannot yet trust you with my thoughts, Rachel, although I respect your motives for what they are. But as your friend of many years I must say one thing: be very careful in the months ahead, and in particular be careful of François Dupont."

* * * * * *

The snoring beside her was gradually becoming unbearable.

"Shut up, Tom!" she ordered, and with a grunt he turned heavily over between the covers and fell still.

For a long time Rachel lay motionless and listened to the silence of the night. Flicking a glance at the bedside table she stared with grim disbelief at the luminous hands of their alarm clock: nearly five-thirty in the morning; for five hours she had lain there praying for sleep, and for five hours sleep had refused to come.

The last two weeks had been like a whirlwind. Every day new orders had arrived from Vienna, orders which invariably had to be adapted to the local circumstances of the London office. It dawned on her that she had been so frenetically busy with the reorganisation that she had not had time to stop and think. But now André had forced her to do just that.

It was not that his words had surprised her; in fact she had been expecting every one of them. But the note he had passed to her at the end of their brief conversation had confused her far more than any verbal exchange could ever have done, a fact which André had presumably known full well.

Again she turned over in her mind the various possible explanations for the note. André knew something of great significance, or at least suspected something, that much was clear. She suspected he had had two chocolate bars concealed in his pocket, each with a different message written on its wrapper. He had always been obsessed with secrecy, an obsession that had stood him in good stead during some of the difficult and sensitive documentary work he had undertaken over the years, and she knew he would never have spoken to her freely about sensitive matters in a public park where any number of simple listening devices could have overheard their words. So, as she had suspected from the outset, his sole objective in meeting with her face-to-face had been to decide whether she could be trusted with instructions for a further, more secure, rendezvous. And she had failed the test.

What really disturbed her now was that she knew she could have passed the test if she had only tried. If she had expressed slightly more hesitancy about her actions, or if she had chosen to question her orders from Dupont in Vienna, André would almost certainly have spilled the beans. After all, he had already known that she was still working for the European Broadcasting Corporation – he hadn't needed a meeting to discover that. Yet she had pretended to a confidence about her role in recent events which had never in fact existed.

She cast her mind back over the momentous events of the previous two weeks, trying to slot the circumstances of her encounter with André into their proper context. So much of significance had happened and so much of even greater significance was about to happen. It was hard to keep up.

It was clear that François Dupont was a key member of a group of conspirators located at the very heart of the European institutions.

On Nicklaas Vintner's instigation, they had reluctantly decided that Europe's democratic mechanisms were completely incapable of handling the impending crisis created by the White Death and that a barely-disguised coup was the only way of imposing the draconian measures they believed to be necessary. Rachel was not yet sure of the exact identity of all the central conspirators – Dupont had been less than clear on that point – but she had surmised that several senior members of the European Defence Force were involved, including its brash Italian Commander-in-Chief, Marshall Bignoletto.

The evidence of early military involvement in Vintner's takeover was overwhelming. From the outset, the armed forces had accepted without demure the new orders emanating from the Commission building in Vienna, even though it was an open secret that those decisions were being taken under duress. They had also given the Commission vital support in its struggle to 'persuade' Parliament to ratify Vintner's position and powers, surrounding the Parliament building with troops at a critical juncture in order to prevent 'disturbances' and arrest 'terrorist elements'.

The generals' apparent support for the coup was relatively easy to understand. The armed forces had been something of an embarrassment ever since the Treaty of Brussels had created the European Defence Force out of the diverse military units of the old nation states. The Defence Force, like any army, was designed to fight enemies, or at the very least deter enemies, but the end of the Cold War and the effective policing of Third World nuclear capabilities by the Security Council of the United Nations had created a situation in which enemies had become a rather scarce commodity. As peace triumphed, the generals of Greater Europe had watched their power wane and their armies dwindle. And most frustrating of all, in the absence of a convincing bogey-man they couldn't even seem to find any sensible arguments to explain why their power should not continue to decline indefinitely.

The White Death provided the answer. At last the generals had found the enemy they needed in order to survive.

And they had already been put to work. Three days previously Vintner's new puppet Commission had announced plans to construct a massive new system of border defences. Greater Europe was to become a disease-free zone, secured by a new Berlin Wall that looked in most particulars remarkably similar to the one that had crumbled to dust during the 1989 revolutions. The only difference, of course, was that whereas the earlier Wall had been designed to keep people in, this one's central purpose was to keep people out.

For if the Commission's horrific forecasts were right about the likely future course of the disease, it seemed likely that the defensive structures were going to be put to the test within a few years. As the rest of the world woke up to the severity of the epidemic there were likely to be attempts to break into the safe zone of the advanced European state, both by individuals and by large quasi-military units that might even have the backing of foreign governments. The new government was not taking any chances.

But the external defences were not the only building operation planned. For the logical corollary of the compulsory registration and screening which had been the new Commission's first major policy act was that all carriers of the White Death would be securely isolated, thereby preventing any further spread of the disease within the safe zone. Work had already started on creating secure 'Care Centres' to which all carriers, sick and healthy alike, could be transferred.

Rachel finally gave up trying to sleep and quietly slipped out of bed, taking care not to disturb Tom. He had just started snoring again, and this time she decided to let him continue without interruption. But the sight of him reminded her of the sixteen-year-old boy of whom André had spoken. It could so easily have been her Tom. Or it could have been Rupert, or Jane, or even little Sam. The knock on the door, the men waiting while the bags were packed and final goodbyes said. And if it had been her family, would she view herself and her role in constructing the new disease-free Europe any differently?

Two weeks before in Dupont's office it had all seemed so straightforward. It was a harsh but logical utilitarian position; the age-old principle of the greatest good for the greatest number. Dupont had persuaded her that in view of the highly infectious nature of the illness, Vintner's policy of segregation was the only decent way to protect people from themselves. Yet now, with the policy beginning to bite and the first carriers being rounded up and taken away, it was hard to come to terms with the dreadful human misery it was bound to cause for the afflicted and their families.

She tiptoed downstairs to the lounge and turned on the ornate artificial log fire. Curling up in her favourite armchair, she studied the dancing flames, seeking their help in explaining why André had warned her about Dupont. Why Dupont in particular? Why not any of the other conspirators?

In truth there was a lot about François Dupont that didn't make sense, particularly as regards his relationship with her. Why had he chosen to call her to Vienna in that melodramatic fashion on the crucial night before the coup? The takeover itself did not require her active participation and although she was an important employee of the European Broadcasting Corporation she was no more important than a dozen other regional bosses. She could easily have been 'consulted' after the event.

She suspected already that she knew the truth. She had glimpsed it when she had seen his pleading eyes, seen how much he appeared to need her approval for his role in the night's events. For some reason she did not yet understand, she had become personally important to him.

The flames seemed to leap more vigorously in the fireplace, dancing their exotic dance with incandescent fury. It was certainly not the first time during her marriage that she had become aware that another man was attracted to her. As a successful and passably attractive woman, frequently apart from her husband for lengthy periods of time, it was hardly surprising that men had tried to begin affairs with her. But she had always resisted their advances, not because she knew it was wrong, but simply because she had no wish to get involved. It was enough to love one man.

But this time she knew it would be different. For although Dupont had not yet made any open move to win her, she knew in her heart that it was only a matter of time before he did. And what frightened her was not that she would begin an affair with him – her loyalty to Tom was too great for that – but that this time, for the first time, she would find it hard to refuse.

And now, suddenly, everything began to fall into place. Now she knew why she had held her old friend André at arms length, deliberately letting him walk away without telling her what was preying on his mind. For even though she trusted her intellect sufficiently to make at least provisional judgements about the politics of the new regime, she was as yet too uncertain of her own emotions to risk creating a dangerous conflict of interest between two men she cared for very much.

She lay back in the armchair, enjoying the warmth of the fire seeping through her body, and before very long fell sound asleep.

OLD VIENNA, AUSTRIA, APRIL 2005

A thick blanket of smog hung over the city as she stumbled through the narrow streets of the Old Quarter towards the café where she had agreed to meet him. It was only three-thirty in the afternoon, but the visibility was so poor that it already seemed like late evening. The particularly high pollution count must have detered people from venturing forth, because the streets along which she was walking were nearly deserted.

He had asked her to meet him privately at a meeting of regional broadcasting controllers convened that morning to review the reforms within the European Broadcasting Corporation since Vintner's accession. The Corporation was organised into twenty-two different regional transmission centres, each broadly corresponding to the different language zones within Europe, and Rachel had been asked to attend as head of the London office.

On her arrival that morning at the Corporation's headquarters she had realised how few of her former colleagues had survived the transition to the new order: of the twenty-two regional offices, some eighteen had fallen under new management, although it seemed impolite to enquire too closely as to the circumstances behind the change of staff. She could only surmise that the sackings for which she had herself been responsible in London had been matched by a similar bloodletting at the highest level.

Against this rather inauspicious background, she could not help but be impressed by the way in which Dupont had managed the meeting. His grasp of detail amazed her, and it was clear that he possessed considerable independent knowledge of the changes that had taken place within each regional organisation. When somebody questioned his actions, his eyes would flash reassuringly across the room at his interrogator with a warm and reassuring smile before he would savage their arguments with his customary hard cold logic. But the very moment he sensed the criticism was doused, the danger passed, the charm would return, reassuring his adversary that they continued to enjoy his continued and undying confidence.

Dupont had explained the overall media strategy of the new regime. He summed it up in three words: control, conviction and concern. Control was to come through incorporating all the different media under a single umbrella organisation called the European Information

Office, of which he – François Dupont – was to be the head. Independent television and radio stations, newspapers and magazines would continue to exist separately from the European Broadcasting Corporation, but editorial control would be tightened in 'sensitive areas'. When asked what the term 'sensitive areas' meant, he had explained that this covered all matters relating to the difficult political situation or the measures required to control the spread of the White Death.

Conviction was to be achieved through ensuring that all staff in positions of influence within the organisation, from the most junior journalist through to the most senior managers, believed wholeheartedly in the objectives of the new administration. Regional controllers were urged to be particularly vigilant of members of staff harbouring secret doubts, with a view to replacing them with trustworthy staff as soon as possible. As he had explained this point, Rachel could not help but feel a flicker of relief that André had resigned, for if he had stayed she might have felt under pressure to sack him herself.

And concern. All staff without exception should be sympathetic to the worries and fears of ordinary people in the difficult new circumstances. Programme-makers should wherever possible seek to allay people's fears and reassure them that the new government had everyone's best interests at heart.

She turned a corner and glanced casually into the display window of a travel agents. A huge poster of a mountain view in the heart of summer stared out optimistically into the bleak Viennese smog, promising better days to come. She would have walked straight past had she not noticed the words at the top of the poster. For there, printed in large blue italic script, was the caption: 'Care Centres: the Best Place to Be!'

She flinched and took a closer look at the building. For the sign over the door showed that this was not a travel agents at all but one of the new-fangled Care Centre Information Bureaux. She had known that these Bureaux were going to be established but was surprised that the Viennese city authorities had managed to move with such admirable efficiency. Glancing at her watch to check that she had time before her rendezvous with Dupont, she stepped hesitantly through the door.

For all the world it really did look like a travel agents. On every available inch of wall space there were posters of happy mountain scenes, many showing smiling people enjoying tranquil rural pursuits, while the middle of the room was filled with tastefully arranged display shelves and several deep sofas. The display shelves were laden with beautifully printed full-colour brochures containing yet more glossy pictures of mountain paradise.

When she entered the room it was completely empty, but within seconds of her arrival a door at the back swung open and a rather plump middle-aged lady with a concerned look emerged.

"Good afternoon," the lady said, her strong Viennese dialect difficult to understand even by a fluent German-speaker such as Rachel.

Rachel paused for a moment.

"Good afternoon," she replied in High German, all hesitation vanished. "Can you help me, I wonder?"

The dialect vanished as the woman switched instinctively to High German. "Of course, my dear. What is troubling you?"

"I've flown into Vienna to see a close friend of mine. I've just been to her flat to visit her but ... but her neighbours said she'd been taken away."

The lady did not look at all perturbed by this news. She moved closer to Rachel and steered her gently by the arm to one of the sofas.

"Is she the first you've known?" she said sympathetically.

"Yes," Rachel murmured. "I'm so frightened for her. The neighbours said she was perfectly healthy."

The lady nodded.

"She probably is healthy, my dear. If she's only recently contracted the illness she'll have at least six months before anything shows. And some lucky people don't seem to get ill at all. She's probably been taken to one of the new Alpine Care Centres where she can be looked after properly."

"Where will they have taken her?" Rachel asked.

"Ah, that depends where she lived."

"In the thirteenth district."

"Well in that case I expect she's been taken to Oberstein. It was only opened last week but when it's finished it'll have a capacity of over fifty thousand. I've heard it's very nice. But of course, when things settle down people will be able to choose."

"Choose?" Rachel asked with genuine surprise.

The middle-aged lady laughed merrily.

"They're not prisons, you know. Oberstein is in the Alps. Wonderful if you like skiing in winter and nice invigorating mountain walks in the summer but not much fun if you're scared of heights! If you are you might be happier at, say, one of our nice sunny Sicilian Care Centres. Transfers are easily arranged."

The lady rose with some considerable effort from the sofa and waddled over to one of the display shelves, selecting a brochure and handing it to Rachel.

"Here you are, my dear, it tells you all about the facilities planned for Oberstein. They're not all open yet, of course, but everything should be ship-shape in about three months time."

Rachel flicked through the brochure, which seemed to project much the same holiday image as the posters on the wall.

"You mean they can choose which one they go to."

"Of course. That's the whole point of the government's new programme. These poor people are ill. Unless we're lucky enough to find a cure, most of them are going to pass away within a year. The least those of us who are uninfected can do is make sure they have a good time so long as they're still healthy and proper medical attention if they develop symptoms."

"Can I visit my friend there?" Rachel asked suddenly, curious to know how the councillor would handle the question.

"Oh no, dear, that's the whole point, isn't it. Only essential personnel are allowed in. They're specially trained and protected. It'd be defeating the purpose to allow the rest of us to wander in and out, wouldn't it?"

"But we were so close. She can't just disappear like this."

"You can talk with your friend whenever you like, my dear. Just use the videophone – the number of the reception desk is in the brochure. Whichever Care Centre she finally opts for, however far away, the calls will only be charged at the local rate."

Rachel's eyes returned to the brochure, trying to imagine how she would be feeling at this moment if her own family had been taken away.

"I know what you're thinking, dear," her companion interjected. "It seems very hard to take someone away who appears to be perfectly healthy and lock them up, even if the place they stay is as nice as Oberstein. But it just has to be done, you know, it has to be done. Two years ago nobody in Vienna had the disease. Now there's at least enough carriers in this city alone to fill somewhere like the Oberstein Centre to overflowing. If the President hadn't taken these steps, soon we'd have had so many sick people to look after that the whole system would have broken down. There wouldn't have been enough healthy to care for the sick. Now you know that's true, don't you?"

Rachel nodded glumly and rose to her feet.

"Thanks for your time. I'll think about what you said."

The lady stood up and opened the door for her.

"Keep the brochure, dear, and pop in and see me again if you feel the need for another chat. We're open day and night, seven days a week."

Rachel stepped back out into the cold, dank air, watching discreetly through the window as the lady scuttled back to her lair behind the little door at the back to wait for her next customer. She was just about to walk on when a hand touched her arm.

"Rachel."

She jumped and turned to find François Dupont staring at her.

"What were you doing in there?" he asked, indicating the Information Office with a jerk of his thumb.

"I was curious. Never seen one before."

He grunted.

"I nearly went in myself a few days ago for the same reason, but my face is too well known."

He leaned up against the window and peered inside.

"Looks a bit like a travel agents, doesn't it?"

"The analogy is not totally misplaced, François. Did you know they're planning to let them move around from one centre to another? The woman in there made it sound like a vast system of interlinked holiday camps."

Dupont flicked a sly glance at her.

"I know," he whispered. "That was my idea."

Rachel turned and stared at him. It was the first time she had heard him claim personal credit for any policy.

"You?" she asked.

Dupont took her arm and started steering her along the street in the general direction of the café.

"Don't sound so surprised, Rachel. I was involved in this thing from the outset. I do have a certain influence, you know."

She said nothing, but Dupont seemed eager to take the opportunity to drive the point home.

"Some of my colleagues think of these places like prisons," he continued, "as if these poor people have done something wrong by getting ill. They need to be reminded that we are taking a huge responsibility by denying the carriers their liberty and that we owe them the very best conditions we can possibly provide."

"And who exactly are your 'colleagues'?" Rachel asked.

Dupont chuckled.

"Those of us who were behind the changes. We are still in charge, despite Vintner's formal position as President."

"A kind of oligarchy?"

"You might say that."

"I didn't say anything at the meeting this morning, François, but is this stifling blanket of censorship descending over the European media your idea too?''

For a few paces he said nothing.

"You don't approve?" he asked solemnly.

"It doesn't seem totally necessary. Vintner's in charge. The army appears to be solidly behind the new government. There's even a fair measure of public support for a firm line against the disease. Why not let people air their opinions freely if they want to?"

Dupont stopped. Since he had started holding her arm, Rachel had no choice but to stop too.

"Do you think I like these measures? Do you really think I do? What have I been doing in my career for the last twenty years?"

She looked into his eyes. They appeared angry at her implicit criticisms, but lying alongside the anger was that same look of fear she had seen before, a deep lingering fear that she would reject his actions and his thoughts.

Rachel smiled gently.

"No, François, I don't think you are enjoying this any more than I am. Really I don't."

His face relaxed.

"Of course it's censorship. I nearly used the word this morning but I couldn't get it past my lips. And of course I have had something to do with the government's media policy. But again we have to choose the lesser of two evils. We have to recognise honestly and openly when deeply-held principles conflict and act in a logically coherent fashion. Media dissent will create dissatisfaction, dissatisfaction will create disturbance, disturbance will create violence and violence will create more violence. In the end we have to accept that freedom of speech is the natural bedfellow of democracy and that democracy has failed us in this particular crisis."

They turned a corner and emerged into the Stephansplatz. Ahead lay the mighty form of St Stephan's Cathedral, the multicoloured tiles adorning its roof almost hidden from view by the smog.

"Shall we step inside?" Dupont asked. "It is very beautiful."

Rachel cast a cautious sideways glance at him but followed obediently as he pushed open the huge wooden door and entered the long nave. Far away the cathedral organist was practising, filling the huge cavern with echoing sonorous tones.

Without a word Dupont steered her to a pew near to one of the massive columns.

"Thank you for coming to meet me this afternoon," he said, his words so quiet they were almost imperceptible.

She looked at him and knew the struggle she had feared was soon to be upon her. It would have been easier to refuse his invitation to share a coffee with him in the clinical surroundings of a modern conference room earlier in the day, but her courage had failed her.

Dupont had lapsed into silence again and appeared to be concentrating on the organ music. She thought of Tom, struggling bravely along the road with little Sam to meet the kids from school, and felt disgusted with herself at the thoughts passing through her mind about François Dupont.

"You don't have to thank me for coming, François. The pleasure is mine."

Inwardly she winced. A woman of her experience should know better. She was sending out the wrong signals, signals that would only serve to make the final rejection more bitter when it came.

"Do you know why I asked you to Vienna on the night before the take-over?" he asked quietly, turning his face towards her.

She hesitated.

"Not really."

"It was because I value your opinions. I value the freshness of your thinking. I value your support. I didn't want to risk losing any of those things by not consulting you before I acted."

Rachel smiled.

"You hardly did that, François."

She couldn't be sure, but she thought she saw him flinch. Again, the same apparent insecurity, the same incongruous signs of weakness in a man who seemed so very strong.

"I didn't dare involve you until I was sure it would succeed. We could all have ended up in jail if things had gone wrong." Rachel refrained from asking him what he would have done that night if she had told him two hours before the change of policy was announced on breakfast television that she found his actions repulsive.

"I don't know what I would have done if you had told me that everything I was planning was evil," he said slowly, as if he had heard her thoughts, "but I'm very relieved I didn't have to find out."

Rachel stared at the stained glass window high above her.

"But why me?" she said slowly. "Why is my opinion so important to you?"

Dupont picked up a small prayer-book that lay on the pew in front of him and started flicking through the pages.

"You probably didn't know that my father died when I was only five. My mother died shortly afterwards. Perhaps I have been looking ever since for a replacement."

"For a mother and a father?"

"For someone I can trust."

"And you think you can trust me?"

"I sense I can. Never before in my life have I sensed that about any woman."

The organ stopped and suddenly the tension broke within her. Rising from the pew, she turned to face him, her face cold and accusing.

"I'm a married woman, François. A married woman with three children. I think – so far – that I can support the policies you are advocating. But I can't do more than that for you. I'm sorry, but can we forget the coffee, please?"

And without waiting for an answer, she swung on her heels and hurried away down the aisle. Only when she had reached the ancient wooden door at the end of the nave did she allow herself a quick glance back in Dupont's direction.

He was kneeling exactly where she had left him, and to her complete amazement he appeared to be deep in prayer.

SURREY, ENGLAND, APRIL 2005

"Mummy's home, mummy's home!"

Suddenly the hall was filled with happy faces, happy smiling faces that knew little about the growing agonies of the world outside. They surrounded her and welcomed her, and she rejoiced in her heart that she had had the strength to push Dupont away.

Tom emerged from the kitchen, drying his hands on an old dish-cloth.

"Hi, love," he called over the incomprehensible hubbub of three simultaneous children's voices. "How's things?"

She kissed the children one by one and then took Tom in her arms.

"Fine," she lied, kissing her husband warmly on the cheek. "It's great to be home again."

Tom threw the dishcloth over his shoulder with a flourish that always reminded her of a French wine waiter at a first class restaurant.

"Coq au vin," he announced proudly, lifting up Sam in his arms and tossing him into the air like a pancake. "Not bad going for a busy man about the house with three small kids, eh? We hope she's hungry, don't we kids?"

Rupert, at twelve years old their eldest child and proud of it, stood by his father's side.

"And I did the trifle for afters," he added. "It's got sherry in it."

Ten-year-old Jane elbowed her way into the throng.

"And neither of them could have done anything if I hadn't looked after Sausage Dog."

It had been Jane's idea to call Sam Sausage Dog, and somehow the name had stuck.

Rachel took Sam from her husband and followed him through into the kitchen. Rupert and Jane scampered away to finish watching a television programme.

"Anything exciting happen while I was away?" Rachel asked.

Tom grunted.

"Not much," he replied. Oh yes, your father telephoned. I told him you were abroad."

Rachel lowered Sam carefully down to the ground.

"What did he say?"

"He asked when we're coming up to see him again. Says the fresh air would be good for the children." Tom's face became serious. "He's missing the kids and he's missing you, Rachel. It's been nearly three years."

Rachel could imagine it all too well. Her father, now in his late seventies, was still living alone in his remote cottage in the Highlands. Admittedly, the local council had built a road right past his front door since the days when she had lived there, but it still seemed an excessively hard life for such an elderly man.

"I don't suppose we can persuade him to come down here, can we?" she asked, knowing that holidays – at least for her – were out of the question for the foreseeable future.

Tom shrugged.

"I tried," he replied. "But you know what he's like – 'I spent the first forty years of my life down there and that was more than enough for me.'"

Rachel sat down on the floor and started building a tower of bricks with little Sam. There was absolutely no doubt from whom she had inherited her bloody-mindedness, but the thought of her father up there all alone still made her feel guilty.

"Could you go, Tom?" she asked at last. "Take the children up to see him during the holidays."

Tom looked at her.

"No chance of you getting away for a few days, I suppose?" he said.

33

Rachel frowned.

"I only wish I could, love, but with all the high drama at the office it's hardly a good time for the boss to disappear on holiday."

With a slightly forlorn look, Tom removed the dishcloth from his shoulder and turned towards the cooker.

"O.K. love, if you like. We'll go up for the whole of next week."

ONE WEEK LATER

The house seemed so empty without them. She walked moodily from one room to the other, trying to console herself with the thought that they would only be away for another four days, but every room reminded her of their absence and only served to magnify the cloud of depression that had descended upon her.

She realised with a shudder how much she had come to take her family for granted. She would sometimes disappear from home for weeks at a stretch, never really missing them, in truth hardly noticing they were not with her. But she always knew where they were, she knew they were safe, and she knew they would be there to greet her just as soon as she took it into her head to grace them with her presence.

Giving up her pointless travels around the house as a bad idea, she sat down at the desk in the living room to write Tom a letter. She would have videophoned, but her father regarded videophones as the work of the devil and refused to have one in his house.

She looked fondly at the photograph of her husband on the desk, but as she did so her eye fell on the information booklet they had been given after their blood tests the previous Thursday, just before Tom and the kids had set off for Scotland. It was lying where Tom had left it, thrown casually onto the desk, but the sight of it was sufficient to remind her of the carefully masked trauma of their visit.

Rachel had thought she knew what to expect from the blood tests. The new law made a test compulsory every three months, and there was therefore no stigma attached to going to the clinic. When they had gone as a family to the hospital that Thursday afternoon she had supposed, as had Tom, that the whole thing would be over within minutes.

They had entered the building at the appointed time and joined the queue of those waiting to have their blood samples taken, but when they got to the front of the queue, instead of being taken into a room with a doctor or a nurse present, they had been shepherded into a room with a policewoman sitting behind a desk.

The woman's manner had not been unfriendly. With a rather bored expression on her face, she had carefully inspected their identity papers and checked them against some kind of list before embarking upon what turned out to be a lengthy interrogation, asking all manner of personal questions that seemed to bear little relationship to the purpose of their visit. All the answers were recorded carefully on paper and, Rachel suspected, by a hidden microphone.

After about half-an-hour the interrogation had finally come to an end, and they were chaperoned into another room containing a desk behind which sat an elderly man in a white coat. Unlike the policewoman, whose manner had been rather officious if not actually rude, this chap was going out of his way to be warm and friendly, albeit in the slightly artificial manner that people who have to be warm and friendly for a living generally adopt.

This then was to be the councilling session. The man had reminded them that every single person in Europe was having the test and that it would soon become a regular part of life. Soon the disease would be virtually eradicated within the safe zones, but they had to realise that the first test was going to throw up a substantial number of carriers who were not aware of the fact that they had contracted the illness. He was therefore charged with explaining the rationale of the testing programme to each citizen who passed through his office, while at the same time carefully outlining the steps that would be taken if a positive result was detected.

He had done his job as well as possible under the circumstances, almost making a positive result sound like something to be hoped for, an opportunity to relax from the stresses and strains of everyday life and let the rest of society look after you for the rest of your days in relative luxury. At the end of the interview, he had asked them to state exactly where they would be staying for the next few days before thanking them for their time and passing them through to the nurse in the room next door for the blood test itself.

Rachel leant back in her chair and thought how terrifying that interview must have been for someone in one of the high risk groups. For young people experimenting with sexual contact for the first time, for middle-aged businessmen used to cavorting with mistresses and prostitutes in overseas hotels, for the promiscuous both heterosexual and homosexual, for anyone living the kind of communal lifestyle where body fluids could pass freely back and forth, the interview must have sounded like an instruction manual for a compulsory game of Russian roulette.

She knew it was wrong to be smug and she also knew it was wrong to point the finger at those who were less careful than she and Tom and say they had only themselves to blame if they got nabbed. But however hard she tried, she could not help but feel relief that she had sat through that quarter of an hour as an observer of events rather than a likely carrier.

With a jolt, she remembered her letter to Tom and glanced hastily at her watch. If she wrote it quickly, she could fax it through to the local post office near her father's house before they closed down for the night and it would be on the mat at the cottage first thing in the morning.

The minutes ticked by and the words flowed forth from her pen in a fluent stream. Perhaps it was her thoughts of the recent interview at the hospital or perhaps it was the fact that she was still inwardly trying to fend off her suppressed feelings towards François Dupont, but now, for the first time in seventeen years of married life, she found herself writing a love letter to her husband. She told him of the guilt she felt for taking him for granted and of the pain she felt that he was not with her. She told him how much she valued his undying love for her and how passionately she reciprocated that love. And finally, with tears by now flowing freely down her cheeks, she promised him that soon – as soon as she possibly could – she would free herself of some of her responsibilities at work and devote herself to a man who deserved better from her than he got.

She finished the letter and quietly laid the pen down on the desk. Then, without reading her words through, frightened almost by the emotion she felt within her, she carried the sheet through to the kitchen and flicked through her diary for the fax number of the post office near her father's home.

The fax machine next to the videophone was already humming quietly, waiting patiently to receive its tiny cargo, when her mood was abruptly broken by the doorbell.

Leaving the letter lying on the kitchen work surface, she walked to the hall and swung open the door.

"My God," she exclaimed, and already as the words passed her lips she could feel her stomach screwing up into a tight ball.

Strangely enough, the old man before her looked younger than his years. In fact he looked younger than she had seen him look for a very long time.

"Can I come in?" her father asked, leaning slightly on his walking stick as he walked past her into the hall.

She stared at him in horror.

"Father!"

He turned to her and their eyes met. Inwardly, she already knew what he had come to say, the reason for the journey he had so recently sworn he would never again make.

Her father enclosed her in his arms. Even now they were strong arms, strong from half a lifetime surviving in the bleak outdoors.

"You at least are safe," he said quietly.

She pushed him roughly away, refusing in her own mind to believe what she already knew in her heart to be true.

"You don't know yet, do you?" he murmured.

Her eyes pleaded with him to speak.

"They came yesterday morning," he said without any trace of emotion in his voice. "I was in the kitchen fixing the breakfast while Tom was down by the loch with the children trying out a little toy boat I had built out of a log. They took one look at me and followed my eyes to the lochside where the children were playing. Then, without so much as a word of explanation, they walked off over the moors and spoke to Tom."

Suddenly, without warning, images out of the distant past reared uncontrollably from her subconscious; the crudely-made carts piled high with dead bodies, the roughly-clad men ringing a bell to warn of the coming of death. But had it been any more terrifying for them than it was for her now?

"I couldn't hear what they said to Tom," her father continued, "but after about ten minutes he left the children playing by the boat and came up to me with the two men. There was a woman with them, and she stayed down by the loch with the children. Tom took me into the cottage and told me that the tests had proved positive."

Rachel could feel herself spinning, fighting to retain control as her whole life was ripped out from beneath her.

"Who? For God's sake who?"

Her father held her closely to his chest, making a futile attempt to shield her from the pain.

"All of them, my dearest child. Tom and all the children."

LONDON, ENGLAND, MAY 2005

An unseasonal wind lashed at her coat as she forced her way along Harley Street towards the consulting rooms of Sir Francis Morley. She knew what she was doing was improper, a gross misuse of her position of authority within the European Broadcasting Corporation, but frankly she didn't care any more. She simply had to know the truth, and Sir Francis Morley was well placed to give it to her. Arriving at the imposing Georgian mansion where he practised, she pushed open the front door and, with a deep breath, entered the building.

"Can I help you?" came a sonorous voice from somewhere within a mousy lady sitting behind a large mahogany desk.

"Rachel McNie," Rachel muttered, removing her coat and hanging it purposefully on the coathanger.

"Ah yes, Mrs McNie. Sir Francis is expecting you."

The mousy lady with the deep voice rose to her full five feet and ushered her upstairs past an impressive array of expensive furniture and old paintings.

"This is Sir Francis' office. Do please go in."

The furniture in the room she had entered made the pieces in the hall look like cheap junk. This was the inner sanctum designed to impress the most opulent of clients, no doubt to reassure them that their exhorbitant fees were going to a good cause.

Sir Francis, although not himself a particularly impressive physical specimen, made up for his inadequacies with his fine display of plumage. His finely cut Saville Row suit, his old Etonian tie, his heavy gold ring, all served to complement and reinforce the tangible surroundings of his private parlour.

"Mrs McNie," he said, rising from his chair and approaching her with a warm smile. "How good of you to come and see me. I do not believe we have ever had the pleasure."

With a broad flourish of his arm, he invited her to sit in one of the two Queen Anne chairs carefully positioned by the fireplace. When they were settled he looked at her steadily over his pince-nez for several seconds before speaking.

"I expect you have come to discuss with me the new groundrules for media coverage in my capacity as chairman of the Committee of Independent Medical Advisors on the White Death. Am I right?"

Rachel shifted uncomfortably in her chair.

"No," she said bluntly.

Sir Francis looked at her with surprise.

"No," he repeated at last. "Then to what do I owe the pleasure?"

"I have come to seek your advice on a personal matter."

"I see," he said calmly. "But I had understood from my secretary that your visit was in your professional capacity."

Rachel braced herself.

"I lied," she said bluntly.

Sir Francis raised one eyebrow slightly.

"Mrs McNie, I wonder if you could explain yourself?"

"I want your help. I can't get any real answers from anyone else and so I've come to you. It's about my husband and children. They've contracted the White Death under circumstances I do not fully understand."

All doubt vanished, Sir Francis rose imperiously to his feet and moved purposefully towards his desk.

"I'm sorry to hear that, Mrs McNie. But I'm afraid that in my position I am not at liberty to discuss the matter with you further. I'm sure your family practitioner, or perhaps one of the new Care Centre Information Bureaux, will be able to provide you with councilling in your difficult personal circumstances. And now, if you'll excuse me . . ."

His hand reached out for the buzzer to summon his secretary.

Rachel took a deep breath.

"Don't!" she ordered.

Sir Francis froze, as if she had produced a pistol and was pointing it straight at his chest.

"I beg your pardon?" was the best he could manage.

Rachel rose from her chair. It was a trick she had learnt early in her career – never stay seated when your adversary is standing. Fixing him with an icy glare, she pulled a single sheet of paper from her handbag and held it up. On the paper, written in large capital letters, was a name: 'Jessica Greenbaum'.

Sir Francis resumed his seat and studied her carefully for a few moments.

"The case was closed over ten years ago. You know that. It was an absurd accusation in the gutter press. My name was cleared and I was awarded substantial damages in the High Court."

Rachel's lips cracked into a thin smile.

"The case was closed because of lack of evidence. As you may or may not recall, I was assigned to investigate the allegations, and I believe I now have the evidence that would convict you in court."

Sir Francis snorted.

"Nonsense," he muttered. "If you had found any evidence, my dear Mrs McNie, I am sure you would have produced it at the time."

Rachel smiled grimly. This was going to be a long shot.

"Oh, you're so touchingly innocent of our little ways in the news industry, Sir Francis. Journalism's a tough business these days. You have to keep one step ahead of the competition. I thought you might be useful one day, so I withheld some evidence I'd stumbled across. After all, I'm not a police officer, am I? It's not really my business."

"You're lying. There is no evidence. You're making the whole cock-and-bull story up as you go along."

Rachel smiled sweetly.

"It's been a pleasure, Sir Francis. I'm flying to Vienna tonight, so I'll mention our little chat to François Dupont and see if we can fix up some prime time for a special feature. Perhaps an edition of 'Justice Hotspot'. My feeling is the public would enjoy a little light relief in these trying times."

Sir Francis rose from his chair and moved swiftly to block the door.

"My dear Mrs McNie," he said in the most obsequious tone he could muster. "On reflection, I am sure I will be able to help you with your personal difficulties. Do please sit down again."

Rachel turned to face him but remained standing. Her voice was icy cold.

"You suggested earlier on that I go to my family practitioner or to one of the Information Bureaux for advice about my situation. Well, I did go. I went to ask how it is possible that a woman can be married to a carrier, having regular and highly participative unprotected sexual intercourse with him, and not catch the disease. I also tried to establish how probable it is that all three of my children should become infected while I did not. But wherever I went, I was met by a wall of silence. Sympathy, yes, but answers, no. Now I ask you the same questions. The background to my case is written down here."

Sir Francis took the sheets of paper she handed him and read them through several times before speaking.

"You asked me two questions and I will address them in reverse order. Looking through this, I note that your husband had the main responsibility for the children's welfare. As such he could have infected all three of them relatively easily. I do not see that it is particularly improbable that this should have occurred. But on the other question, if as you say you were engaged in regular unprotected intercourse with your husband, then I must admit that I am puzzled at your failure to contract the disease from him. Although it seems a cruel kind of luck, it would simply appear that you have been a very lucky lady."

"How lucky? Just how lucky am I? In what percentage of cases under these circumstances would a man fail to infect his wife?"

Sir Francis rose to his feet.

"You will excuse me, please, but I must refer to my records if you require an exact answer."

He walked over to a small computer terminal beside his desk and remained deep in concentration for what seemed like an eternity. But eventually, he raised his head.

"As I say," he said slowly, "you appear to be a very lucky lady indeed. This computer terminal is directly connected to the data banks of the Central Disease Monitoring Unit in Warsaw. Across Europe in the weeks since systematic screening began, many million cases have been reported where the disease could plausibly have been passed on through unprotected heterosexual intercourse."

Rachel approached the desk.

"But how many well-documented cases are there of unprotected sexual contact failing to result in transmission?"

Sir Francis pressed the screen several more times, as if he himself could hardly believe the figure he was seeing before him. After a long time he rose slowly to his feet and turned to face her.

"Forty-seven," he murmured in a voice so quiet it was scarcely audible. "As far as I can see you are one of only forty-seven."

SURREY, ENGLAND, MAY 2005

She threw the remains of her cheese sandwich into the kitchen bin and dialled the number for the twentieth time that evening.

A face appeared, the young smiling face of the girl she had spoken to on each of her previous calls.

"Hallo, this is the Aldershot Care Centre. Can I help you?"

Rachel tried to control the anger boiling up within her at the girl's sing-song voice.

"Yes please, I'd like you to help me in exactly the same way as on the other nineteen times I've spoken to you this evening."

The girl focussed her eyes on the image before her, something she apparently found a considerable strain.

"Oh, it's you. Your husband. I'll try and connect you."

She stared to one side, as if looking for the correct extension number on a computer screen.

"It's 46926," Rachel interrupted, "I would have thought you'd have learnt it off by heart by now."

The girl showed no sign of being offended.

"Thanks."

There was a pause.

"Sorry. The line's still engaged."

"What! Still? Are you really sure?"

"Last time I spoke to you I checked with the engineer. He said the line was in order."

Rachel glanced at the clock on the kitchen wall.

"Look. I've been trying to reach my husband for over three hours. Every time I get you on the phone you tell me the line's engaged. It can't be."

"Sorry," the girl's sing-song voice droned on, "but the engineer has checked the line and he tells me it's working fine."

"Couldn't you break into the call, please? Tell him his wife wants to speak with him urgently."

"Sorry. That's not permitted."

"Could you leave a message for him then? Tell him to ring me."

"Sorry. That's not permitted either."

Rachel felt her nerve beginning to break.

"Well, could you give me a call when the line comes free please? Surely you can do something to help. He's my husband, for God's sake, and all I've got is this bloody videophone. Surely you can understand that."

Again the sing-song voice. It would probably have sounded cute to teenage boys at a school dance, but now it began to assume the terrifying menace that is the natural accompaniment of idiocy in positions of power.

"Sorry. It's not permitted. Please can you call again."

Rachel flicked the switch on the videophone and the screen went dead. Another second and she would have screamed abuse at the girl, and that would have achieved precisely nothing.

The blank videoscreen taunted her silently. Perhaps her father was right about videophones. Perhaps they really were the work of the devil.

What on earth was Tom doing talking to someone else all evening? Didn't he know she was trying to speak to him? And why didn't he call her? Not for the first time that evening, she couldn't help

42

but wonder whether he was talking to another woman.

Yet it was a ridiculous notion. The very thought of her Tom with another woman was completely absurd. He couldn't possibly have been with another woman. He must have caught it some other way.

She finished making two mugs of coffee and carried them through to her father. He had opened the French doors in the living room and was sitting out on the patio in a garden chair, gazing silently down the garden into the evening gloom.

Rachel approached him quietly and carefully placed his cup of coffee on the ground beside him. Strangely enough, he was the one redeeming feature of the daily living nightmare she had been enduring since Tom and the kids had gone. In the past, as an adult no less than as a teenager, there had always been a silent barrier between them, a carefully concealed strain that stemmed from what Rachel had always supposed was their different outlooks on life. Only now, in this time of acute personal crisis, had she begun to realise just how close they had always been.

Her father looked up.

"Ah, coffee at last," he said. "I was hoping you'd bring some out when you'd finished." He paused, looking sadly at his daughter's desolate face. "No joy this time either, eh?"

She shook her head, and suddenly she could feel the tears welling up inside her.

"They're just so bloody unhelpful, dad, that's what really gets me. Why can't they be more . . . more human?"

Her father started to rise to his feet, groping at the side of his chair for his stick.

"Don't get up, dad," she said, forcing a smile to her lips. It was strange how his very frailty actually helped her to cope. "I'll be all right."

He slumped back gratefully into his chair and she picked up the coffee and handed it to him.

"Rachel," he said quietly, "I saw something interesting on your television before I came out here. A special report about the disease broadcast live from that data place in Warsaw you told me about."

She looked at him with interest.

"Didn't you tell me that doctor fellow told you there were only forty-seven known cases where the disease had failed to be transmitted by sexual intercourse?"

"Unprotected sex. Yes."

Her father nodded towards the television in the living room.

"Well, that's not what they said on there."

She looked at him sharply.

"They didn't?"

"Not at all. Apparently there's about a one in five chance of not picking it up. That fellow you spoke to must have got his facts muddled."

"Are you sure. dad?"

Her father grunted.

"I know I'm pretty old and infirm these days, my dear, but I'm not senile yet. I still know when something's important."

She looked at her father's face. He so much wanted to take her pain away, it must be hard on him to know there was nothing he could really do. She leant over and kissed him gently on the cheek.

"Sorry, dad. I suppose I should be pleased he got his facts wrong. I've been worried sick about being one of only forty-seven."

"What are you going to do?"

"Do? Do about what?"

"About that doctor? Maybe he was lying to you deliberately."

"Why should he do that?"

"I don't know. But he's chairman of an expert medical committee. He should know what he's talking about."

She remembered the look of surprise on Sir Francis' face as he had checked and double-checked the figure on his computer screen.

"I'm not going to do anything, dad. I'm sure the figure on television is the right one. There's no reason why they should make it up."

Her father looked at her.

"Fancy a wee dram before bed?" he asked. "Take your mind off your sorrows and help you sleep."

She thought of the sleeping tablets upstairs in the bedroom. One day she might mix them with the Scotch, but not yet.

"Not for me thanks, dad, but I'll get one for you."

She rose and fetched the whisky bottle and a glass from the living room. As she returned, she could see that her father was eyeing her thoughtfully.

"Has it changed the way you think, Rachel?" he asked.

She turned and smiled weakly at him.

"Think?"

"About your work. You're part of this new policy, aren't you? You're backing the government line."

She shrugged.

"I didn't make the policy, but you're right that I'm helping to implement it."

She poured out a large whisky, and then poured in a bit more for good measure. It seemed only reasonable to suppose that her father was having some pretty rough nights too.

"Funnily enough, dad," she said, "it makes me feel better about what I'm having to do at work. Stronger. Morally stronger."

She handed him the whisky and sat down again.

"It's odd," she continued, "but I used to feel guilty that others were suffering from the controls but I wasn't. Now I'm suffering as much as anybody. But it makes me even more convinced that what we're doing is right." She laughed drily. "Look at me. How long would I have stayed clean with my whole family infected? It would have got me soon. And the kids. Sooner or later they would have given it to some other kids, and then some other mother would have to go through the same torments as me. No, dad, it may seem hard but it's better this way, it really is."

Her father downed the whisky in one gulp and reached for his stick.

"I'm away to my bed."

She helped him to his feet and watched as he slowly made his way towards the French doors.

"Goodnight, dad," she said, "and thanks for being here."

He reached the door and turned to face her.

"I know it's hard now, but you'll pull through this thing," he said softly. "I was almost exactly your age when your mother passed away. Then it was you that helped me pull through, so now I suppose it's my turn."

And without waiting for an answer he quietly turned and left.

Rachel sat for a while in the chair her father had just vacated. But the warm summer air filled with the heavy scent of Tom's lovingly nurtured plants stirred up too many images of happier times. She rose and returned to the living room.

"On!" she ordered as soon as she had closed the French doors, and the television hummed into life.

"Channel 8!" she commanded, and the television switched obediently to the news channel. Ever since her childhood days news had served as a relief to life's personal crises, a reminder that there was a wider world beyond the private one.

She sat down listlessly in an armchair and tried to concentrate on the image before her. The screen was filled with a shot of the Commission headquarters in New Vienna – the only building taller than the offices of the European Broadcasting Corporation she knew so well. An announcer Rachel knew personally from the days when she had herself worked in the newsroom was just beginning his evening report.

"The new Commissioner for the Environment, Dmitri Alexandrov, today announced sweeping new restrictions on the use of the private motor car as part of a radical restructuring of Europe's transport strategy. As from next September, certain areas will be designated as 'pollution control zones' and cars will require a special permit in order to travel within them. Other zones will be classified as 'congestion zones' and cars will be required to hold a permit in order to enter during peak hours. The timing of these announcements appears to coincide with the major expansion in funding for the rail networks that was announced yesterday by the Transport Commissioner. I spoke to Mr Alexandrov immediately after the changes had been announced."

The picture switched to Alexandrov's smiling face, speaking as usual from the viewing platform at the very top of the Commission building.

"Mr Alexandrov," the interviewer began, "many people, particularly those used to travelling regularly by car in these new zones, are going to find the new restrictions very inconvenient. Were they really necessary?"

Alexandrov smiled reassuringly. He was a Green Party man, brought into the Commission by Vintner partly in recognition of the vital support given by the Greens in Parliament to Vintner's accession and partly in order to give substance to what was being called the 'government of European unity'. But despite being Green, and therefore almost by definition rather eccentric in his outlook, it appeared that power had already knocked off the worst of the rough edges from his manner. As he smiled sweetly at the viewers, he almost looked like a normal politician.

"People who travel by car must now recognise the damage they are causing to the environment, both locally and globally," he began. "For too long we have allowed short term expediency to override our longer term environmental interests."

The smile grew broader and even more reassuring as he switched up into a higher gear.

"This is the beginning of a new age, a new age in which Mankind will live in harmony with nature and not struggle against it. These measures are merely the first steps in a major programme the Commission is proposing to clean up our continent and, insofar as it is within our power, the world at large."

The interviewer changed tack.

"Some people may regard these policies as reflecting an undue

46

amount of Green Party influence over policy within the new Commission. Would you care to comment on that suggestion?"

"The new transport policy we are developing is the result of cross-party consensus."

"Mr Alexandrov, you said we could expect further measures from your department soon. Could you give us any indication of the areas you are currently examining?"

"Certainly. We are particularly concerned about achieving lower levels of industrial pollution, and will be introducing new and more stringent standards in this field. The success of this policy will determine our ability to tackle the major issue of water pollution which is I know an area of great public concern."

"But won't higher pollution standards mean yet higher prices for the consumer?"

Alexandrov nodded.

"They probably will. But again, consumers must be made to recognise the underlying cost of everything they buy and use. We should not simply pass on these costs to other people, irrespective of whether those affected live in Europe or abroad."

"Mr Alexandrov, some people might argue that the epidemic currently sweeping through the world outside the European safe zone will eventually cause such a dramatic reduction in world population that many of our global environmental problems will be allieviated without any further action by governments. Would you care to comment on this view?"

"The White Death is a global tragedy. Nobody in their right minds would welcome the suffering it brings. As you will be aware, the European Community has repeatedly advised other nations to follow our example and introduce rigorous control measures as soon as possible. Without wishing to interfere in their internal affairs in any way, we are extremely concerned at the consequences of their failure so far to do so."

"But given the fact that they have failed to take action, do you not feel as Environment Commissioner that this particular cloud may have a silver lining?"

Alexandrov looked angry.

"As I have already said, the White Death is a tragedy for Mankind. I utterly reject the notion that sensible environmental policies require death on a huge scale."

Alexandrov's image disappeared to be replaced by that of the main news announcer in the studio.

"And now for the latest snooker results . . ."

"Off!" Rachel commanded, leaning back wearily in her chair. Soon, unavoidably, she would have to face the darkness of another night alone with nothing but her sleeping pills.

For several minutes she sat motionless, alone with her sombre thoughts, but then, suddenly, the doorbell rang.

"Exterior view!" she ordered, and the television screen was filled with a closed circuit picture of the person standing by the front door.

"Jesus!" she exclaimed, staring in disbelief at the tall figure of François Dupont. He was standing erect, waiting patiently for the door to be opened.

She had not seen him in person since their bruising encounter in St Stephan's. On one occasion since then, a few days before her father had told her about Tom and the kids, she had spoken to him in connection with work, but neither of them had made any reference to their previous meeting. She had assumed he had taken the hint.

The figure waiting by the door pressed the bell again and she hastened to open it.

"François!" she said. Part of her found his intrusion in her time of suffering tasteless, particularly in the light of the words they had exchanged in Vienna. But she could not help but also feel a sense of relief that he had come.

"I heard the news," he murmured. "I'm so sorry."

She held the door open and let him pass.

"I didn't even know you were in London," she said.

"I flew in tonight."

He looked rather forlorn, as if he wasn't sure whether she'd welcome him or throw him out.

"Well, you'd better come in. Did you come to London just to see me?"

Dupont remained motionless.

"Yes. But perhaps I shouldn't have." He hesitated. "If you object to my intrusion, I'll go again."

He made as if to leave.

Rachel smiled at him. The hangdog look, the hesitation. The man knew he was doing something wrong, but still she didn't want him to go.

"Don't be silly, François," she said. "Of course I'm pleased to see you."

Dupont followed her through to the living room. But still he looked ill at ease, uncharacteristically ill at ease for a man who usually cut such a commanding figure.

"I take it this is a personal call," she asked. "I don't have to call you 'sir'?"

Dupont flashed a weak smile at her.

"I know I've done wrong," he said. "I really should have stayed away."

Rachel watched him as he stared gloomily through the French windows into the garden. She thought of Tom, but Tom seemed a very long way away.

"Maybe you did, François, but I'm still glad you came."

He turned to face her.

"I haven't come to take advantage of this awful situation you're in. Please believe that. I've come because I cared. I thought you might be lonely."

The words cut through her like a knife. For at least thirty-five of her thirty-nine years, ever since she had tired of the sheep, she had been fighting loneliness. Tom had only ever eased the pain, but now Tom was gone for ever, lost from view behind a videophone and a girl with a sing-song voice.

"I am," she said.

Dupont smiled, revealing a gentleness of such extraordinary depth that it would have shocked and astonished the outside world. He sat down heavily in the armchair she had recently vacated.

"That makes two of us," he said. He looked at the empty whisky glass she had brought in from the garden.

"Been taking it out on the Scotch?"

Rachel shook her head.

"Nope. Sleeping pills. If you'd come half-an-hour later I'd have been out cold. My father was drinking the whisky before he went to bed."

Dupont remained silent for a while.

"I frightened you in Vienna, didn't I?"

She hesitated before replying.

"Yes, François, you did. To be perfectly frank I thought you wanted to start some kind of affair."

Dupont looked away.

"Perhaps I did, but maybe not in the way you supposed."

She looked at him with a puzzled expression.

"It's your companionship I value, Rachel. Of all the thousands of people I know, I value your companionship more than that of the rest of them put together. I promise you that's all I'm looking for."

He paused, as if struggling to find the right words.

"You don't need to worry," he said at last, "I'm not looking for any kind of sexual relationship. I know your love for Tom would never allow such a thing."

Rachel flinched. He was right of course. She was still loyal to Tom, even now he was locked away, but part of her still wished he hadn't said it quite so bluntly.

"I'm sorry," she said quietly. "Maybe I jumped the gun."

Dupont looked at her thoughtfully.

"Is there any part of my feelings towards you that is reciprocated," he asked, "any part at all?"

Rachel touched his arm. If Tom had been there maybe she would have reacted differently. But Tom wasn't there. He wasn't ever going to be there again. And she was so terrifyingly alone.

"More than I can say," she murmured softly.

Dupont smiled gently at her. If he had reached out to hold her she would have accepted the embrace willingly, but he remained passively in his chair. Only his face showed the relief he felt that her earlier rejection had been reversed.

"Have you been able to speak to Tom and the children yet?"

She nodded.

"Yesterday. Today the line's been engaged all evening."

"And are they comfortable?"

"Yes, insofar as it's possible to be comfortable in a prison. He's been given an old army flat in Aldershot while he sorts himself out. I've sent on all their stuff to them, even Tom's precious cello."

She thought of Tom, consoling himself and the children by playing his beloved Bach on the cello, and suddenly, uncontrollable, the tears began to flow down her face. Dupont leant forward to where she was sitting and placed his hand gently on her arm while she wept. It was a long, long time before she had recovered herself sufficiently to speak.

"I'm sorry, François. It wasn't fair of me to inflict that on you."

He released her arm and sank back into his chair.

"Of course you will weep. It would be a sign of madness if you did not weep."

For a long time there was silence. Finally it was Rachel who spoke.

"I really can't decide what it is about you that I like so much, François."

"Meaning?"

"I can't decide whether it's your strength or your weakness."

He laughed.

"Do you think I am a strong man, then?" he asked with a wry smile.

"The world does."

"But do you?"

"Yes. Probably stronger than you let on, even to the world."

"Why?"

"The world thinks you're a champion of civil liberties, a champion with a killer instinct for tracking down injustice and misuse of power wherever it appears. Ironic in present circumstances, perhaps, but I still think that's how you're perceived by the public at large. But I think there's more to you than that. A hidden sincerity, perhaps. That's why you've had the courage to face up to the logic of this disease so honestly when others have simply run away."

He grunted.

"Maybe," he muttered, a strangely distant look on his face, "but I often have doubts about the course I am set upon. Grave, grave doubts."

"Doubts you want to share with me?" she asked.

He smiled, as if she had seen through the real purpose of his visit.

"There is so much about the present situation that is not as it seems," he murmured, "so very very much. Who, for example, do you think is the leading figure in the ruling oligarchy we discussed the other day in Vienna?"

"Why, Vintner, I suppose. The President."

Dupont laughed cynically.

"Vintner is just a little fool. A front-man was needed to give Bignoletto and the other generals the constitutional pretext they needed to back the new government. He fulfilled his role well enough, I suppose."

Rachel stared at him in astonishment. The sheepish look with which he had arrived had completely vanished, to be replaced by an expression of taut calculating intellect that must have terrified his enemies.

"You?" she mouthed.

He nodded slowly.

"I'm glad I fooled you. If you didn't see through it then nobody did."

"You mean he was acting as your puppet?"

Dupont shrugged casually.

"It wasn't that hard. I did it years ago, back when he was running around on the fringes of Dutch environmental politics."

"How? Blackmail?"

"You must be joking, Rachel. Oh, I've blackmailed people sometimes, I don't deny it. People like the Commissioner who appointed me as head of the European Broadcasting Corporation, for example.

But not Vintner. I wanted him for something special. Blackmail's
O.K. in its place, but it always brings resentment in its wake. For
a really durable relationship, you need something stronger. Vintner
was ambitious, hungry for a power he would never have achieved
on his own. So I advised him to back away from his hothead colleagues
and become a conventional politician with a genuine interest in environmental affairs. The way the environment was disintegrating in the
late 1990s, I knew it would only be a matter of time before he would
come in useful. It just so happened that he came in even more useful
than I had anticipated."

"So he's not exactly in your pocket, then."

"The trouble with Nicklaas Vintner is that his vaunting ambition
is matched by neither political acumen nor intellectual substance.
But he has believed in me, and as you have probably noticed I am
not short of either of these qualities, although I could perhaps do
with a trifle more modesty."

"You mean he does exactly what you say? Vintner asks you what
to do."

Dupont frowned.

"He did at first. Always had done. But now I'm getting worried.
That's partly why I came to see you tonight."

"About Vintner?"

"Yes. I hope you don't mind." He hesitated. "You see, last time
you spoke to me you were angry because I had organised the coup
without consulting you first."

Rachel looked at him with surprise.

"I wasn't angry with you, François. I just said as a matter of record
that you did not consult with me in the proper sense of the word."

"Perhaps. Anyway, this time I am going to take you into my confidence, and seek your advice before I take any irrevocable steps. And
if you don't approve, I won't go ahead. Simple."

Rachel stared at him in outright amazement. Sitting opposite her
was the man who claimed to be the most powerful individual in Europe
and he was suggesting that she, Rachel Mary McNie, could exert
an effective veto over his actions.

"I don't understand," she murmured. "Why me? Why anyone?"

It was only for a fraction of a second, but she was sure she glimpsed
a look of fear pass across his face. But before she could be certain,
the look had vanished.

"Like I say, I've decided I trust you. I trust your judgement. I
know I'm a persuasive man, and now I want the chance to persuade
you that what I am doing is right. Perhaps it's my way of reassuring

myself that I'm not mad."

Rachel swallowed hard.

"O.K., François, tell me what it is you're proposing. But I warn you, if I don't agree I won't pretend I do. And that will put your words to a hard test."

Dupont sat down again and closed his eyes.

"I'd not reckoned on it, but Vintner is becoming dangerous," he began. "Not only Vintner, but several other people who have been drawn into the ruling group. Marshall Bignoletto, for example. And also Alexandrov, the Commissioner for the Environment."

"Dangerous, you say?"

"Each wields enormous power in his own right: Vintner because he is President, Bignoletto because he heads the armed forces, and Alexandrov as effective leader of the Green Party organisation. I suspect they are on the point of forming a kind of triumvirate with the express intention of excluding me from influence. I fear they may even try to arrest me."

"But why? I thought you were all in on it together."

"Partly because they are frightened of me, partly because they are piecing together a policy programme to which they know I am violently opposed. Bignoletto cares about nothing but turning society into a giant military machine in which everyone is a soldier subject to strict military discipline. He's like a Stalinist throwback, wanting to construct a rigidly hierarchal society in which everybody knows their place."

"But what about Alexandrov. I wouldn't have supposed that he would be too happy with that. The Green Party has always struck me as virulently hostile to the military."

"Oh, but you do them an injustice, Rachel. Remember, they were the only political party prior to the take-over that held together with any kind of cohesion. Their form of democratic centralism was highly reminiscent of the totalitarian parties of the mid and late twentieth century. It was their very cohesion that made it necessary to win their thirty percent block of votes in Parliament when Vintner made his grab for power. That is why Alexandrov and the other Greens were brought into the Commission in the first place, it was the price we had to pay to gain their support. But believe me, Rachel, people like Alexandrov are not opposed to military-style discipline provided that it serves their purposes and not somebody else's."

"So are you telling me that is the deal Bignoletto and Alexandrov have now struck? A highly regimented society based on ecologically sound principles. Is that the future they're aiming for?"

Dupont nodded.

"Yes. Both Alexandrov and Bignoletto are happy to leave Vintner in nominal charge for the moment while they pull the strings between them. But that's not all. As well as sharing a contempt for Western liberal values, I believe they are also planning to use Europe's growing strength as other nations succomb to the disease in order to embark on some kind of crazy military adventure. They haven't discussed it with me, of course, but I fear that Alexandrov has become convinced of the need to extend his power to other continents in order to avert global environmental catastrophe."

"War?" she exclaimed. "But war is the last thing the world needs just at the moment."

"Precisely," replied Dupont gloomily. "But it gets worse, I'm afraid. Bignoletto and Alexandrov are both hardliners on the White Death. I hinted as much when I spoke to you in Vienna. They share highly reactionary attitudes to the carriers of the disease and seem to believe that if Europeans had led a purer, cleaner life they would not have been affected. They regard the disease as a cancer that needs to be swiftly and surgically excised from our society."

Rachel stared at him in horror. In her mind she could see Tom and her children in their tiny flat in Aldershot. They were surrounded by the military, entirely at their mercy.

"At first they were arguing for minimum expenditure on the camps," Dupont continued. "They argued that people who'd become infected didn't deserve better. I used my influence over Vintner to overrule them. Now I'm frightened they've gone one step further in their thinking."

"Oh my God, François, surely they can't be proposing to ..."

"To eliminate the carriers completely. Not wait for them to die peacefully in their beds. I can't be sure, Rachel, because they don't dare discuss it openly, but I very much fear that is what is at the back of their minds. They see the Care Centres as a futile waste of resources which could be better devoted to overseas military campaigns."

"I can see why you're worried, François, but what exactly do you propose to do about it?" Rachel asked.

Dupont looked her straight in the eyes.

"I propose to take absolute power myself."

"What? You mean directly, as President?"

"Yes, until such time as the present crisis is over and the burden can be safely transferred to other shoulders."

"But how can you do that? Surely Vintner and the others won't allow you to."

Dupont eyes flashed menacingly, like a tiger tracking its prey.

"I think I still have time. Many of the Commissioners are my place-men, even though Vintner formally secured their appointment. I think I will have a majority if I act against him resolutely now. And with the vote of the Commission behind me I will be able to oust Bignoletto as Commander-in-Chief of the European Defence Force in favour of a less dangerous general. As for Alexandrov, his support was essential when Parliament still had a say, but now he can be quietly marginalised and eventually removed from office altogether."

"And if you wait? What will happen if you wait and see how things develop?"

"But that's the point, Rachel. If I wait, Vintner will move first. Perhaps he has moved already, perhaps he is moving this very evening while I'm sitting here. I just don't know. But when he does, my place-men in the Commission will be replaced by Alexandrov's or Bignolet-to's. And the moment that happens, their dictatorship will become unstoppable."

Rachel looked at him silently for a while.

"But if you act, François, your dictatorship will become unstopp-able. Is there not a danger in that, too?"

He smiled at her grimly and slowly nodded his head.

"That's the trouble when democracy fails, isn't it, Rachel? Some-body has to play God. But it seems to come down to a simple choice. It's either them, or it's me."

Dupont knelt down beside her and took both her hands in his.

"But like I say, maybe you're the one playing God right now. So tell me, Rachel, do I act, or do I not?"

NEW VIENNA, AUSTRIA, SEPTEMBER 2006

The view on a starlit midsummer night from the window of Europe's highest flat was understandably magnificent. Far, far below, the tiny floodlit carriages of the Big Wheel in the famous Praterstern fair-ground crawled slowly round, taking tourists high above the rooftops of Old Vienna as they had done for over a hundred years. Every few minutes they would pause, allowing passengers to board and alight, before grinding laboriously on their way. From close quarters the fine old iron structure of the Big Wheel still looked as magnificent as on the day it had been opened, but from where she was standing, in Dupont's flat on the top floor of the Commission building, it seemed like nothing more than an insignificant child's toy.

She remembered the day Dupont had come to her house that night so many months before as if it were only yesterday. He had come late, minutes before she had taken sleeping tablets to mask the bitter pain of separation from her family, and he had asked her to play God.

From where she was standing it was easy to believe you were God, looking down from heaven at the tiny mortals leading their insignificant lives in the city so very far below. Her gaze moved upwards into the night sky. The moon, low down on the horizon above the distant expanse of the wide Hungarian plain, was escorted by a pale blue halo of reflected sunlight, and she wondered whether another higher God was looking down on her.

For in all honesty she had to admit she had become a kind of God, if being a God meant having immense powers over the lives of ordinary people. It was not a job she had sought, but Dupont had thrust it upon her with all his inexhaustible charm and logic. He had asked her to act as his conscience, to reassure him that his actions were sane, and she had accepted the challenge. And when he finally wrested absolute power over Greater Europe and become its ruler, she had moved into his Presidential flat in New Vienna in order to be by his side, casting aside her job and all her previous life.

François Dupont had proved himself to be a benevolent despot, steering Europe skilfully through the political minefields of a world striken by catastrophe on such a grand scale. In the more advanced regions of the globe, in North America, in Australasia, in Japan and the other prosperous East Asian economies, something approximating to the European model of disease control had eventually been adopted, but not before the illness had affected a far higher percentage of the population than in Dupont's Europe. And as a logical consequence of delay, the clampdown when it had come in these other countries had been less palatable, the care offered to the sufferers less munificent, and the political repression with which it was associated correspondingly more severe.

But if the world's rich had finally learnt to harness the power of the White Death, the vast majority of the world's population, those unfortunate enough to live in the poorer countries of Asia, of Africa and of Latin America, were not so fortunate. Without the economic resources to contain it, the plague swept relentlessly on its path, becoming ever stronger and more infectious as time went by. Complacency was followed by panic. Panic was followed by violence. And now, finally, it began to look as if violence was being followed by the empty silence of despair.

For the world's poorest people, the disease offered a painfree death, perhaps a better death than the starvation they feared with every new crop failure. And for the others, for the billions of people too rich to be poor and too poor to be safe, the disease at least offered an end to the dull and growing tedium of struggling against life's petty adversities as living standards slid inexorably downwards.

Rachel touched a button and a curtain moved silently across the window before her, concealing the awesome view of heaven and earth that lay beyond. She turned and faced the room in which she was standing. On the far wall, almost filling its vast expanse, was hung a huge ornate map of Dupont's European empire, stretching from the wooded slopes of the Urals to the crashing waves of the Atlantic, from the northern wastes of Scandinavia to the warm gentle beaches of the Mediterranean. Within that area, people were safe, the disease had been held at bay. And although the controls were strict, the screening rigorously enforced, European life on a day-to-day level continued much as before.

Dupont had dealt with the troublesome triumvirate of Vintner, Bignoletto and Alexandrov with his customary ruthlessness. She smiled quietly to herself as she remembered the way he had reacted to her words on that crucial night some sixteen months before. He had knelt patiently beside her and held her hands, he had asked her tenderly for her blessing and she had given it. But the very next second, all trace of tenderness had vanished as he strode into her kitchen and pressed the button on the videophone. Within seconds, he had awoken one of his most trusted allies on the Commission and told him that the plot they had discussed would be sprung at the Commission meeting planned for the following morning at nine o'clock. Then, with a gentle kiss on her forehead, he had swept out of her home to catch the plane back to Vienna. By noon the following day, Vintner, Bignoletto and Alexandrov were all in prison, their fate sealed, and François Dupont was the new President of Greater Europe.

But there was to be no witchhunt. No further arrests followed, and if others had been involved with the plots hatched by the triumvirate, they were given the opportunity to quietly realign themselves with the new master. It seemed a lifetime's examination of the machinations and psychology of Europe's ruling class had given Dupont considerable insight into how to be a ruler himself. He knew that the people with whom he was dealing posed a potential threat to him, they were themselves manipulators with considerable political skills. He judged that a climate of fear would achieve little and jeopardise much, and so he had played on their vaunting ambition instead, promoting those who served him well and demoting those who failed to offer support. And almost without exception they had taken the bait, tripping over each other to prove their worth to the new leader.

It was hard for some to accept it, but in truth Europe had become a better place to live for those who remained clean. Dupont's removal of Alexandrov from the political scene did not bring to an end the measures he had planned to improve the European environment. The water was drinkable now, the power stations were cleaner, the acidity of the rain was falling, tighter controls were reducing the frequency of the tragic environmental 'accidents' which had so bugged European life in the last years of the twentieth century and the first years of the twenty-first. Most experts agreed that the continent was cleaner than at any time since the advent of the First Industrial Revolution.

Rachel walked over to the huge mahogany desk in the corner of the room and picked up the small photograph of Dupont that stood in the corner. She had feared that power on such a huge scale would corrupt him, that he would become arrogant and dismissive of the views of others. She had feared these things even as she had told him to make his bid for power. But strangely enough the reverse process had occurred. Far from becoming overbearing, he had instead become more relaxed in the role in which he found himself. He listened to his advisors carefully before taking decisions, devolving power wherever possible to lower levels. He had allowed criticism of his rule to be articulated through the national and regional media. He had even restored an element of genuine democracy into regional government, albeit within carefully defined limits.

From the beginning of their relationship, Rachel had detected a tenderness in François Dupont. And as she looked at his photograph, she knew she now loved him more than she had ever loved any other man.

Despite herself, she replaced the photograph of Dupont on the desk and picked up the photograph of Tom and her children sitting beside it. None of them had yet developed any symptoms, and after more than a year she had come to hope they would be spared, allowed to live out their full natural lives in a place where they could live a life of decency without fear of bringing harm to others. Tom had decided to take the children to a coastal Care Centre in the south of Spain and whenever they wanted to the children were able to play on the beach and swim in the sea. And nearly every day she would speak to them, listen to their lives and tell them something of hers.

It was typical of Tom, dear sweet Tom, that he was not angered by her feelings towards François Dupont. She had told him of her plans to move to his Vienna flat, of the closeness of the relationship that had developed between them, and he had given her chosen course of action his blessing. He had laughed his kindly laugh and jokingly told her that sleeping with the President of Greater Europe was probably a pretty good second best to sleeping with him.

Rachel swiftly replaced the photograph in its place and moved away from the desk. She had not been able to bring herself to tell the truth to Tom. She knew full well that he would never have believed the truth and that the thought of her deceit would have tormented him beyond endurance. For Tom, the lie became a palatable truth but the truth would have become a bitter lie. And so she had not found the courage to tell her husband that he was still the only man with whom she had ever made love.

A muted chime in the corner of the room announced the imminent arrival of the lift. Seconds later, the door slid silently open and Dupont entered. He looked tired and drawn.

"François!" she said, approaching him and kissing his weary face gently on the cheek. "You're late tonight."

Dupont said nothing. He smiled at her reassuringly, trying without success to conceal his exhaustion, and slumped heavily into his armchair.

"Do you want a drink? Coffee?" she asked.

"A cup of tea, please, my love," he murmured.

Rachel turned towards the door to the kitchen with some distaste.

"Machine! Tea!"

'Machine's' were becoming the vogue these days amongst the more prosperous elements of European society. They were useful things, handling a great deal of menial routine work about the house. Most people programmed them to respond to silly names like Jeeves or Fritz but Rachel had refused to call it anything other than Machine.

Dupont smiled.

"It's your father's stern influence, I think," he said.

Rachel looked at him askance.

"What is?"

"The way you call it Machine. You don't like it very much, do you?"

Rachel shrugged.

"I wouldn't say that. It's just that I don't care much for the way

59

people seem to treat them like pets. It's just a machine, isn't it, so why not call it Machine?"

After a few moments Machine entered from the kitchen adjoining the living room. In a small cavity to one side, it bore a tray on which rested two delicate china cups.

"Tea is served," it announced in a voice reminiscent of a sexy girl with an injured larynx.

Rachel picked up the two cups and handed one to Dupont. She took the other and sat beside him, watching as he slowly sipped his drink. His earlier glum look had reappeared.

"You look like you had a bad day?" she said softly.

"Oh, not particularly," he muttered cynically. "There was a messy breakout from one of the Polish Care Centres that had to be put down by the army. The American Ambassador issued a particularly uncivil ultimatum over the new trade deal just when we thought we'd sewn it all up. The Joint African Congress is threatening to lob a couple of nuclear missiles at us if we don't allow a hundred thousand of their top brass sanctuary. Other than that, and the fact that I've had a lousy headache since lunchtime, everything's just fine."

Dupont attempted a smile, but it turned into a grimace.

"Do you want to talk about the problems, François? Put our heads together?"

"No," he replied. "You will advise me, one, to spend more money on the Polish Care Centre; two, to tell the Americans to get stuffed and; three, to let the Africans have limited sanctuary if they want it but on a somewhat fairer basis than they are proposing. Your reasons for this will be: one, the only reason people try to escape from Care Centres is because of local mismanagement; two, the Americans are greedy pigs who always ask for more when you concede anything to them and, three, Africans are rapidly becoming an endangered species and it would be a pity if there weren't any left. I have already acted on these opinions, which I fully share, and given the appropriate instructions."

Rachel looked at him and grinned.

"We're getting boring, aren't we? Just over a year together and we're starting to think the same way. Some people might say that was dangerous."

Dupont returned her smile. Expressing his problems seemed to have lightened the load somewhat.

"We are dangerous. Always have been. But are the available alternatives any less so?"

Rachel leant back in her chair.

"I've been thinking about that American idea," she mused.

Dupont gazed at her inquisitively. He was always rushing around, busy with affairs of state. It was accepted between them that she would remain on the sidelines, a kind of one-person think-tank on particularly intractable problems.

"We didn't think too much of it at the beginning," she continued, "but on reflection I think it might be the only feasible way forward for those countries."

The Americans had proposed to the Federation of Safe Zones – the talking shop of those rich countries with full disease control measures in place – that their own peculiarly American approach to the disease should be extended to the Third World. Instead of locking infected people into camps as the Europeans had done, the Americans had run the process in reverse. As growing panic had spread across the continent, the corporations had independently developed safe zones to which only those who could prove they were free of the disease could gain access. At first small enterprises – factories, schools, leisure centres – but later whole communities – had been organised to exclude the carriers. The government, heavily influenced by big business, had lent its support. At the end of the process the carriers, the sufferers and those who simply didn't want to be tested found themselves rather in the position of the Red Indians after the arrival of the White Man several centuries before. They were free to roam, it was just that there weren't many places left for them to go.

The Americans had now suggested to the Federation that their method be extended to the rest of the world. Corporations, backed if necessary by the military might of the rich countries, should be permitted to move into the Third World and set up miniature safe zones.

Dupont sipped his tea.

"They're materialist bastards, aren't they?" he said drily.

Rachel shook her head.

"Say what you will, François, continued supplies of raw materials from these countries are under threat. Properly controlled zones will guarantee continued production."

"But who's going to get in? Even if the zones are angled at raw materials rather than simply extracting surplus cash from frightened people, there's going to be a lot of pressure to get in. Every crackpot tribal leader, every corrupt drugs dealer, every military boss. Anyone with enough money and influence. You'll have to pay a hell of a price just to get a job cleaning the toilets in those places."

"The corporations won't do it at all if they don't make any money.

However, you could argue at the Federation for a strict code of practice. Safeguards. A reasonable proportion of places within the zones that are not rationed by money. It's better than nothing, isn't it?"

Dupont rose from his chair and walked silently towards the window. Pressing the button, the curtain slid silently apart to reveal the majestic view beyond the glass. It was something he often did when a new policy was taking shape in his mind.

"Genetic intelligence profiling," he said softly, speaking more to himself than to Rachel. "That's what we'll go for at the Federation. Even the corporations will like that; they want bright people out there working for them. Many of the rich and influential in those countries will slip through the net simply because they're bright. But everyone will be able to have a go. At least it'll be a kind of fairness."

Rachel moved closer to him.

"And the money. What if they can't pay?"

Dupont turned and kissed her gently.

"Then we will, my love. Like you've said, they're an endangered species out there." He jerked his thumb towards the kitchen. "And if we can afford those stupid housework machines, then surely we can afford to help save a few million of the world's underprivileged from the clutches of this disease."

Rachel took his arm.

"What will you do if they find a cure?" she asked suddenly.

Dupont turned and gazed at her.

"What prompted that?"

"I don't know. I was just wondering. You seem to thrive on danger, François. You're in control. You're strong. You're decisive. But sometimes I wonder whether you're like Winston Churchill. Only good in a crisis, hopeless when things get easier. Sometimes I wonder whether you're capable of living a normal life."

Dupont studied her with curiosity.

"And what, my dear Rachel, do you understand by a 'normal life'?"

She thought of Tom, the cello, the kids at bedtime. It all seemed so very long ago.

"Maybe the kind of life I lived before you swept me away," she replied.

Dupont turned away from her and gazed through the window.

"The kind of life they lead?" he asked, no trace of contempt in his voice, pointing at the city lying far below.

"Yes, I suppose so."

"Do you envy them so much?" he asked softly.

Rachel hesitated.

"François. Tom's not coming back. I know that now. My future lies with you. François . . ."

He turned to face her again, saw the tears forming in her eyes.

"Yes, my love."

She stood by the window and took his hands in hers.

"Make love to me tonight," she murmured. "For over a year I've stayed loyal to Tom, even though he believed you to be my lover. Now I want . . . I want to consummate our relationship."

Dupont remained silent for several minutes, gazing steadily into her eyes. It was almost as if he were trying to make some kind of internal calculation, although what it could be she could not grasp. She said nothing, holding his gaze for as long as she could and then looking away. He frightened her sometimes when he was like this, as the burning intensity within his soul seemed to penetrate her deeply, probing for answers to questions as yet unasked.

Then, without a word, he drew her towards him and she lost sight of his eyes. She relished the warmth of his body against hers as he pushed her back against the smooth cold glass of the window-pane. Slowly at first, but then with increasing urgency, she could feel him removing her clothes and his, but never for a moment did he release her from his grasp, never for a moment did he allow his eyes to meet with hers. And then, suddenly, he lifted her from the ground and was within her, thrusting her back against the glass so powerfully that she was fearful at first that it would break behind her, throwing them both out into the summer night beyond. But as the thrusting continued she found she no longer cared. She was already beyond the glass, flying high towards the distant moon with its pale blue halo and the stars beyond that. And now they were truly like two Gods, bound together in the life beyond the world, floating interlocked in the timeless eternity of space.

The thrusting slowed and finally stopped. Dupont lowered her to her feet and sank down on his knees, his breath heavy, his body dripping with sweat. For a while Rachel stood motionless, trying to steady her own breath, and then she too knelt down.

"François," she whispered softly.

He raised his head and briefly met her gaze before turning away and staring out into the night sky.

"One day I believe you will know me for what I really am, Rachel," he said. "And I hope . . . I pray . . . that the beauty of your love for me will withstand the terrible pain that knowledge will surely bring."

CHIEMSEE, BAVARIA, SEPTEMBER 2006

The water shimmered brightly in the late morning sun as the brightly-painted steamboat began heading out across the lake towards the Presidential summer residence. A respectful distance to one side another less picturesque craft steered the same course, piled high with the security personnel and telecommunications equipment that habitually followed the President of Greater Europe wherever he went. Rachel glanced briefly at her fellow travellers in the other craft before walking swiftly to the far side of the boat, from where she could look out over the wide expanse of the lake towards the dense pine forest on the far shore and, beyond that, the distant peaks of the northern limestone Alps rising high into the brilliant blue autumnal sky.

In her new life, her life as Dupont's mistress, it was difficult to attain the tranquil peace of obscurity. But here, standing on the deck of this graceful nineteenth-century wooden paddleboat as it chugged gently across the wide Bavarian lake of Chiemsee, it was almost possible to pretend that she was back on a summer holiday with Tom and the children.

Since she had moved in with Dupont she had understandably become the object of a great deal of media attention, some of it favourable, more of it not. After one particularly tasteless report, Dupont had asked her if he should extend the tight but limited censorship rules to cover her role in his life. But she had smiled and refused the offer, on the largely spurious grounds that the report had said nothing that wasn't absolutely true.

She glanced back at the small lakeside town from which they had just departed. The crowd which had greeted them was slowly starting to disperse, but as they had been driven in their bullet-proof car to the tiny jetty, she had been struck by the obvious sincerity with which they had greeted their unelected President. In the absence of any formal opinion polls it was difficult to obtain any fully objective measure, but the indications of his growing popularity were all too apparent to anyone with eyes to see.

Dupont approached her silently and touched her arm.

"You were surprised by the kindly reaction of the townsfolk?" he asked jokingly.

"'Kindly reaction'! That's a bit of an understatement. Those people back there were going crazy. All that cheering and flag waving. I've never seen any elected President get that kind of reaction."

Dupont said nothing, but she could see he was quietly pleased with himself. Suddenly a terrible thought passed through her mind.

"You didn't ... did you?"

Dupont gently pretended to smack her bottom, an affectionate mannerism he had allowed himself to adopt since they had begun their physical relationship.

"I have better things to do with my time than organise cheering crowds in rural villages, my love," he said.

Rachel glanced anxiously around.

"François. Not in public, please. There might be someone out there with a high resolution camera. I really don't want to be plastered all over the six o'clock news having my bottom smacked."

"But you told me quite distinctly you didn't want any censorship on these matters."

"François! You know perfectly well that's got nothing to do with it."

Dupont hung his head over the side of the boat and watched the water surge past the enormous paddle that was driving them along.

"Do you think we should stick with this summer residence, Rachel, or ask them to look out for something a bit less ostentatious? If it had been up to me, I would never have chosen a place like this."

Rachel looked at him and grinned. Sometimes, when he was relaxed like this, he reminded her of a little boy.

"François, don't lie. You know this place is perfect. It's a large château with plenty of space; it's on a secure island, and it's not too far from Vienna. The real reason you don't like it here is because it was built by Ludwig II, and you're worried that some of his lunacy might rub off on you."

"Maybe you're right," he grunted moodily, picking up a leaf that was lying on the deck and throwing it into the lake. He watched intently as the force of the water from the paddles thrust it violently aside.

"I wish to God I knew the real reason he's pressed for this summit," he muttered, his face suddenly serious.

Rachel looked at him out of the corner of her eye. She was well aware that Dupont had been fretting about something ever since James L. Goldberger, President of the United States and the only man in the world able to challenge François Dupont on equal terms, had approached him to arrange the private meeting that was to be held on the island the following day.

"I thought it was about their proposal for setting up protected zones in the Third World?" she said.

"That was the excuse. But he could have left that until the full Federation summit in two months time. I think there's more to it."

"Something he doesn't want to discuss through advisors. Something for your ears only."

"And yours. You'll be there."

Rachel turned to face him.

"What! You want me in on the summit! But I have no formal position."

"So what. You can attend as my personal advisor."

"But I haven't attended a meeting with you since we worked together at the European Broadcasting Corporation."

Dupont jerked a thumb in the general direction of the shore in a manner that seemed to indicate the rest of the world.

"They seem to have worked out our relationship. So why disappoint them."

Rachel remained silent. A change had come over François Dupont in the last few weeks. It wasn't as if he had become easier to understand, for she still frequently found his actions unpredictable, but he seemed to feel closer to her now, a closeness he clearly wanted to demonstrate publicly to the outside world.

"Like William and Mary, the monarchs who shared the British throne after 1688?"

He smiled.

"And why not?"

"Don't you think it'll make you a laughing stock?"

Dupont shrugged impatiently.

"Anyone who likes laughing will be laughing already," he muttered.

For some reason his remark hurt. She looked away.

"But why me, François?" she whispered. "I still don't really understand why you've chosen me for all this."

He looked up from the water and saw that his words had wounded her.

"Isn't it obvious why I've chosen you, Rachel?" he said. "Isn't it painfully obvious that you are the first woman I have ever loved?"

* * * * * *

The diminutive figure of James L. Goldberger stepped cautiously down the red-carpeted steps from the helicopter and shook the outstretched hand of François Dupont. Television cameras whirred and stills cameras clicked as the two most powerful men in the world shook hands for the first time and approached the podium. As the select gathering of the world's press and leading officials of the two countries clustered around and applauded politely, François Dupont approached the assembled barrage of microphones.

"It is with great pleasure," Dupont began, speaking in the casual and relaxed tone with which he habitually addressed the television cameras, "that I welcome the new President of the United States to Europe for this our first summit meeting. As you will know, the United States has been our good ally through many hard and difficult times ..."

Rachel stood patiently by Dupont's side, but instead of listening to his formal words of introduction she found herself carefully eyeing the man she already perceived to be her partner's adversary. Goldberger's surprisingly small stature was not matched by his flashing eyes, eyes which seemed to generate a kind of electricity, a nervous energy which threatened to set everything about him on fire. And now, while he awaited his opportunity to respond to Dupont's words of welcome, his eyes flicked eagerly around the assembled crowd, as if silently identifying and classifying the people he saw around him.

It had been with some considerable surprise that Vienna had received news that the United States' President was seeking a private summit with François Dupont. For although the Americans shared with Europe the rare distinction of having developed an effective strategy for containing the White Death, the rapid political developments of the last few years had given rise to a considerable degree of conflict between the world's two military giants.

American public opinion had reacted with pronounced antipathy to the coup which had swept Nicklaas Vintner to power in New Vienna. At that time, political institutions in the United States were still suffering from the general paralysis against which Dupont and the other conspirators in Europe had fought so hard. The Americans, with their powerful traditions of political liberalism and democracy, were outraged by the suppression of democratic rights and freedoms in a region of the world that numbered amongst its major cities Moscow, Warsaw, Bucharest and Prague. For while the tightly controlled European media sought every opportunity to legitimise and justify the take-over, the as yet uncontrolled US networks ruthlessly exposed the unfolding coup in Vienna for what it really was, and made frequent references to the totalitarian legacy of the countries of eastern Europe. To many on the far side of the Atlantic, it seemed as if the democratic traditions Greater Europe had inherited from its western regions had suddenly and unexpectedly been overthrown by Stalin's ghost, affording a bloodless victory to a totalitarian ethic that decades of struggle during the twentieth century had failed to achieve.

Despite some early rumblings, however, it soon became apparent that the United States' government was in no real position to influence the unfolding drama taking place in New Vienna. US land forces in Europe had long since been withdrawn, and the new rulers of Europe were careful to offer no provocation to American sensitivities that would have justified retaliation. A nuclear strike could have been threatened, but Europe's own potent strike capability, incorporating the nuclear arsenals of Britain, France and the Soviet Union, would have rendered any such threat implausible. For a while a trade embargo was considered, but it was soon realised in Washington that such a policy would have achieved little besides serious damage to the already ailing US economy.

But perhaps the biggest argument against any intervention in European affairs was the traumatic effect developments across the Atlantic were having on US public opinion. It was as if the scales were suddenly falling from people's eyes as they watched the new government in Vienna start implementing its draconian approach to the White Death, leaving Americans fearful that their own government was failing to take effective action to protect them. And so, while the government dithered, the powerhouses of American life – the giant corporations – suddenly woke up to the fact that the White Death offered an excellent opportunity to make some money. The principles of laissez faire capitalism on which the United States had prided itself for so long began to triumph once again.

American citizens began to find it increasingly hard to get around without a 'Clean Bill', as the forgery-proof certificates stating that the bearer was free of the White Death were called. Clean Bills became more important than dollar bills in daily life, offering the bearer a sense of security whenever they entered what became colloquially called a 'bug-free zone'. Try taking your children to school: no way without a Clean Bill. Try going swimming: no way without a Clean Bill. Try getting a job: no way without a Clean Bill. Try getting into a department store: no way without a Clean Bill.

But a major problem remained outside the 'bug-free zones'. People still had to live in houses where bugs might be holed up next door, they still had to walk the streets where the bug might be lurking in a passer-by. People might feel safe at work, they might feel their children were safe at school, they might feel they were safe in a restaurant or in a leisure centre, but they still didn't feel truly safe. And as the disease spread throughout the world and people watched with growing envy the relative security enjoyed by their European cousins, the pressure gradually mounted for further change.

Once again, it was the corporations which took the lead. They started buying up whole blocks and then whole towns, offering hefty financial inducements to residents to obtain a Clean Bill and even larger financial inducements to carriers to move away to other areas.

Predictably, a political backlash against these developments soon got underway, and before very long the 'Don't Get Tested' campaign was launched, organised by a number of leading politicians and civil rights groups. As the campaign gathered speed, it looked for a time as though the corporations would be frustrated in their plans for total segregation. But all predictions of imminent defeat crumbled to dust as big business fought back, publishing the names and addresses of each and every citizen who had refused their generous invitation to undergo a free test.

Shortly afterwards the shootings began. As fear stalked the land, people with Clean Bills fought back, first by smashing windows and daubing paint, later with more violent methods. The corporations denied all responsibility and condemned the attacks, but used every opportunity to transfer the blame to the supporters of the 'Don't Get Tested' campaign. Gradually the campaign lost ground, as more and more people succumbed to pressure from their fellow residents and took the test. And as first one civil rights campaigner and then another was handed a Clean Bill it was curious to note just how speedily they recanted their previous heresies and transferred their allegiance to a new campaign which proudly called itself 'Keep America Clean'.

The United States soon became a pitiful sight, for the delay in dealing with the disease had allowed a far higher percentage of the population to become infected than in Europe. And once inside their comfortable and spacious bunkers, Americans showed little collective will to care for the large numbers stranded outside. Vast stretches of the country became semi-deserted no-go areas, abandoned by all except the sick or the very brave, and as the death toll rose in those areas, so their capability to deal with the horrendous logistics of survival began to decline.

Throughout this process the Federal institutions, in the hands of a weak and vacillating Democratic President and a bitterly divided Congress, had talked much but done little. But then, as a new Presidential election loomed, one man had broken cover and run with the issue, a hitherto little-known Republican Congressman by the name of James L. Goldberger. Correctly identifying that a majority of the public were not only in possession of Clean Bills but also proud of the fact, he had come down firmly on the side of the corporations. And he had won.

Dupont finished speaking and moved away from the podium to a polite ripple of applause. Goldberger, carefully adjusting his horn-rimmed spectacles, stepped smartly forward to take his place. The applause died away and the world listened attentively.

"The American people thank you for your welcome ..." he began, articulating every word in his usual dry clinical manner. Rachel watched as she saw Dupont squirm. Superficially it sounded polite enough, but the sub-text of the remark was a barbed reference to the fact that he, James L. Goldberger, was a democratically-elected President, entitled to speak for his people, while his European counterpart was not. The rest of his brief opening remarks continued in much the same vein, adding insult to injury behind a thin veneer of civility.

Goldberger finished speaking and turned to face Dupont. Again the handshake, again the artificial smiles, another heaven-sent opportunity for a photo-call. A few moments later the two men descended from the podium.

"May I introduce Mrs Rachel McNie, my personal policy advisor," Dupont said, turning to Rachel.

Goldberger stretched out his hand and shook Rachel's, and she couldn't help but wonder how such a tiny man could have such a powerful handshake.

"My pleasure," he said mechanically in the manner of one used to shaking hands with people of no importance whatsoever.

"I hope you will have no objections to Mrs McNie attending our private sessions as my advisor," Dupont added abruptly.

The plastic smile vanished from Goldberger's face.

"I beg your pardon," he said.

"I said I hope you do not mind if Mrs McNie attends the private sessions of this summit. You will of course be welcome to bring in an advisor from your side."

For a few seconds Goldberger's face went blank, as if he were trying to work out the full implications of Dupont's bizarre and wholly unexpected request.

"As you wish," he said drily, and as his small grey eyes met hers she suddenly felt as if she were standing naked before a man who could read her most intimate thoughts.

* * * * * *

The small room set aside for the summit had once been the private office of Ludwig II, the inner sanctum in which he had planned the crazy extravaganzas which had finally led to his downfall. One side of the room was still dominated by Ludwig's original mahogany desk, the desk from which for several years the Presidents of Greater Europe had conducted their affairs when in residence at the palace. But today the desk itself was empty, and the focus of attention was the three symmetrically-positioned dark leather chairs placed facing each other on the deep-piled Chinese rug in the centre of the room.

Despite Dupont's offer, Goldberger had decided to attend the summit alone, and he watched with a frozen smile on his face as the last of the cameramen responsible for the latest photo opportunity departed, carrying with them their odd assortment of lights and equipment. Finally, the door swung closed and they were left alone.

Rachel had expected talk, but what followed was silence. Perhaps Dupont and Goldberger had initially met each other's gaze by accident, but now their faces appeared to have become frozen, as they looked intently into each other's eyes as if attempting to outstare one another. In normal circumstances she would have found the spectacle amusing, but this was plainly no normal circumstance. The two men were like two chess players, each trying to get the measure of other before the match began.

After what seemed like minutes but was probably only seconds, Goldberger turned to Rachel.

"Mrs McNie, may I be so bold as to ask you to explain your role at this meeting?"

Rachel flinched and flicked a glance across at Dupont. He nodded as if to indicate she should answer.

"I am here as advisor to the President."

Goldberger's lips cracked into a thin smile.

"But what I am driving at is this. Am I to treat you on an equal footing to the President?"

Dupont stepped in.

"Yes," he said drily. "For the purposes of this meeting Mrs McNie is to be treated on an equal footing. You may speak plainly in her presence, if that is what you mean by your remark."

Goldberger nodded.

"I must thank you to agreeing to this meeting at such short notice," he said.

"I confess we were surprised at your request," Dupont replied, "especially in view of the sorry state of relations between our two countries in recent months."

71

"There are historical reasons for the coolness in our relations, as I am sure you ..."

"Reasons we are presumably not going to waste time rehearsing today," Dupont interjected sharply, his face showing the growing anger he clearly felt.

"Of course," Goldberger said slowly, but the tone of his voice suggested he considered Dupont's words to be an admission of weakness. Dupont could not resist a riposte.

"I am all too well aware, President Goldberger, of the sharply hostile tone you adopted towards the current political arrangements in Europe during your campaign for President. And throughout your introductory remarks before the television cameras today you continually referred to 'the American people' as if you personify them by right of the knife-edge victory the corporations bought for you at the polls. Needless to say, it would be easy enough for me to join you in drawing invidious comparisons between the United States and Europe, comparisons for example concerning the type of treatment offered to those unfortunate enough to be carriers of the White Death. Without wishing in any way to criticise you personally I hope you will accept that if we had allowed due political process to occur in Europe as it did in America, the process of containing and controlling this dreadful disease would have been as brutish and uncivilised here as it has plainly been in your country."

Goldberger removed his spectacles and placed them carefully on his lap. Once again, the thin smile spread slowly across his face.

"Shall we call it quits?" he asked.

Dupont stopped in his tracks and peered at him.

"O.K.," he replied. "Quits it is."

"The reason I have asked for this summit," Goldberger continued quietly, "is to ask you personally if you have any information on the origins of the White Death."

Rachel looked in surprise at Goldberger, but his expressionless face gave nothing away.

"The evidence suggests it originated in Europe," Dupont replied slowly. "We are inclined to the view that it was a genetic mutation originating within a Danish bio-chemical research establishment. But I am quoting a number of published academic papers on the subject of which you are no doubt fully aware. You presumably have some additional information to hand which you wish to corroborate privately."

Goldberger fidgeted uncomfortably in his chair, nervously fingering the spectacles that lay on his lap.

"I have no information. Merely a disturbing rumour. That is why I have come to see you."

Rachel felt the time had come to speak. Having been invited to attend by Dupont and cross-questioned about her role by Goldberger, she had no intention of sitting there for the entire duration like some kind of stuffed turkey.

"President Goldberger," she said with a reassuring smile, "perhaps you should tell us the nature of your information."

Goldberger turned to face her, returning her smile.

"Certainly. The rumour that has reached my ears, and I stress it is no more than a rumour, is that we have been the victims of a deliberate disinformation campaign about the origins of the disease."

He paused, allowing the full force of his remarks to sink in.

When Rachel had taken over the conversation, Dupont had slumped back in his seat. Now he sat forward again, a look of taut concentration on his face.

"Are you implying that the European government is involved in some kind of disinformation campaign on this matter?" he asked sharply, making no attempt to disguise his irritation.

Goldberger looked genuinely taken aback.

"Goodness me no," he said quickly. "Whatever made you think that?"

A look of immense relief spread across Dupont's face as he relaxed back into his chair.

"What kind of disinformation campaign?" Rachel asked.

"A clandestine communication has been received in my office from a European source to the effect that the Danish story is an attempt to cover up true responsibility for the disease. The source claims that the Danish establishment would have been extremely unlikely to have been able to generate this infective agent."

Rachel and Dupont both looked at Goldberger, expecting him to continue, but he said nothing.

"That flies flat in the face of the research papers I've read on the subject," Rachel said.

"I know it does," Goldberger added. "And that's why I'm here."

Dupont, who had temporarily closed his eyes, opened them again.

"I don't suppose your source gave you any particulars of the true origins of the White Death, by any chance?" he asked.

Goldberger shook his head.

"Nope," he added. "Not a clue. He just says it couldn't possibly have been the Danish plant and that any research papers to the contrary are part of a deliberate disinformation campaign."

"By whom?" Rachel asked.

Goldberger shrugged, but Dupont rose suddenly from his chair and walked over to the window. As the others watched in silence, he stared out into the sunny formal gardens beyond the glass.

Then he whispered something, a single word, but his voice was inaudible.

"Sorry?" Goldberger asked. "I didn't catch that."

"Alexandrov!" Dupont repeated more clearly, returning to his seat. "It's just possible, I suppose. The full enquiry into the disease's origins was organised within his ministry when he was Commissioner for the Environment."

Suddenly, Rachel remembered a night long ago, a night so very long ago that it might have been during a previous incarnation. The kitchen of their old house. Tom reading a recycled Green Party newsletter which had dropped on the mat. The wild claims that the disease was a wicked by-product of an evil and misguided pesticide research programme.

Goldberger was looking a little puzzled at Dupont's assertion.

"Alexandrov was one of the leaders of the Green Party before the . . . before the transition of power," Rachel explained. "The Greens put out what seemed at the time like a rather fanciful story about Danish pesticide research. It looked to most of us like a plug for one of their favourite hobby-horses . . ."

"And you think that Alexandrov may have used his position in Vintner's government to confirm the story?" Goldberger asked.

"It's just possible," Dupont said. "He did bring in a lot of his own people as scientific advisors. Some of them were sound enough, but others were blessed with considerably more ecological zeal than scientific reliability."

Goldberger looked at him askance.

"Didn't you check the research when you took power?"

"No," replied Dupont with a shake of his head. "We had no real reason to doubt it. And even if we had doubted the veracity of the work, it would have seemed like a rather pointless exercise. Wherever the disease sprang from, we're all living with the consequences of it, aren't we? That seemed to us the main priority, as indeed it still does."

Rachel looked in Goldberger's direction.

"He's got a point, hasn't he?" she added. "It does seem a trifle academic."

A look of relief had spread across Goldberger's face as Dupont had offered his explanation of events.

"I guess it is a trifle academic in the light of what you've said. But if this story is true I'd sure love to be able to tell the folks back home about the true origins of this goddam disease. Do you think you could look into those research papers organised by Alexandrov again and see what you can come up with?"

Dupont nodded.

"No problem," he said with a smile. "Unfortunately Alexandrov died in prison a few months back, or we might have been able to extract the truth from him."

"Some guy, that Alexandrov," Goldberger muttered. "I remember thinking that at the time of his trial."

"Shall I tell you something interesting about Alexandrov?" Dupont asked with a smile. "Something that never came out at the trial."

Goldberger looked up in surprise.

"You mean there was more. The revelations at the trial were bad enough."

"He had territorial ambitions concerning the U.S.A."

"What!"

"Yes," Dupont said, pleased that his words had had the desired effect on his opposite number. "You see, I am a man of parochial European concerns, President Goldberger. But Alexandrov, he had wider ambitions. Together with Marshall Bignoletto, he was planning a progressive take-over of just about the entire world, starting with environmental criminal number one, the United States of America. And in the state of acute disarray that prevailed in Washington until your timely election, he might even have managed it."

Goldberger took the judiciously placed compliment for what it was. His lips cracked into a smile.

"With my predecessor in charge at the White House I guess you might even be right about that, President Dupont."

Dupont leant forward again in his chair with a broad smile. And when he spoke, Rachel was sure she could detect the slightest drool of an American accent behind the Parisian lilt of his English.

"What say you we drop all this 'President' business? The name's François."

Goldberger held out his hand.

"James L. Goldberger," he said, "but you can call me Lionel. Can't stand the name my dear old Mom and Pop gave me."

Rachel stared in astonishment at the transformation before her eyes. Some ten minutes earlier these same two men had been snarling at each other as if the Third World War was about to begin. Yet now they appeared to be old friends, exchanging anecdotes about their respective careers, chatting merrily about the common acquaintances and shared experiences of a lifetime in public life. And as for her, it was as if she had disappeared from view. Neither man took the slightest bit of notice of her presence as they bantered, an observation reinforced by the increasingly coarse language into which the two men gradually slid.

After half-an-hour or so the conversation became more serious again, but the tension of the earlier part of their encounter did not return. They began to turn their minds to the many serious problems affecting Euro-American relations, and as they did so solutions seemed miraculously to emerge. Complex deals were struck involving trade-offs between totally disparate aspects of government policy, as reductions in European agricultural tariffs were traded for advanced military hardware and agreement reached on coordinated policy towards non-Federation members.

Two hours later the two men both sat back in their chairs and exchanged self-satisfied glances.

"Well," Goldberger said with a broad smile. "That just about seems to sew up the world for the next ten years or so, François."

"Certainly does, Lionel, and I must say it's been a pleasure doing business with you."

Goldberger rose to his feet.

"I guess we'd better get ready for that big feast you've planned for tonight, guys. My people were expecting me out over half-an-hour ago."

He shook Dupont warmly by the hand and held out his hand towards Rachel. And as he did so she suddenly remembered something.

"There's one thing I forgot to ask you earlier, President Goldberger," she asked, accepting the proffered handshake.

"Fire away," he replied.

"That rumour you told us about at the beginning of our meeting. Could you by any chance let us know the name of your source?"

Goldberger nodded.

"Sure thing. Should have told you right at the beginning since you folks probably know him. We didn't actually meet the guy in Washington. He was having some trouble getting over to us from your end that he didn't want to go into. But he approached one of our people at the Embassy and explained the whole thing to him. I understand he used to work for the European Broadcasting Corporation as a reporter until a couple of years back. My man in New Vienna says his work used to be quite highly regarded this side of the Atlantic, which is really why we took him so seriously. His name was André Rostropov."

NEW VIENNA, AUSTRIA, SEPTEMBER 2006

Rachel had taken charge of the President's private roof garden on the top of the Commission building the moment she had moved in. She looked around fondly at the plants which filled the tiny patch over which she now had command. The roses which had dominated her old garden in England were absent, of course, since the top of a fifty-five storey building in the heart of central Europe was hardly conducive to such delicate plants. But she had to admit that the fine collection of alpines she had amassed was a more than satisfactory recompense. With the hot sun of the summer months and the biting winds and swirling snow of winter, the conditions seemed an ideal reconstruction of the high mountain pastures which were their natural habitat.

The garden was located on one of the neat corners excised from the top storey of the Commission building. On two sides, the exterior walls of their Presidential flat offered not only some shelter against the elements but also provided an excellent framework for her collection of delicately-scented climbers. The walls also offered some protection against the psychological stress that would undoubtedly have resulted if a garden so high and exposed had been surrounded on all four sides by empty space. But despite the protective shield of the walls, Rachel had to admit this was no place for agrophobics, especially when high cross winds caused the top of the building, including the garden, to sway gently back and forth like a cruise liner in a strong Atlantic swell.

Rachel carefully placed a little mat on the soil in one of the flower beds and started to pluck out the weeds. Today there were no winds buffeting the building, only the hot September sun beating down relentlessly from high above. She plucked the tiny unwanted intruders deftly from the ground and placed them neatly into a small wicker basket she had brought with her from the kitchen. And as she worked she thought of André.

Of course it had been André. Who else could it have been? After all, André had been researching the origins of the disease at her own request when the terrible rift had come between them over her role in the coup. She plucked the weeds from the ground and played

77

back in her memory every word of their fateful conversation. In the end it had been André who physically walked away, but in reality it had been she who took the decision, deliberately tricking her old friend into departing without telling her of his fears. She had understood too well her growing loyalty to the new regime – or was it really to François Dupont – and had not dared seek out information that would ultimately have forced her to make a painful choice between an old friendship and a new loyalty.

She moved the little mat and started weeding a new patch of soil. The motion of her hands not only helped her to think, but also helped to prevent the conflicting emotions within her from flying out of control. Above all, the situation that confronted her now required clear judgement and a cool head.

But that was precisely the trouble, and the cause of her deep disquiet. André's judgement had always been crystal clear, the judgement of a man of measured sentiment in an industry riddled with intemperate enthusiasms. Yet she had neither listened to his words nor heeded his warning. Instead she been swept along into a new life of which she had never dreamed in her wildest dreams. In François Dupont she had found a man she could love in every sense, a man who was more than Tom could ever be, a man of rare destiny who had chosen to share that destiny with her.

'Be very careful in the months ahead, and in particular be careful of François Dupont.' André's words echoed within her over and over again. He had written them on the back of a chocolate wrapper, but now he seemed to be standing in the garden with her, bending down low and whispering the words into her ear.

She looked round.

"Bloody hell," she said, realising immediately what she had done and quickly rising to her feet. With a glance up at the sun, she realised that only a reckless Scot would go out and work in the full glare of the Viennese sun. And when you started hearing ghosts it was certainly time to go inside and drink a glass of water.

She put the mat and the basket of weeds to one side of the garden and strolled into the cool air-conditioned atmosphere of the kitchen. She glanced at the little box-like device sitting quietly in the corner of the room and for the first time felt almost pleased to see it.

"Machine!" she ordered.

The box clanked reassuringly. They were apparently programmed to do that, it was supposed to give them a certain quaintness which the market researchers had discovered added significantly to their commercial appeal.

"Yes, Mrs McNie," the machine replied politely.

"Bring me a large glass of iced water through to the lounge, and also the portable videophone."

"At once, Mrs McNie," it replied, scuttling off to connect itself to the relevant utilities.

Rachel walked through to the lounge and sat down beside the large picture window overlooking Vienna. After a few moments Machine clattered in merrily from the kitchen carrying the glass of water and the videophone in two of its oddly-shaped recesses.

"Shall I wait?" it asked.

Rachel took the glass of water and looked at it.

"Yes," she said. "Find the number of André Rostropov's home in London and make the connection."

She sipped the glass of water and waited, watching as the machine whirred gently. 'Whirring' was another deliberate design feature, another way of trying to make the machines more approachable to their all too human masters.

The whirring stopped.

"The last recorded number listed in the London directory is unavailable, Mrs McNie."

Rachel flinched. Quite deliberately, she had made no attempt to contact André since their last conversation.

"What is the address of the last number listed?"

The merest hint of a whirr.

"46, Queens Gate, Kensington, London, W1."

That was André's old address.

"When did the last number become unavailable?"

"April, 2005. One year, five months and three days ago."

"What was the reason for disconnection?"

"Non-payment of rental premium."

Rachel stared at the machine. That didn't sound like André, even if he was moving house.

"Are you sure of the reason?" she asked.

This time a prolonged whirr, almost a clatter. It was another design feature, of course, the machine was sure the first time. But the programmers knew that when a statement was queried it was only polite to think before replying, and that the information should invariably be repeated to the customer in different words.

"Computer centre confirms that a bill and two reminders were sent before termination of line."

Two possibilities were forming in Rachel's mind. She decided to try the more palatable of the two first.

"Check global listings, starting with full European listings. If no record exists check full address listings where available."

This time at least she knew the delay was genuine.

"No listings refer to André Rostropov."

She refrained from asking the computer to repeat itself. Instead, she tried the second possibility.

"Check main carrier list," she ordered.

Poor André. He always had been one for the ladies. Perhaps it was predictable that one of them would have infected him early on. She had originally supposed that he had arranged to meet Goldberger's man in New Vienna in person, but he could always have contacted the Embassy by videophone from one of the Care Centres. It would certainly explain the difficulties Goldberger had suggested he was encountering in getting to the United States.

The machine stopped whirring. It always did so a few seconds before speaking in order to warn its owners it was about to address them.

"There is no listing of André Rostropov on the main carrier list," it muttered.

Rachel stared at the machine in disbelief.

"Repeat," she whispered faintly.

The whirr. The pause.

"I'm afraid there is no listing of André Rostropov on the main carrier list, Mrs McNie."

Rachel rose silently from her chair and walked slowly towards the giant plate glass window. It was hard to believe, even harder to accept.

André Rostropov. Sane, rational, cultured André Rostropov. The André Rostropov from whom she had so often sought advice and support throughout her career in broadcasting.

That same André Rostropov had chosen to join the ranks of the living dead.

* * * * * *

"I still can't understand why he's done it, François, I really can't."

Dupont looked at her with exasperation. He was trying to keep his patience, but she kept asking the same question over and over again.

"Don't you think we could talk about something else for a change?" he asked. "We've been over all this before."

Rachel slowly picked up the newspaper beside her chair and pretended to read. Dupont looked at her with despair.

"All right, all right. I get the message," he said.

Rachel knew perfectly well that Dupont hated her reading the paper when he wanted to talk. And Dupont knew that she knew. She looked at him expectantly.

"It's not really as surprising as all that, Rachel," he began. "We all know there are living dead around. It's no great secret. Only last week we picked up another bunch of them holed up in the Latvian forest."

The 'living dead', as Europeans had come to call them, were either people who had refused to take the compulsory blood tests or people who had been discovered to be positive but had subsequently managed to give their captors the slip. They constituted a new kind of underground in Europe, hiding away from the authorities, living from hand to mouth, eking out a pathetic existence from day to day in the desperate hope of living another few hours in freedom.

Some of the living dead remained in towns and cities, usually hiding away in the back rooms of houses in order to remain close to their loved ones. But the majority had formed themselves into roving bands, living in remote parts of the countryside and only rarely emerging into populated areas. Due to their isolated lifestyle, they were not perceived as any great threat by the authorities, but occasionally an unexpected outbreak of the disease would spring up as one of the living dead reintroduced the infection into a healthy population. Needless to say, whenever this happened police squads would speedily move in and flush them out. The Latvian forest group to which Dupont had just referred had been detected in this way, and had proved to be one of the largest so far discovered, numbering nearly a thousand men, women and children. All except twelve were found to be positive, with many close to death.

"But André?" Rachel persisted. "Why André?"

"Why not André?" Dupont replied with a yawn. "He never even went for his blood test. You told me yourself he was a randy operator. He must have known for sure he was positive."

"But there was no point. André was so immensely rational. If he had become infected he would have known perfectly well that he needed proper medical care. Most of the living dead are crazy. If they're not positive to start with, they soon will be in these bands they join. And if they are positive, they're much better off in a Care Centre. André would have understood that."

"O.K. Maybe he's not in a group. Maybe he's a love bird."

Rachel shook her head firmly. A 'love bird' was the slang used to describe people who were so terrified of the pain of separation from their loved ones that they were prepared to break the law and go underground.

"Not André. Definitely not André."

Dupont looked down cautiously at the paper as if wondering whether it might not after all be better to let her read it.

"O.K., then. If he wasn't crazy and he wasn't a love bird then he just must have been a political."

A 'political' was a person who didn't believe in getting tested on grounds of principle, perhaps because they refused to accept the fundamental infringement of human liberty they believed it represented. The politicals were the most dangerous amongst the living dead, convinced of their mission to bring down what they regarded as an oppressive and dictatorial regime and quite prepared to undertake terrorist actions against the state. Moreover, when they developed symptoms of the disease, which they frequently did, they had a disturbing tendency to say their farewells with a suicide attack. On several occasions since taking office, Dupont himself had nearly been a victim in such attacks. On one occasion, Rachel had been by his side at the time.

She nodded reluctantly.

"I suppose it's just about possible," she murmured.

Dupont must have sensed that her defences were about to cave in.

"After all, he did resign from the European Broadcasting Corporation on grounds of principle," he added. "It does seem true to character."

Rachel looked at him sadly.

"Poor André," was all she could manage to say.

Dupont remained silent. He knew Rachel was clever enough to follow the logic of the argument for herself, to deduce that one possible reason for André's intervention with the Americans had been a crude attempt to destabilise the Dupont regime.

Rachel stared out from her armchair towards the old city of Vienna far below. It was dark, and the lights in the city were shining brightly, but cutting through the built-up area between the Commission building and the old city was a twisting snake of blackness, an empty void where the Danube crept stealthily through the city and on towards the Black Sea. The empty void was like André, another treasured part of her earlier life which had now died and would never again return.

There was no denying it made sense. André had been her closest colleague in the London office, other than Tom the nearest thing she had to a personal friend. Was it possible he had felt a twinge of jealousy at her decision to back Dupont's judgement rather than his in the heady days after the coup, a twinge of jealousy which had prompted him to warn her so vehemently against taking François Dupont's advice? Had he hatched up some story about the project on which he was involved to try and weaken her resolve to support the coup, hoping perhaps to persuade his wavering friend to come over to his side? And had he now given up all hope of democratic reform originating within Europe and decided to use the very same story to win support from the Americans, the only outsiders with sufficient military might to put a check on François Dupont?

James Goldberger may have been right to believe he had been the victim of a disinformation campaign. But perhaps the disinformation campaign was not instituted by Dupont, nor by Alexandrov and the Greens, but rather by André Rostropov himself in a cunning and desperate attempt to bring down a regime he had always loathed.

EPILLION-SUR-MER, FRANCE, SEPTEMBER 2006

The tiny fishing settlement of Epillion-sur-Mer lies some five kilometres to the south-west of the major French port and industrial centre of Dunkerque, close to the Belgian frontier. It is a nondescript sort of place, windy and desolate in winter, passably picturesque on a fine summer's day, one of those sleepy French villages which time has seemed to pass by. Behind the sea defences abutting the shingle beach, a few rather dreary hotels and boarding houses attempted to draw tourists to the limited attractions of Epillion-sur-Mer, but the inadequacies of the beach and the close proximity to the giant and rather smelly chemical plants at Dunkerque meant that the villagers' main activity remained the diminishing number of fish they caught in their tiny brightly-painted fishing vessels.

Rachel flicked a glance at François Dupont as they drove along the coast road from Dunkerque airport and wished too late that she had had more sense than to suggest this crazy visit to the place where he had spent the first five years of his life.

Although this was to be a purely private trip, they had been invited to stay at the home of the Mayor of Epillion-sur-Mer, a small French château lying just inland of the village. The Mayor must have tipped off the locals about their imminent arrival, because as the convoy of black limousines swept into the village streets the villagers had come out in force to greet them. The enthusiastic welcome seemed to lift Dupont's spirits somewhat, and he waved his hand graciously through the bullet-proof glass at the crowds.

"Remember anything?" Rachel asked.

Dupont continued to wave but offered no reply.

"They seem enthusiastic today," he said drily. "More than usual, don't you think?"

Rachel studied the smiling faces lining the side of the road, waving their little blue flags covered in stars, each star representing one of the original member states of the European Community.

"They're probably proud of you," she said with a smile. "By the looks of it, I shouldn't think Epillion-sur-Mer has very much to be proud of."

Dupont looked at her.

"It's got a quaint little port," he said non-committally.

"You remember it?" she asked.

Again Dupont looked away. There was a sadness about him today that the crowds were only partially relieving. And once again, Rachel felt the twinge of guilt at suggesting they visit the place during a part of their all too brief summer holiday.

"François?" she said quietly.

He turned.

"We don't have to stay if you don't want to. We could make some excuse about pressing affairs of state and go straight on to Scotland."

He smiled quietly, although it seemed more as if he was smiling to himself than in response to her remark.

"No," he murmured. "Now we're here we'll see it through."

The car swept into the crowded village square and a small brass band started to play, its rhythmic but chaotic thumping totally at odds with the chime of the bells in the tiny church on one side of the square. They drew up at a small raised dais decked out with flags and climbed out of the car to greet the Mayor.

Claude Charles Maurisseur was a burly man of about sixty, dressed in a smart light suit which looked as though it had been specially purchased for the occasion. He held out his hands in welcome, rough hands which showed ample evidence of half a lifetime at the helm of a fishing boat, and ushered them up the makeshift wooden stairs onto the platform.

Maurisseur held up his hands for quiet and the waiting crowd fell silent. He turned to Dupont with a triumphal gesture.

"He has returned!" he cried exultantly. "At last he has returned!"

The crowd exploded into rapturous applause, and then, quite spontaneously, started to sing the European national anthem. And as they sang, Rachel looked in astonishment at François Dupont's face. He was holding his gaze in the middle distance, his eyes focused somewhere near the top of the squat tower rising above the nave of the church, and she could see that he was fighting hard to control his emotions. There was a distinct moistness in his eyes, and he was gently biting his lower lip as if to prevent tears from running down his cheeks. Others watching the occasion would have easily understood the emotion he felt at his homecoming, but only Rachel knew the true significance of his behaviour. For in all the long months she had lived with François Dupont, this was the very first time she had ever seen him cry.

The singing died away and Maurisseur turned to face the crowd again as another hushed silence descended.

"It has been too long since François Dupont has walked the streets of Epillion," he began, to a murmur of approval from the crowd. "We have been sad at the loss, but we have been overjoyed to know that our loss was Europe's gain!"

A ripple of applause from the crowd.

"We are simple folk in Epillion, but François Dupont has proved to us that greatness can come even from humble roots like this. Only he had the foresight to deliver us from the folly of the politicians we ourselves had chosen. At first we were unsure, but now we can say, François, that we understand your actions. We were wrong, you were right. We thank you for delivering us from the evil menace of the White Death. We thank you for making us clean again. We thank you, François, and we welcome you home!"

The crowd erupted again into applause. Children and adults alike waved their tiny flags, clapped and stamped their feet. The applause continued for several minutes, but then the crowd gradually began to chant.

"Speech! Speech! Speech!"

Dupont glanced at Rachel with a smile and stepped forward to the microphone. As he did so, the applause faded away and the crowd stood in absolute silence waiting for his words.

"I thank you with all my heart for the welcome you have given me today," he began, carefully controlling his voice to prevent the emotion he clearly felt from choking his words. "As I think many of you know, I was born here and lived here for the first five years of my life, five happy carefree years that I wish could have gone on for ever. I left Epillion at the age of five when my parents died, and I was sent to an orphanage far away. And I can tell you that for many long years afterwards I used to dream at night of Epillion, of the little ships smelling of fish in the harbour, of the sound of the waves pounding the sea shore, of the church bells on a Sunday morning, of the man who sold ice cream from the little kiosk that I rejoice to see is still standing today where it always stood in the corner of this very square . . ."

He stopped and pointed at the tiny ice-cream kiosk and the crowd erupted once again. And then, incoherently at first but soon with growing force, another chant arose.

"Ice cream for François! Ice cream for François!"

A hush descended. From somewhere in the midst of the crowd, an open space appeared around a frail upright old man with a grey moustache and a walking stick. He started walking slowly towards the ice cream stand, and as he walked the crowd stood respectfully back to either side, making an open avenue along which he could pass.

Dupont tried to open his mouth to speak, but then he closed it again. Along with the rest of the crowd, he watched in silence at the old man's slow progress through the crowd.

Eventually he reached the kiosk and disappeared inside, but he was only gone for a few moments, soon reappearing with an enormous multi-coloured ice-cream on a cone. This time he left his stick behind, and walked proudly down the wide avenue lined by his respectful fellow villagers towards the platform.

After what seemed like an eternity, he reached the podium and started to climb the wooden steps. Slowly, painfully, he clambered to the top, pausing only to shake Dupont's hand before proudly handing him his gift.

Dupont wiped his eyes and took an enormous lick. And as soon as his tongue touched the ice-cream, the crowd before him once again exploded into rapturous applause.

* * * * * *

Claude Maurisseur described it as his 'humble home', but in reality it was a château of some considerable proportions, a grey stone building complete with battlements, moat and drawbridge to which each and every one of its owners over a continuous period of some six hundred years appeared to have contributed. And if this continual process of adaptation and improvement had done little to enhance the architectural integrity of the structure, it had certainly resulted in a fascinating mix of styles.

Its present owner, Epillion's current mayor and owner of its largest

fishing fleet, showed every sign of following in his predecessors' footsteps. Once again the château was in the throws of building work,
this time in the form of a new sports complex, complete with indoor
squash court, heated swimming pool and the latest variety of high-tech
gymnasium. And it was while Maurisseur was proudly showing his
important guests around the new sports wing that he first brought
the subject up.

They were by the swimming pool, standing amidst a collection
of exotic indoor plants which had been cunningly back-lit in different
coloured lights so as to create a soothing yet entrancing effect, when
their host suddenly swung round to face Dupont.

"Did you know," he began, "that your father was a wonderful
swimmer? One of the very few in Epillion who could beat me at
freestyle."

Dupont looked shocked, caught completely off guard by the unexpected nature of his remark. Maurisseur was admittedly a man in
his late sixties, some twenty years older than François Dupont, but
neither of his two guests had previously been aware that he had known
Dupont's parents personally.

"You knew François's father?" Rachel asked, secretly delighted
to have found a person who could reveal something about his early
life. For although she knew that his parents had died when he was
roughly five years old and that he had subsequently been dispatched
to a remote orphanage somewhere high in the French Alps, she knew
very little else. He had always been reluctant to discuss what had
understandably been a painful and difficult phase in his life, and she
had hoped that the mere sight of his birthplace would help lay to
rest some of the ghosts of those distant childhood years. But to find
a surviving personal friend of his parents was better still.

Maurisseur turned to Rachel.

"I knew him well," he said. "But then, everybody knew Maurice
Dupont. He was a very likeable man."

Dupont remained silent, standing with his face partially hidden
behind a tall overhanging plant as if he were shrinking away from
the conversation.

"Do please tell us about him," Rachel said. "François can't remember very much, can you, François?"

Dupont looked down at the swimming pool.

"I think, if you do not mind," he said suddenly with one of the
disarming smiles he frequently used to conceal his nervousness, "that
I will take a short swim. The water in your pool looks most enticing."

Maurisseur glanced at him.

"Of course," he said. "In this respect at least you are really like your father. Do you wish to borrow a costume?"

Dupont smiled.

"No need," he replied simply, pulling off his clothes and diving naked into the water.

Rachel and Maurisseur watched in silence for a few moments as Dupont attacked the water. He swam fluently and fast, his face submerged except for when he came up for air, speeding through the water with impressive speed for a man of his years.

"I'm sorry." Maurisseur said at length. "I did not mean to cause any upset."

Rachel turned to face him.

"François doesn't like talking about his parents. Or about his childhood at all, really. I think they are painful memories for him. When he became President somebody asked him to agree to a television biography covering his childhood, but he refused to allow anything other than the barest outline of that period in his life to be made public."

Dupont had reached the far end of the pool and thrust himself energetically back in the direction from which he had come.

"I'm sorry," Maurisseur muttered. "Perhaps it is better that I talk of other things."

"Oh no," Rachel interjected. "Please don't do that. I'd very much like to know something of his early years. It might help me to understand him better. Perhaps even to help him come to terms with it. It can't be good for him keeping all those memories bottled up the way he does."

Maurisseur took her by the arm and led her to a small wooden bench set amidst the plants.

"I will tell you what I know, then," he began thoughtfully, as soon as they were seated. "Or rather, first I will tell you what is generally known amongst the people of Epillion. Then I will tell you some things of which only I have certain knowledge."

He paused for a moment, as if collecting his thoughts.

"As you know, I am of the same generation as François's father. We were in the same school as each other and became good friends, largely because we shared a common passion for sports of all kinds. But although he was never boastful about it, I always knew that Maurice Dupont was far cleverer than I. He would organise debates at our school, but they were never very successful, largely because he would always trounce the poor boy charged with presenting the opposing point of view. And at his studies of course he was brilliant, gaining the very highest marks in all the examinations. So when we left school, he did not become a fisherman like the rest of us, but went off instead to university in Paris in order to develop his growing interest in chemical engineering.

Maurisseur looked out across the pool and smiled.

"I can tell you that many of the young men in Epillion were quite pleased to see the back of him. You see, Maurice Dupont was always a great success with the ladies. With his good looks, his sophisticated charm and his restrained intelligence, he simply swept our village girls off their feet. I would guess that a fair proportion of the older women you saw in the village square lost more than their hearts to Maurice Dupont.

"But we thought we had seen the last of him when he left. Most people who leave Epillion for the wide world beyond don't venture back. But Maurice was the exception. After he had finished his studies in Paris, he picked up a research job at one of the huge chemical concerns in Dunkerque and bought one of the brightly-painted fisher-men's houses you can see in the centre of the village."

Rachel smiled.

"That must have worried the young men," she said.

"It did. Quite a few men had used the opportunity offered by his departure to marry the disappointed young ladies he had left behind. But it seemed we had no cause to be concerned, because the Maurice Dupont who came back to Epillion was a very different man from the Maurice Dupont who had stepped onto the Paris express some four years before."

Maurisseur's face became serious as he remembered the transition that had occurred.

"He had met a girl in Paris, a pretty thing no more than sixteen or seventeen years of age, and he had married her there. So when he returned to Epillion, he naturally brought his young wife with him and they moved into their new home together ..."

Maurisseur fell silent, studying Dupont's powerful body as he thrust aggressively through the water. Then he turned to Rachel.

"I am not one hundred percent sure that I should be telling you these things," he muttered.

Rachel looked at him in surprise.

"But why on earth not?"

Maurisseur fixed her for a few moments with a penetrating gaze.

"As I say, Maurice had changed. Before he left, he had been as I told you, an outgoing figure bursting with energy and enthusiasm. But on his return he became a recluse, staying indoors when he was not at work, refusing all offers to join in with the social life of our little community."

"Perhaps he was happy," Rachel said. "The insularity of young love."

"Perhaps."

"But you don't think so, do you?"

He paused before replying.

"There is an indefinable quality about two young people who have fallen deeply in love with each other. To be sure, they may refuse invitations because they prefer their own company, but they have a radiance in their eyes, a sparkling vitality which seems to resonate with the exquisite beauty of their emotions. But with Maurice it was different. His love seemed more like a chain, as if some hidden power had strapped him to his wife against his wishes."

Dupont came surging up for air, and as he did so Rachel noticed his eyes flick in their direction before his face disappeared from view beneath the surface. He had already completed several lengths, but it was clear that he had not the slightest intention of ending his swim before they had finished their present conversation.

"Tell me about François's mother," Rachel asked.

Maurice sighed.

"She was very young and very pretty, but her eyes were always filled with sadness. When she went out, which she did as infrequently as possible, she would carry herself erect but with a downcast expression, as if she were carrying some terrible burden within her."

"Did you ever find out what it was?"

Maurisseur looked down into his lap.

"I didn't know her well, Rachel, so I can't be sure. But I am not aware of any objective reason for her sorrow."

"Did it make any difference when François was born?"

"Perhaps she became sadder still, I don't know. She came out even less frequently than before. Usually Maurice would do the shopping and take little François out for walks. But I do think Maurice became happier again at that time, almost as if the smiling face of his baby son had restored a faint echo of his previous good spirits.

"Around that time we started to swim together again. He didn't speak about his wife but once I plucked up the courage to ask him why she seemed so sad. He told me she was sad because she knew her love for her husband could never last. It seemed as if she was tormented by the thought of his inevitable death."

Rachel took a deep breath.

"Jesus," she murmured.

90

Maurisseur looked at her.

"You know about the accident, I suppose?" he said.

"I know his father died in an accident at the chemical plant and that his mother died shortly thereafter. That's all he told me."

"One day there was a blast in the laboratory where Maurice worked in Dunkerque. The whole building went up in flames and Maurice was killed along with several other people. François was five years old at the time. Of course, those of us in the village knew it would have a devastating effect on François's mother and we tried to help. A place like Epillion does not permit a young bereaved mother to mourn alone."

"But she died," Rachel added.

"Yes," Maurisseur replied bluntly. "Six months later, she died."

Rachel looked up at him, the unspoken question written on her face.

"The inquest recorded a verdict of accidental death. That is what you will find on the death certificate."

"But you don't believe that, do you, Claude? You think she took her own life."

A look of sorrow passed across Maurisseur's kindly old face.

"I don't think," he said slowly. "I know."

Rachel stared at him.

"But how could you possibly know?"

"Because I was there."

For a few moments neither of them spoke.

"But if you knew, why did the inquest record a verdict of accidental death?"

Maurriseur remained silent for a long time before replying.

"What I am going to tell you now I have told nobody in forty years?" he said. "But I am old enough to make up my own mind about whom I trust and I have decided to trust you. I believe you have François's best interests at heart and that you will use the knowledge to help him live with himself."

He paused.

"Have you seen our fishing port?" he asked.

Rachel nodded.

"Today, as we drove in."

"It happened there one night shortly before Christmas, on the harbour wall where it juts out into the sea in order to break the force of the winter storms. I had a pet alsatian at the time that needed regular exercise. So, ignoring the rapidly worsening weather, I went out with the dog before turning in and strolled down in the direction of the harbour. On such a night I expected to meet no one, but suddenly I became aware of a solitary figure walking along the harbour wall. At first I couldn't make out who it was, but as the figure approached the red flashing beacon at the end of the wall I realised that it was François's mother. And then I saw that she was not alone. Walking beside her, clutching her hand with the total trust of a dependent being, was a tiny child wrapped in a winter coat.

"Of course I knew immediately something terrible was happening. Nobody takes a child out on the harbour wall during a winter storm. So I ran as fast as I could towards them. By the time she became aware of my approach she had lifted François up onto the highest part of the wall overlooking the sea and had started clambering up beside him. Suddenly I knew she was going to jump. I yelled and screamed at her to stop. But she didn't stop, she just climbed more quickly, hurrying to join her son on the top of the wall ..."

He stopped talking for a moment and Rachel could see in his eyes the emotion he felt as the memory flooded back.

"That's why I let go of the dog," he said at last. "The animal rushed at her on my command and pulled her down from the wall, holding her coat securely in his powerful jaws. And as he did so, I jumped up onto the sea wall and dragged little François down to safety.

"I tried to reason with her, but to no avail. She was totally insane. And all the time the boy was standing by my side, looking on with a strange bemused expression at his mother. She pleaded with me to allow her to die as she thought she must die. And all this time, I could see that she cared for François in a mad sort of way. She feared for him being alone in the world, she feared he would suffer the same torments she had known, she genuinely thought that throwing him to a certain death in the Atlantic breakers was the kindest thing to do.

"I wasn't going to allow it to happen, of course. I had hoped that the commotion would bring help, but the waves were crashing so violently against the harbour wall that no one could hear. By now she had fallen silent, so I commanded the dog to release her while I tried to comfort the child. It was enough. Before I could do anything she had leapt into the water. There was a small fishing boat tied up beneath us, and as she fell she smashed her head badly on the prow of the boat before crashing on down into the water.

"François was beside me staring blankly after his mother. I thought he might jump in after her, so I didn't dare try to fetch her out. I just watched, hoping that by some miracle she would rise to the surface."

Maurisseur fell silent again and watched as Dupont completed yet another lap, pushing himself deep beneath the surface on the turn.

"But she didn't come up," he said at last. "With the blow she received to her head, she was probably already unconscious by the time she hit the water. The boy was shivering, although whether it was because of the cold or the fear in his heart I could not tell. He didn't cry. He didn't react in any obvious way to the terrible scene he had witnessed. And my first instinct was to wrap my own coat around him and carry him back to the warmth of my cottage.

"His mother was dead. The boy was cold and frightened. There was no possible purpose to be served by going straight to the police station. I was planning to dry him out and calm him down before taking him there. But later, after I arrived back home, I changed my mind. I looked at François's innocent face and wondered what was best for him. I tried to think ahead, to think of how he would cope with the fact that his own mother had not only committed suicide but had also tried to take him with her. Such a thought, it seemed to me, was not an easy one for a young child to grow up with.

"If I had told the truth there was no way I could have protected François in a community like this. It would have followed him around like a shadow for the rest of his childhood, perhaps for the rest of his life.

"It wasn't easy to know what to do. A five-year-old is aware of his surroundings. François knew something terrible had happened, although he didn't understand what. But he knew his mother was dead. So I told him it was very important for him that nobody knew about what had happened, that he was to say that his mother had put him to bed in the usual way and that he knew nothing. I told him to forget everything he had seen. Then I took him home.

"The rest was straightforward enough. When he finally fell asleep I slipped out of the house, fetched my dog and walked down to the harbour as I had done before. I was already lying, so I thought a little further lie would make no moral difference. I told the police that I had seen his mother walking alone along the inside of the harbour wall towards the beacon. Unusual at that time of year, perhaps, but not out of character for a woman such as François's mother. Then I explained how I had seen a stray dog scavenging amongst the lobster pots jump up at her, grabbing her clothing and causing her to slip and fall into the water.

"They had no reason to doubt my words. François played his part well. He kept his own council then as he appears to have kept it ever since.

"The boy had no living relatives so he naturally became a ward of court. At that time he suffered from asthma, and I think those charged with his welfare decided that the Alpine air would be good for him, certainly better than the chemical fumes that frequently drift over from the Dunkerque factories. But perhaps they too thought it would be good for a boy who had lost both parents in such tragic circumstances to have a completely new start."

Rachel looked at Maurisseur.

"Is that why you never visited him or wrote to him at the orphanage? François once let slip that nobody from this village ever contacted him after he left."

"Yes. You see, I was a part of his nightmare, wasn't I? Seeing me would only have forced him to relive the terror of that night. But you can imagine my joy when I heard that he had accepted my invitation to stay during your visit to Epillion."

Maurisseur watched Dupont thoughtfully as he made yet another turn.

"Does he remember still, do you think?" he asked.

Rachel thought for a long time before replying.

"He remembers something, some shadowy image of the past, although I suspect he doesn't understand the significance of what he remembers. But I think from what he has said that he loved his mother very much."

"And will you share my secret with him now that you know?"

Rachel looked at Dupont. He was still swimming strongly, but she could just detect the first signs of exhaustion setting in. And as she watched him swim she could feel an overwhelming desire to hold his naked body in her arms, to comfort him and protect him from the terrible nightmare he had borne alone for so very many years.

"I don't know," she said simply. "I'm afraid I just don't know."

KNOYDART, SCOTLAND, ONE WEEK LATER

"A referendum!"

François stopped dead in his tracks.

"Yes," Rachel replied, sitting down on a large boulder. "Why not?"

For a moment, Dupont looked flustered. Then he sat down heavily on an adjacent boulder and nervously scratched his head.

From where they were sitting the view over the heather-clad hills and shimmering lochs of Knoydart inspired original thinking, and the idea had occurred to Rachel half way up the path towards one of her favourite childhood vantage points. Now, pulling off her knapsack and removing a small bar of Belgian chocolate, she split the bar in two and handed half to Dupont.

"Do you know what they call you out there, François?" indicating with a sweep of her arm the European continent that lay beyond the hills.

François shrugged.

"Some of them call me a dictator," he muttered.

Rachel jabbed him gently in the ribs.

"Prove them wrong then," she said. "You know damn well that most people simply call you François. It's a term of endearment. Don't you realise how grateful people are for what you've done?"

Dupont shrugged again. Despite all the evidence, he really didn't seem to grasp just how popular he had become.

"But a referendum would be dangerous. For one thing, we'd have to allow free speech."

"Why? You wouldn't have to relax any of the important controls on anything. A referendum doesn't imply an election. Give 'em a straight choice. Keep it simple. You want François, tick here. You want François to retire, tick here. That sort of thing. At least it would give you some kind of democratic legitimacy."

François nodded.

"It would give me a greater moral authority, I suppose."

"And it would shut the Americans up."

He thought for a moment.

"Perhaps you're right," he said eventually, rising to his feet. "I'll think about it."

Rachel knew better than to pursue the topic. Once an idea had been planted in his head, it was generally best to leave it there for a few days. By that time, it would have become his idea rather than hers.

Dupont had started climbing again, stepping gingerly over the rough heather in order to avoid twisting an ankle. But the appearance of isolation on their rural walk was deceptive, for at a respectful distance on every side, groups of secret service personnel carefully monitored their progress up the hillside.

"Your father isn't one of my fan-club, is he, Rachel?"

Rachel had hoped he hadn't noticed, for her father had behaved with perfect courtesy throughout their stay in his cottage. But perhaps it was too much to hope that a man as perceptive of human nature as François Dupont would fail to draw the correct conclusion.

"It's really me he doesn't approve of, not you. He thinks I've betrayed Tom."

Dupont fell silent for a while.

"Rachel," he asked presently, without stopping or turning to face her, "what would you do if there was a cure? What would you do if Tom came back?"

There was an edge to his voice that didn't quite make sense. But the question itself was reasonable enough.

"I've often wondered that. But it doesn't seem very likely at the moment, does it? Nobody's saying they're on the brink of a break-through."

"No. But hypothetically. You must be able to answer the question hypothetically."

They walked on in silence. Their trip to Epillion and her knowledge of the trauma of his early years had strengthened yet further her feelings for François Dupont. A long time ago, during their early encounter in the nave of St Stephan's Cathedral, she had sensed his fear about the past, but now she probably knew more about that past than he knew himself. It was almost as if she was his subconscious memory, and she knew she wouldn't have the strength to leave him now.

"Would you share me?" she asked with a laugh.

Dupont stopped and turned.

"With Tom?"

She nodded.

He thought for a moment.

"Yes," he said decisively. "But would he share you?"

She thought of Tom, of the cello, of the long hours he had spent alone while she had pursued her precious career.

"Tom's nicer than you are, François. Not as exciting, perhaps, but nicer. He shared me with my job. I think he'd share me with you."

It was an intriguing thought. The three of them, together with the kids, living in the Presidential flat on the top floor of the tallest building in New Vienna. Suddenly a wicked thought crossed her mind and she couldn't resist a snigger.

Dupont flicked a glance at her.

"What's so funny?" he asked.

"A funny thought occurred to me, that's all. Nothing important."

For all the love she felt for François Dupont, she still had sufficient loyalty to her husband not to tell him what that funny thought had been. For while she was pretty confident that Tom would share her body and her mind with the President of Europe, there was absolutely no way he would share household management with a silly robot. So while François Dupont would be allowed to stay, poor old Machine would simply have to go.

NEW VIENNA, AUSTRIA, OCTOBER 2006

Rachel picked over the remains of the lunch she had eaten alone and looked disconsolately into her coffee. A copy of the European Gazette was lying on the table beside her plate and she picked it up, idly flicking through the pages in the vain hope that some item of news would distract her from the nagging worry that had been creeping into her thoughts ever since their return from Scotland.

The trouble was, most of the news these days was so terribly depressing, especially if you turned away from the domestic European pages to the extensive coverage of the rest of the world. For across most of the globe the White Death had left a trail of destruction in its wake the like of which had not been seen since the great plagues of the fourteenth and seventeenth centuries, cutting a huge swathe through areas that had entered the twenty-first century with inflated populations and even more inflated hopes and ambitions.

Much of Africa had virtually ceased to exist except as a game reserve, Latin America was reeling, while much of Asia – protected in the early years of the disease by differing social customs – was now succumbing fast to the ravages of a disease that was becoming more virile by the hour. Governments struggled against impossible odds to put a check to its spread, but without sufficient economic resources they could do little more than arrange for the dead to be buried.

In some of the Latin American countries with more violent traditions, the rich minority which had traditionally governed the region had tried to emulate their mentors in the United States, isolating themselves from the vast masses of the urban and rural poor in a desperate attempt to stay healthy. But although they had used all their considerable political and military might to achieve their ends, the odds were heavily stacked against them. As fear turned to desperation, the outsiders attacked and isolated the insiders, mercilessly ripping away their protective walls and and forcing their leaders to share in their sorry fate. Before long the Latin American powerbrokers had begun to do what they always did in time of crisis – emigrate to the United States – where the corporations and Lionel Goldberger's government were always willing to allow safe haven to the healthy holder of a foreign passport if only they could find the cash.

But at least the Latin American states had tried to make some kind of internal response to the illness, albeit a response which only sought to protect the rich. The African model, although not universally followed on the continent, was much more despairing. Most African governments simply chose to close their eyes to the reality of the calamity that was befalling them. They simply prayed it would go away, and while the governments prayed many ordinary people sought to return to their rural roots in the hope that they could sit it out. The towns and cities which had seen the original growth of the disease had gradually emptied, but as people returned to their villages the disease had followed them back, its invisible tentacles stretching out across the continent to even the most remote human settlements. As time passed, all attempts at administering the crisis seemed to collapse, as people waited and hoped they would be the exception that proved the general rule.

The vast Indian sub-continent had chosen to accept the inevitable in a different manner. In some indefinable way that no one could really grasp, the disease became tangled up in the religious conflicts of the region, almost as if it represented some sign sent by the relevant god to justify a particular political position. For a while, the sheer ferocity of the resulting war between Hindu and Muslim resulted in a greater death toll than the disease itself, wasting precious energies that would in any case have been insufficient to make much impact on an already impossible situation.

In China, the authoritarian grip of the Communist Party – in so many ways a throwback to an earlier era – had seemed to promise a hope of adequate administrative machinery to contain the illness. But here something strange had happened. The authorities chose to remain inactive, the leaders waiting and watching inside secure zones to see what would happen to the vastly overpopulated lands within their control. Indeed, rumours abounded that certain of the Chinese leadership regarded the White Death as a heaven-sent opportunity to implement a new population policy in place of the failed initiatives of the late twentieth century.

But despite the gloom, there were certain rays of hope. It wasn't just Europeans and Americans who were finding ways to live with the White Death. In East Asia, the booming economies of the Pacific fringe were succeeding in copying the Japanese model of containment, combining tight political control and traditional social attitudes in order to isolate and deport the victims of the disease with a ruthlessness that shocked even the Americans. Japan had been a full member of the Federation of Safe Zones from the outset, but already South Korea, Taiwan and Singapore had applied for candidate membership.

Another ray of hope concerned the disease itself. Like its predecessors in earlier centuries, it seemed choosy about whom it devoured. It would sweep though a population group touching every member of it, but a small minority of people would not just remain healthy but completely free of it. This natural immunity gave rise to the distant hope that some people at least would be left behind in order to repopulate even the most seriously affected areas.

Rachel laid the newspaper back on the table and rose from her chair. Whenever her thoughts turned to the world beyond the Federation countries she felt a wave of guilt pass through her mind about the utter triviality of her own personal concerns. Life was treating her too kindly at a time when others had to suffer so much, and she had no right to feel the growing sense of unease she was feeling about her relationship with François Dupont.

She slumped down in her armchair and gave up trying to think of something else.

The Scottish holiday had been a blissfully happy time for them both. For the first time in two years, he had allowed himself the luxury of putting aside affairs of state and relaxing. They had walked. They had talked. And once they had even made love together on the open moors after telling the security guards to stand discreetly behind a rock. It was as if their relationship had suddenly reached a full maturity in which for the first time they felt completely comfortable in each other's company. But only two days after their return to New Vienna something had definitely changed. It wasn't anything definable, but a sudden reticence had descended upon Dupont, an unwillingness to talk freely that she found hard to square with his earlier verbosity.

At first she had put it down to the strain of returning from a holiday to the problems of the world. But now, after his sombre mood had continued without a break for some ten days, she was forcing herself to recognise the possibility that something had gone catastrophically wrong with their relationship.

But what? However hard she thought, she could not think of any obvious answer.

A soft chime from the direction of the lift interrupted her thoughts and she swung her head round in surprise. Dupont had told her he was going to be away until the evening, and she should have been consulted by the reception desk on the ground floor before any other visitors were admitted.

The lift door slid silently open and a pretty young girl of no more than twenty years of age stepped confidently out.

Rachel rose to her feet.

"Hi, Rachel!" said the girl simply, before Rachel had a chance to speak. "I'm Justine. Nice to meet you."

If anyone else had arrived in the flat in this unannounced fashion, flouting every single security rule in the book, Rachel would immediately have used the code word to summon the security guards. But something about the girl's confident manner made her hesitate.

"How on earth did you get in here?" she asked.

The girl grinned.

"By the lift," she said sweetly. "I'd have got puffed out if I'd climbed fifty-five flights of stairs."

The joke made Rachel angry.

"But you had no pass. Tell me how you got in without a pass immediately or I'll call security."

The girl walked straight passed Rachel towards the window.

"I've got a pass," she said simply, fishing a small piece of plastic from a pocket in her plain cotton frock and chucking it across the room to Rachel. Then she sat down in Rachel's favourite armchair and gazed out admiringly at the view.

Rachel looked at the complex geometric design on the pass. It was exactly like the one she possessed herself, and entitled the holder to free access to the Presidential flat without prior notification.

"But..."

The girl swung round and looked at Rachel with a serious look on her face.

"Bloody hell. He hasn't discussed it with you yet, has he?" she said, rising to her feet with an apologetic expression.

Rachel stared at the girl in utter astonishment. Various possible explanations for her arrival were beginning to form in her mind, but none of them were particularly palatable.

"Who hasn't told me what?"

"Why, François, of course. It was François who arranged for the pass."

The girl smiled sheepishly.

"Look," she said. "I'm sorry about the way I arrived. It must have come as a bit of a shock. I assumed François would have told you all about it ages ago. I thought you'd be expecting me."

"François hasn't told me anything." Rachel said drily. "But I'd be very grateful if you would."

"So he didn't tell you I'd be moving in."

Rachel's mouth dropped open. If the girl's manner had been different, she might have reacted more angrily, but the childlike simplicity with which she announced her intention caught her completely off guard.

"You're not his daughter, are you?" she asked abruptly.

Justine chuckled merrily, flicking her head to one side to dislodge the hair that had fallen across her eyes.

"I could be, I suppose, but I'm not."

She rose to her feet and moved towards the lift.

"Look," she said, "I think you'd better talk this through with François first. I'll come back later. Are you expecting him soon?"

"I wasn't. But don't you worry. I'll get hold of him somehow."

"Good idea. I'll come back when you've had a chat."

Before Rachel could reply the lift door had closed and the girl was gone. She swung round and strode towards the kitchen.

"Machine," she ordered, anger finally gaining the upper hand over curiosity, "where is François?"

A faint whirr followed by a clunk.

"François is attending a meeting with the South Korean Ambassador on the thirty-third floor to discuss the South Korean application for Federation membership."

"Get him!" she said menacingly.

Silence.

Utter confusion was one of the few ways to reduce the machine to silence. But even that could possibly have been a deliberate design feature.

101

"Sorry?" asked the machine politely.

"I'm telling you to send someone into that room to fetch him out of that meeting immediately. I want to see him up here this minute."

A pause.

"Secretarial computer tells me that he has left instructions not to be disturbed until his meeting with the South Korean Ambassador is over."

Rachel hesitated, trying to decide whether or not to use it. But then she remembered the pass. François had issued the pass, François had chosen to say nothing, so François had only himself to blame.

"Emergency code 5381. Override secretarial computer and relay my request."

Without waiting for any further backchat she stormed back into the living room and stared at the huge map of Europe spread across one wall. He might be President of Greater Europe, but if he was really proposing to chuck her out on the street for a younger woman, the least he could do was to give her the chance to move out before her replacement arrived.

Several minutes later the bell in the corner of the room chimed, and Dupont stepped nervously out of the lift.

Before he had had a chance to speak she was on her feet glowering at him.

"Hi! I'm Justine," she mimicked. "I've just popped in to tell you that François Dupont has given me a pass and asked me to move in."

Dupont's head hung low, taking the verbal blows with quiet resignation.

"Rachel ..." he began.

"Don't 'Rachel' me, mate. She's young. She's sexy. And for the last ten days you've been trying to get the guts together to tell me you've fallen for her. Am I right, or am I wrong?"

Dupont remained motionless by the lift.

"I wasn't expecting her yet. Not for a few days at least. That's why I hadn't told you about it."

Rachel braced herself inwardly.

"You've got every right to change your mind about our relationship, François," she said calmly. "If you want me to go, please just say so and I'll pack my bags."

Dupont looked up at her in panic.

"No, Rachel, please don't go. Please don't."

Rachel stared at him silently. It was apparent from his reaction that her initial simplistic explanation of Justine's arrival did not make complete sense. For any other man, perhaps, but not for François Dupont. And as she watched him standing by the lift, his head lowered, alone and unprotected, she could feel the anger within her subsiding almost as fast as it had arisen.

"François," she murmured. "Is something wrong? If it is, why don't you tell me about it? We've always talked."

"What did she say?" he asked.

"Exactly what I said. Nothing else. She said she'd come back when I've had a chance to talk to you alone."

Dupont moved over to the sofa and slumped down heavily. For several seconds he closed his eyes and said nothing.

"Her name's Justine Medoc. I knew her before, while you were still with Tom. We had a relationship of sorts."

Rachel looked at him in consternation.

"But she doesn't look a day over twenty now. And you say you were with her two years ago."

Dupont stood up and walked over to the drinks cabinet in the corner of the room. He didn't normally drink, but today he helped himself to a large cognac.

"She's eighteen, coming on nineteen. I said I had a relationship with her before. I didn't say it was sexual. We were . . . friends."

Rachel watched him as he slumped back in the chair with his cognac.

"And now?"

"Tell me, Rachel, do you want a child?" he asked abruptly, his eyes suddenly alert and probing.

"You know I don't. We've talked about that before. I'm too old to start another family."

Dupont fixed her with one of his most penetrating looks, challenging her to work out the rest for herself.

"And you do?" she said slowly.

Dupont nodded.

"But you always said you didn't. When we spoke in the past about it you always said you had no time to look after children."

"I don't have the time. You don't have the time. But she does."

"And so you're proposing to move her in here to carry your child. Is that your plan?"

Dupont nodded slowly.

Rachel started pacing up and down the room.

"Is she pregnant, then?" she asked.

"No. Not by me at any rate. I haven't slept with her, so she couldn't be, could she?"

103

Rachel stopped in her tracks in front of Dupont and swung to face him.

"I'll say this, François. You certainly are a man full of surprises. Two weeks ago in Scotland I thought I was finally beginning to get the measure of you, but now you've thrown this in my face."

François looked up at her towering over him.

"Do you mind?" he asked.

"Jesus! What a question. What if I say yes? What if I do mind?"

Dupont didn't take his eyes off her for a moment.

"Do you remember that day up on the moors in Scotland. I asked you what you'd do if Tom came back. You asked me if I'd share you with him and I said yes. Now it's my turn. Now I'm asking you."

Rachel's head was spinning. Dupont's question had been hypothetical, as had been her answer. But Justine Medoc was right there in Vienna waiting to move in.

"Tom's not the same!"

"Why not, Rachel? Why is Tom not the same? I would have thought Tom was exactly the same."

Rachel looked at him in exasperation and knew he was right. Why had she ever married Tom? What was she looking for, if not for a man to bring up her children and look after them properly?

"You never loved him, did you?" he said without a trace of malice in his voice.

She thought of Tom, thought of all the kindness he had shown her during the seventeen years of their married life together, and with all her heart she wanted to contradict Dupont's accusation.

"No," she said numbly, tears coming into her eyes. "I love you, François. Tom deserved it far more, but it's you I love."

Dupont rose and took her face gently in his hands.

"And it's you I love, Rachel, not Justine Medoc. Please believe me when I tell you that. I want her to stay, I want her to bear my child, but I want you to stay too. I need you to stay. Surely we can find a way to work it out."

Rachel dried her eyes and stepped back. If Tom had really returned it would have been her at the centre of a crazy ménage à trois, sleeping with two different men to avoid sacrificing either of them. The only thing Dupont was asking was that she fulfil a role she had constructed in her mind for him.

"But I don't see how it can work. Not in practice."

Dupont smiled one of his sheepish smiles.

"Look. I've got the South Korean Ambassador waiting downstairs, my love. He's been waiting for weeks for this meeting and if I don't get back soon it's going to cause an international incident. Why don't you talk to her, get to know her, see if you can work something out."

Rachel looked at him numbly and nodded.

Dupont kissed her on the cheek before moving towards the lift.

"I know where she's staying," he said with obvious relief, before pressing the button to close the door. "I'll call her from my office and ask her to come over straight away."

Rachel walked silently over to the window and watched the sunlight glinting on the windows of the surrounding skyscrapers. It did seem a remarkably strange thing to do, but if he really did want to have children perhaps it wasn't such a crazy way to proceed as she had at first supposed. After all, other men in his situation would simply have stepped up the pressure on their reluctant partner to agree. Perhaps Dupont – always a man to seek original solutions to intractable problems – had judged it was better this way. And maybe, just maybe, he would be right again.

Two hours later Justine Medoc stepped once more into the room.

"Hallo," she said.

Rachel walked over to her.

"I'm sorry about the way I greeted you before," she said, holding out her hand.

Justine laughed.

"That's all right. Hardly surprising in the circumstances, I suppose."

"Tea?" Rachel asked, uncertain how to proceed.

"Please," said the girl, flashing a warm smile in her direction.

"Machine!" Rachel ordered, and the thing hurried in from the kitchen.

Justine threw her head back with laughter.

"You don't really call it Machine, do you?"

Rachel looked at it for a moment.

"Yes, and why not?" she asked.

"It's so formal. I won't be able to keep that up for long. What about calling it 'Johann'? You know, like the composer."

Once again her bright innocent laughter filled the room.

"You call it Johann if you like," Rachel said drily. "I think I'll stick with Machine, if you don't mind."

Justine walked to the window and gazed out.

"Great view," she commented admiringly.

"Two teas!" Rachel ordered, and then walked over to join the newcomer by the window.

"François has told me you're going to bear his child," she said.

"Yup. I'm going to try. François said you'd already had a family and weren't too keen on starting another."

Rachel swallowed hard. Then she nodded.

"I hope you'll play Auntie, though," Justine said with a grin, once again tossing the hair away from her eyes.

Try as she might, Rachel couldn't find the correct words to express herself. Again she nodded. But Justine must have taken her silence for anger.

"I'm sorry I said that about your machine. I think Machine is a cute name, really I do."

Suddenly, without being able to help herself, Rachel couldn't help but burst out laughing.

"I'm not angry," she said when she had managed to control herself. "It's just that this has come as a bit of shock to me. I'm still trying to get used to the idea."

Justine smiled affectionately.

"If you really want I suppose I could live somewhere else. But François thought you'd prefer it this way. He thought it'd be more honest."

Machine clanked in with the tea and Rachel passed her a cup before taking one for herself.

"Why don't we sit down for a bit before we decide anything," Rachel said with a smile. "And while we're drinking our tea, why don't you tell me how you got to know François."

Justine sipped her drink and nodded.

"Known him since I was a kid, actually. To tell you the truth, I've always been rather keen on him, ever since I was about twelve years old."

Rachel looked at her thoughtfully.

"Just friends?" she asked.

Justine giggled.

"Afraid so," she said. "It wasn't for lack of trying on my part, mind you. But François always said I was too young for him."

"Did he ask you to bear his child, Justine?" Rachel asked.

"I hadn't seen François for about two years, not since he became President. Then, a couple of weeks ago, we met by chance and got to talking. We just sort of decided it between us."

Rachel eyed her suspiciously. Presidents don't just bump into people. Their security personnel don't give them the opportunity. But she decided to drop the subject.

A serious look came over Justine's face.

"Are you going to be jealous of me?" she asked.

Rachel gulped.

"I don't know. I should be, I suppose."

"Please don't be. It's you he really loves, you know."

Rachel said nothing. She didn't really doubt that François loved her, at least on a cerebral level. But the young girl sitting next to her, her slender body scarcely concealed beneath the light cotton frock, couldn't help but make her aware of the ravages time and three babies had inflicted on her own looks. She may well still be good-looking for a forty-year-old, but she certainly wasn't eighteen any more.

The girl must have read her thoughts.

"He really enjoys you sexually," she said sheepishly, "so you don't need to worry about that."

Rachel gulped again. If somebody had told her a few days before that this conversation was going to happen she would have laughed in their face. But the most extraordinary thing about the situation was that however hard she tried to be angry, however hard she tried to hate the girl sitting next to her, she couldn't summon up the relevant emotions. In fact, she had to admit she was beginning to find certain aspects of the whole thing tremendously amusing.

"What are we going to do, then?" she said. "Take turns?"

"I'm easy," Justine replied. "However it suits you."

Rachel hastily took another sip of tea, wishing she hadn't raised the subject. But Justine had obviously got interested.

"Is he any good in bed?" she said with a snigger. "I've always wondered? Ever since I was twelve."

Rachel stared at her intently for several seconds. A thought had suddenly occurred to her, an evil thought perhaps, but certainly an excellent way of getting her own back on François Dupont for inflicting such a bizarre shock on her without any warning.

"I've just had a good idea," she said, a broad grin spreading slowly across her face, "an idea that will determine whether this little cohabitation plan of François's is really going to work."

* * * * * *

It was nearly ten o'clock in the evening when Dupont finally arrived back at the flat. Casting his eye warily in the direction of the two women sitting beside each other on the sofa with their backs to him, he stepped gingerly out of the lift and moved towards them.

"I'm back," he said, a distinctly nervous tone to his voice.

Rachel turned to face him, smiling reassuringly.

"We can hear that, François. Why don't you come and join us?"

He moved cautiously to an armchair opposite the sofa and sat down. Justine smiled.

"Good day?" she asked, a sly grin spreading across her face.

Dupont sat forward in his chair, reluctant to relax until he had assessed the situation before him. He had been expecting to find considerable tension in the flat on his return, perhaps even a full scale row of some sort, and with his usual forethought he had prepared a strategy to deal with such a contingency. But Rachel and Justine were leaning back on the sofa almost as if they were old friends.

"I'm sorry about the mix-up earlier today," he said, ignoring Justine's question. "It was all my fault."

Rachel and Justine turned to each other and smiled. But they said nothing, preferring to enjoy the unusual sight of François Dupont visibly squirming.

"Had a chance to talk things through yet?" Dupont asked.

Rachel looked at him sweetly.

"Tea?" she asked. "We were about to have some."

Dupont nodded.

"Johann!" Rachel called in the direction of the kitchen, and Dupont swung round quickly to see who was there.

"Don't worry, darling. It's only Machine's new name."

Dupont looked at her dumb-founded.

"But ..."

"Justine and I decided Machine was too boring. So we re-programmed it, didn't we, Justine?"

Justine laid her hand affectionately on Rachel's lap as Johann clattered into the room and awaited their instructions.

"Rachel did it for me, really," she said. "You see, François, we've spent the last eight hours trying to work out how we can all live in this admittedly spacious flat without getting on each other's nerves."

Rachel turned towards the machine.

"Johann, three teas please. Oh, and when you've done that, pour François a nice hot bath with lots of pine essence."

If it had been possible for Dupont to look more anxious still he would have done so, but he was already approaching total stress asymptotically.

"I'm not sure I want a bath tonight, my love," he said. "To tell you the truth, I've had a rather tiring day. I was thinking of getting to bed early."

Justine giggled.

"But François, darling," Rachel said, "a bath will do you a power of good. Help you to relax."

"We both understand how important it is for you to relax," Justine added, tossing the hair away from her brow. "We've decided that's going to be our central concern."

Dupont was frantically trying to recover his composure. If indeed the idea of having two strong-minded ladies living simultaneously in his flat had ever appealed to him, the appeal seemed to be fading fast.

Rachel watched his discomfort with pleasure.

"I suppose we ought to fill you in on what we've decided, François," she said.

She paused to allow the force of her words to sink in. From her tone it was clear that he was going to have to accept the agreed arrangements without consultation.

Dupont nodded quietly. Only when she was sure he had grasped the point did Rachel continue.

"Justine and I have decided to act as company for each other during some of the long hours when you are concerned with affairs of state. At first we weren't too sure, but after talking it through, we think we can get on perfectly well..."

"Rachel's going to act as Auntie when the baby comes, show me what to do," Justine chipped in.

Rachel looked askance at Dupont. Somewhat to her surprise, the thought of a tiny baby in his flat only seemed to increase the air of despondency that hung over him. But he must have noticed her looking at him, because his face broke into a rather strained smile.

"Good idea," he said brightly. "That's what I thought."

Justine jumped to her feet.

"Where did you put it, Rachel?" she asked. "We can probably fit another one in while François has his bath."

"Third drawer down in the desk," Rachel replied, picking up two of the teacups from the waiting Johann. "And Johann, take François's tea through to the bathroom."

Dupont watched Justine walking over to the desk, deliberately swinging her slender hips as she went.

"What's going on now?" he asked.

Justine stopped in her tracks and approached the chair where he was sitting.

"You're going to take tea in the bath," she said, kissing him gently on the cheek, "while we have another game of Scrabble."

Richard Coward

His lips moved but no sound came forth. Instead, he quietly rose to his feet and passively followed Johann off towards the bathroom.

As soon as he was gone, Justine turned to Rachel with a grin.

"This is more fun than I'd ever imagined," she said. "I've never seen him like this before."

Rachel looked at her with curiosity.

"What was he like with you? Years ago, I mean, when you were a child."

Justine collected the Scrabble from the desk and started distributing the pieces.

"Quiet, I suppose," she said. "Quiet and thoughtful. A man of dark but irresistible charm."

Rachel pulled up a second chair to the desk and sat down.

"That's what I don't understand about you, Justine," she said. "I mean in my case I can see what I like about François. I'm forty years old, well past the first flush of my youth. A mature woman, you might say. A man of dark charm in his mid-forties might be expected to appeal to a rather serious-minded person like me. But you, you're young and vibrant, you've got a positively impish sense of humour. I can't for the life of me imagine what you see in him."

Justine placed a word on the Scrabble board and noted down the score.

"I think it's because he's a challenge," she said.

"A challenge?"

"Yes. He's so dour. When I was a kid I used to do all sorts of tricks to try and make him laugh. I suppose you could say it became a bit of an obsession with me."

Rachel picked up five letters and put them on the board, neatly interlocking Justine's opening move.

"It's a funny reason to have somebody's baby," she commented.

"Maybe," Justine replied non-committally, carefully studying her pieces. "But maybe I'm a funny person."

Rachel thought of Dupont sitting in the bath. Part of her almost pitied him, but then he only had himself to blame by moving Justine in like this.

"Do you suppose he's got any idea what we've got planned for him once he's finished in there?" she asked,

"You should know better than me, Rachel. After all, you've lived with him."

Rachel shrugged.

"It's never been central to our relationship. Maybe that's why I think I can cope with all this. We lived here for nearly one and a

110

half years without doing anything at all. A totally platonic relationship. But he's not really on his home ground when it comes to sex, that's for sure."

"And you're certain you want to do it this way," Justine said, her face growing serious.

Rachel hesitated for only a second before replying.

"Oh yes," she said. "In fact, this is the only way I think we can do it."

Away in the distance, they could hear the bath water running away. Justine flicked a glance at Rachel and started to pack away the Scrabble things. A few minutes later, Dupont returned. Usually he returned from a bath naked, but this evening he had carefully put all his clothes back on.

Rachel walked towards the wall and touched a small recessed panel. As she did so, the lights dimmed and changed tone, flooding the room with a softly seductive tone of pink.

Justine waited by the desk, watching as Dupont first slowed his pace and then came to a complete halt. For a while, none of them said a word. Then Rachel moved back towards the desk and stood beside Justine.

"We forgot to explain something before, darling," Rachel murmured softly. "We think there should be a new house rule around here. In a ménage à trois like this, jealousy between Justine and I could rapidly turn life into a living hell for all three of us. So since it seems you want both of us, we've decided to oblige."

Dupont looked at them in consternation.

"Oblige . . .?"

Rachel turned to Justine.

"Justine, could you help me with my zip, please."

Justine threw a grin in the general direction of Dupont's frozen expression before turning towards Rachel.

"Certainly," she said, and as soon as she had drawn down the zip Rachel let the dress fall silently to the floor. She stood there naked, wearing nothing but a bra and one of her briefest and most seductive pairs of white silk knickers. Reaching behind her, she silently undid the catch on the bra and let that too fall to the ground.

Dupont was staring in horror at the scene unfolding before his eyes. Unperturbed, Rachel turned and lowered Justine's zip, standing back to allow her plain cotton frock to drop neatly to the floor. Then, without a word, Justine too removed her bra.

Wearing nothing but their knickers, the two women gradually approached the frozen figure of François Dupont. And as they came

111

closer, Rachel could see the horror in his eyes gradually being replaced by a look of quiet resignation.

"I think you're beginning to get the idea," Rachel murmured.

Dupont nodded, his eyes flicking apprehensively backwards and forwards between Rachel and Justine. If he could have stepped backwards he probably would have done so, but he had been foolish enough to allow himself to become helplessly trapped between the the approaching women and the sofa.

Rachel held back.

"If it's all right by you, François, Justine's going to undress you today," she said with a smile.

Dupont nodded slowly.

Justine started work on his shirt buttons, her fingers savouring an experience she had craved for many years. Rachel stood and watched as she worked, and as she watched she found herself surprised by her own reactions to an experience she had never in a million years imagined she would have. Although it had been her idea to tackle Dupont openly together, she had expected to find it harrowing, particularly at first. But instead she realised by the quickening pace of her heartbeat that she was actually finding the occasion rather exciting.

"François," Justine said coyly, "you don't need to look so worried. It's not the first time I've seen you naked, you know."

He looked down at her with surprise.

"No?"

"No. Sometimes when you came to visit I used to climb up into the attic. I drilled a little hole in the ceiling of your bedroom so I could watch while you undressed."

Dupont passively allowed her to remove his shirt.

"You did?" he asked numbly. "Why?"

Rachel laughed.

"Because she fancied you, you stupid man," she said.

"The trouble was," Justine added, pulling down his trouser zip, "that the hole wasn't very big. I only ever saw you from the top, when you walked underneath. You can't see terribly much from the top."

She pulled off his trousers and then his socks before kneeling down in front of him and taking a firm hold of his pants in both hands.

"At the time," she added with a grin, flicking a friendly glance at Rachel, "I always wanted to do this."

And with a sharp tug she pulled his pants down to the floor before pushing him gently back onto the sofa.

There was no denying that the experiment had proved to be an extraordinary success. Perhaps it was the difference in their ages or perhaps it was some strange similarity of purpose or personality, but Rachel had experienced absolutely no difficulty in coming to terms with Justine Medoc.

The younger girl seemed to accept Rachel's overall authority as senior consort to François Dupont without demur, welcoming her advice on practical matters of which she had very little understanding. Now, just as before, Dupont would spend many of his free hours in conversation with Rachel, discussing the continuing development of the Europe under his control and jointly planning the referendum which Dupont now firmly claimed as one of his most brilliant ideas. During these conversations, in which Justine generally displayed little interest, she would either sit and read in the corner of the room where they were talking, or quietly slope off to her bedroom in order to watch a video.

To the outside world the whole episode had been greeted with considerable amusement. The three of them had jointly decided to maintain the policy of allowing their domestic arrangements to be covered in the media, and so Europe's citizens were well aware that their leader was now in possession of a small but growing harem. In fact, it had been Rachel who had gone on television to make the official announcement, explaining that she had no wish to bear another child and that she welcomed Justine Medoc into her home in order to do so.

But today, Rachel found herself alone in the flat. Dupont was at work and Justine had gone into Old Vienna to officially open a new art gallery. Unlike Rachel, Justine seemed to have developed something of a taste for ceremonial duties, and with her youth and flamboyant personality had developed a considerable reputation with those in the media concerned with fashion and social events.

Johann clattered noisily into the living room, a small letter lying in one of its recesses.

"This arrived by special courier," it stated blankly, one of its arms picking up the package and holding it out for Rachel to take.

Rachel looked at the silent machine.

"By special courier?" she asked.

"Yes, Rachel. It is addressed to you by name and is marked 'strictly private and confidential'."

"Has it been security scanned?" she queried.

"Of course, Rachel."

Rachel nervously picked up the envelope and examined it. And as she did so, she could feel a tight knot beginning to form in the pit of her stomach. For there could be no mistaking the spiky writing in which her name had been scrawled. It was a letter from André Rostropov.

For a moment she hesitated, reluctant to risk opening up once more the fears she had experienced at the time of President Goldberger's visit. But despite her attempts at restraint, her fingers silently pulled open the letter and she started to read the contents.

'My dear Rachel,' it began. 'You should know as you read this letter that I am growing weaker by the day. As you are no doubt aware, since I last met you I have become one of what are euphemistically known in contemporary Europe as the living dead. And although I did not have the disease when I saw you last, I have unfortunately contracted it since. Soon, very soon perhaps, I will be dead.

'When I met you nearly two years ago I was hoping to tell you of the terrible fears that were beginning to form themselves in my mind as I investigated the White Death. At that time, my dear Rachel, my thoughts were only hunches, vague feelings of unease that I would have been completely unable to substantiate even in normal times, never mind against the increasingly oppressive political environment in which I found myself forced to operate.

'I had hoped to share these feelings, these hunches, with you. But when I met you that day I confirmed my sad suspicion that you had firmly appended yourself to François Dupont's camp. I was afraid that if I were to tell you what I believed, you would not only have discounted everything I said as a desperate ploy by a political opponent, but also prevented me from continuing with my investigations by informing the new authorities. I have to say that nothing in your conduct since then has caused me to doubt that I made the correct decision that day.

'Suspecting that the authorities would not be far behind me, I therefore opted to continue my work underground. It was for that reason, and that reason alone, that I joined the living dead.

'I was determined to investigate my hunches in my own time and in my own way, retaining my freedom for long enough to be able to prove beyond doubt that I was right. Sadly, however, although I have made some progress since I met you, the disease has now

114

caught me firmly in its grasp. Although I have no pain, my skin has lost all its colour, and I am now certain I do not have long to live.

'I have tried everything and come full circle. So now I am back to you, my dear Rachel, and I calculate you are my final chance.

'I am not going to tell you what I now believe to be true in this letter, Rachel, in case, either by chance or design, it falls into the wrong hands. But as a friend of many years standing, I implore you to come and speak with me one more time before it is too late.

'If you will come, find a reason to visit your father in Scotland. When you arrive, you will be contacted.

'For ever yours, André.'

KNOYDART, SCOTLAND, NOVEMBER 2006

The car sped along the road beside the loch, closely followed by another. Rachel flicked a glance into the rear view mirror and silently cursed the two ever present security men who accompanied her every time she left their New Vienna flat. She had nearly tried to persuade Dupont to let her travel alone to visit her father, but such an unusual request would only have aroused his suspicions unnecessarily. Better to act as normal and let André make his move when he was ready.

But even as she drove she wondered why she was making the journey at all. When she had heard several months before that André had approached the Americans, her instinct had been to trace him and find out exactly what had prompted his concerns. But on that earlier occasion Dupont had successfully managed to divert her from her purpose and convince her that the exercise was pointless.

As she reflected on the way Dupont had achieved his objective, she could not help but feel a vague sense of unease. For he had actually postulated two plausible explanations for André's behaviour, not one. To the American President, he had argued that André's beliefs might have been well-founded, but that it was the Green Party during their brief control of the Environment Commissioner's ministry who had constructed a false report to substantiate their claims about the disease's origins in the Danish bio-chemical industry. But later, Dupont had convinced her that André was himself the liar, deliberately throwing together a disinformation campaign to destabilise his regime. Although at the time she had not really noticed it, the two versions did not really tie up properly.

When she had first received André's letter, however, she had still been inclined to disregard it. In fact, she had carefully placed the letter on the desk, intending to discuss its contents with Dupont on his return that evening. On an objective level, the letter added nothing to what she knew already. It could have been simply another ruse by a political opponent to influence the course of events. She knew Dupont would have argued just that if he had seen the letter.

It had taken Rachel two hours heavy gardening to convince herself that she should remove the letter from the desk and hide it amongst her things. As once before, André's ghost seemed to live amongst the plants, pleading with her to meet him and make for herself a judgement about his worries. Eventually, personal loyalty had forced her to allow him that at least before he died.

Dupont had returned that evening shortly after Justine and they had all sat down to a meal. While they were eating, Rachel had asked him in passing whether a reply had yet been sent to President Goldberger about the origins of the White Death. Dupont had replied casually that the re-examination of the data by his own scientists had found nothing to seriously challenge the findings of the original report, and that a great deal of evidence still pointed in the direction of the Danish laboratory. Lionel, as Dupont now referred to Goldberger, had been sent a copy of the report and had apparently accepted its main conclusions.

So that at least had ruled out one of Dupont's two original explanations of André's approach to the Americans. All she had to do now was confirm that the other one was correct, and that André himself was the true source of the disinformation.

The heather-clad hill country through which she was passing was becoming increasingly familiar. To either side, away beyond the loch to her right and immediately above her on her left, she could see the craggy peaks of the mountains she had climbed as a child. So much had happened to her since those days, but the hills were exactly as they had been then, looking down on those who passed along the narrow valleys beneath with a timeless tranquility.

Suddenly, she indicated right and pulled into a small lay-by overlooking the loch, nearly causing the car behind her to overshoot. But the driver, a thick-set man in his early thirties by the name of Mike Flannery, was pretty nifty in these circumstances. He just managed to scrape into the lay-by behind her.

"Jesus, Mrs McNie," he said, climbing out of his car, "that was a bit sudden. You got problems with the car?"

Rachel, who had already got out of the car and was walking out onto the moors, looked at him.

"Sorry, Mike," she said. "I was suffering from nostalgia pangs, that's all."

Mike Flannery was a friendly enough sort of chap, a former night-watchman who had successfully applied for late entry into the security service. These days he was often attached to Rachel as one of her personal security guards, a role he seemed to relish.

"Yeah, you grew up in Scotland, didn't you?" he asked, standing beside her but flicking his eyes around continually in the reflex manner of a trained security man.

"Yup," she said.

"Brought my kids up here for a holiday a few years back," he said. "I'm afraid they hated it. They said there was nothing to do."

"They were right," she said, turning to smile at him, but before he had had a chance to reply she could see his flicking eyes freeze, staring intently at a point on the hillside above the road some way ahead.

"Get down!" he yelled suddenly, pushing her roughly with one arm into the heather while with his other he started to grab his gun from its holster inside his jacket. His colleague, standing by the car, instantly swung round and began to pull out his own revolver.

The round of automatic fire was brief but intense, throwing Flannery back into the heather beside Rachel and ramming the other guard up against the side of the car. Then there was silence.

Rachel twisted in the grass and stared in horror at the lifeless face that had once belonged to Mike Flannery. Even in death his gun was in his hand, almost as if he were still trying to protect her from the afterlife.

The tall heather provided relatively good cover against their assailants. Rachel gently pulled Flannery's gun away from his fingers and lay absolutely still, trying unsuccessfully to see what was happening on the hillside through the undergrowth.

"Stand up with your hands raised!" came a sudden order. It echoed around her from the steep surrounding hillsides, making it hard to tell exactly where it was coming from.

She looked down at the gun in her hand and back at the corpse beside her, wondering whether to try and crawl away, but her situation was obviously hopeless. There was no one to help her, only mile after endless mile of moorland stretching away as far as the eye could see in every direction.

"We're not going to hurt you, Mrs McNie," the echoing voice called out. "Simply stand up with your hands raised above your

117

head."

Rachel lifted up her dress and pushed Flannery's revolver inside her underwear, pulling her jumper down low to conceal the bulge. Then, slowly and deliberately, she raised her hands high above her head and stood up.

As she did so, two men emerged from behind a rock on the far side of the road and approached. One of them, holding a light machine gun, remained where he was, while the other started clambering rapidly down the hillside towards the road.

As he approached she could see he was a handsome man, scarcely more than twenty, with chiselled features and long blonde hair which suggested Scandinavian origins. But his fresh young face already bore the unmistakable marks of one used to leading a rough outdoor life.

When he reached the road he stopped cautiously and looked at Rachel.

"Are they dead?" he asked.

Rachel turned to look at the lifeless body of Flannery's partner lying by the car.

"I think so," she replied. "Look for yourself."

He circled round her and inspected the bodies, carefully removing the gun from the man lying beside the car.

"Mrs McNie," he said when he had finished, "I'm afraid I'm going to have to ask you to stand with your legs astride and your hands on top of the car. But before I search you perhaps you could hand over the gun you took from the guard."

Rachel reached into her clothing and pulled out the gun before doing as he had asked.

"I'm sorry about this," the man said as he thoroughly frisked her, "but we have to be careful."

"Who are you?" she asked.

"You can call me Bjorn. I work for Rostropov."

Suddenly Rachel remembered Flannery. She had met his kids once, three delightful little girls who would now have to grow up without a father.

"You bastard!" she said, swinging round to face the man. "Didn't you realise I'd come of my own free will to see André. You could have contacted me without murdering my escort."

Bjorn looked at her thoughtfully.

"That's what André said," he muttered. "But André was outvoted."

* * * * * *

After what seemed like hours the jeep in which they were driving pulled sharply to a halt and the engine fell silent. She heard the sound of doors slamming as her two escorts climbed out of the car. Then her door was opened and a hand caught hold of her arm.

"Follow me," Bjorn said. "I'll take the blindfold off as soon as we get inside."

Rachel allowed herself to be steered along. She had already guessed that they were somewhere in the remote hill country, because the jeep had been travelling for some time over a rough pot-holed track, but her suspicions were now confirmed by the springy grass underfoot.

After a short walk Bjorn led her over a step and onto a solid stone floor. Behind her, she could hear a door slamming, and then the blindfold was removed.

She looked around. They were standing in some kind of rough log cabin, an open fire crackling away merrily in the hearth. Several pieces of ancient wooden furniture were scattered around the room, including a bed with a rough straw mattress. The windows had been boarded up to prevent anyone seeing out, and the only light came from an ancient gas lamp in the corner. Apart from Rachel, only Bjorn was in the room.

"I'm sorry about all this," he said apologetically. "I know you probably did come of your own free will."

Rachel sat down on the bed.

"What do you mean 'probably'?" she asked.

"It might have been a trick," he replied.

She thought for a moment.

"I suppose you're right," she said.

Bjorn hesitated.

"And maybe it's better for you this way. Officially you've been kidnapped."

Rachel looked at him sharply.

"And 'unofficially'?" she asked.

"Unofficially you're our guest."

Rachel picked up the blindfold lying on the bed beside her.

"Some hospitality," she muttered.

Bjorn shrugged, sitting down beside her on the bed.

"Look," he said, "you're not a prisoner here, Mrs McNie. If you want to go, just say so."

She looked at him blankly.

"Are you serious?" she asked.

"Perfectly. If you want, I'll put the blindfold back on right now and I'll drop you off somewhere suitable where you can be picked up. That was the deal we struck with André."

Rachel thought for a minute.

"First I want to see him. Is he here?"

Bjorn stood up and warmed his hands by the fire.

"Not far. But before you see him, I've got to explain some of the ground rules of our community."

Rachel suddenly remembered the White Death. Instinctively, she edged away from where Bjorn was standing.

"You know us as the living dead," he continued, "but we prefer the phrase 'free community'. Just how much do you know about us, Mrs McNie?"

"I know enough to know you're dangerous," she said. "I know many of you are infected with the White Death."

Bjorn laughed.

"Is that why you moved away from me just now, Mrs McNie? You suddenly realised I might be infected."

Rachel remained silent.

"Allow me to introduce myself. Dr Bjorn Haverstamp, formerly senior research associate at the Stockholm Institute for Infectious Diseases. And in case you're still wondering, I know what I'm talking about when I tell you I'm definitely not a carrier."

Rachel rose to her feet.

"You're a doctor?" she said with surprise.

Bjorn laughed.

"Yes. I'm twenty-nine. People generally think I look much younger. It's a common mistake with fair-haired Scandinavians."

For some reason, Rachel couldn't help shuddering. She had been expecting André to be surrounded by fanatical terrorists, not research scientists.

Bjorn's face grew serious.

"Although I'm not a carrier there are plenty in this community who are, and you've got to be careful if you want to stay clean. So if you want to stay alive, I suggest you follow my guidance to the letter."

Bjorn swung one leg over a wooden bench and sat down.

"As you know, the White Death is transmitted by body fluids, most easily through sexual transmission, but also via other routes. Therefore you must avoid mixing up your body fluids with anyone else's unless you know they're clean. It's really a simple matter of rigorous hygiene."

"What do you do then, segregate them?" Rachel asked.

Bjorn smiled.

"No, Mrs McNie. It's you who believes in segregation. We believe in education."

Rachel allowed the remark to pass.

"Anyway, as I say, it's hygiene you've got to watch around here. We test in this community. By and large, we know who's infected and who isn't. Toilets, cooking, water, washing, laundry and so on are carefully separated. But most living areas are mixed, with one important proviso: whenever you enter a mixed environment, you always wear a mask."

He rose from the bench and pulled open a cupboard.

"Here's yours," he continued, throwing her a rough face mask fitted with some kind of filtration device.

Suddenly Rachel remembered the Latvian group of living dead who had been picked up recently. Nearly all of them had been infected, despite any precautions they took. She picked up the mask.

"And all these precautions," she asked, "do they really work?"

Bjorn nodded.

"Six months ago fifty percent of us were infected. Now it's down to nearer thirty percent. Mind you, we're pretty strict in this community, much more than in some of the others."

Rachel looked up at him sharply.

"Strict? What do you do if someone breaks the rules."

"Not many try. If they do, we hold a hearing to establish the circumstances. If they're guilty, we shoot them."

Rachel flinched.

"What! Even children?"

Bjorn laughed.

"No, children we segregate. You can't expect children to behave as responsible adults."

"You seem pretty thorough. I always thought you people were supposed to be soft in the head."

Bjorn smiled.

"We're not stupid here," he said. "In fact, I'd say that if we want to survive we have to be cleverer than you do in your society. But whether we tackle it your way or ours, this disease is a killer, and anyone who forgets that fact might as well jump off the nearest convenient cliff."

"So how many of you are here?" she asked.

Bjorn shook his head.

"You don't need to know that, do you, Mrs McNie? All you need to do is put on the mask and the blindfold and come with me. I know André's looking forward very much to seeing you."

Rachel rose and carefully fitted the mask. But as Bjorn raised his

121

arm to put on the blindfold, she caught hold of his arm and looked intently at him.

"Before we go, tell me how he is. Is it true he's near to death?"

Bjorn flinched.

"Yes," he said bluntly, "I'm afraid he is."

He led her out of the hut and guided her by the arm over the springy grass to another building. It must have been larger than the one she had just left, because she could hear the sound of many voices. After a few minutes they must have entered an inner room, because the noise of the other people faded somewhat.

"Take the blindfold off whenever you're ready, Mrs McNie," Bjorn's voice said, and then she could hear the sound of a door closing behind her and footsteps retreating into the distance.

She pulled off the blindfold. The room in which she found herself was much the same as the previous one, with rough wooden walls and rougher wooden furniture. But she took little notice of the inanimate surroundings, for ahead of her, some ten feet distant, a thin skeletal-like figure was lying slumped on a bed, his head turned away from her.

"André?" she said.

The head turned slowly to face her and she felt herself shudder. It suddenly occurred to her that it was several years since she had seen a victim in the last throws of the White Death. Media rules in Dupont's Europe were very strict on that point. The sallow features of the figure lying before her were completely devoid of skin pigmentation, creating the impression of some kind of weird ghost in a cheap horror movie.

"Rachel," André murmured. "You came."

Rachel remembered the robust man he had once been.

"How could I not come?" she said, trying without success to ignore the terrible effect his appearance was having upon her.

André smiled weakly.

"I'm not a pretty sight, am I?" he said.

Rachel bit her lip.

"It's not your fault," was the best she could think of.

This time André tried to laugh, but the disease seemed to have affected his vocal chords, because all that came out was a nasal croking noise.

"Yes it is. I could have followed your route, stayed in the main stream."

Rachel hung her head and remained silent. She found no pleasure in telling a dying man she had told him so.

"What did you make of Bjorn?" André asked presently.

"He's clever all right and vicious when he wants to be."

André made a huge effort to raise himself up in the bed. Without thinking, Rachel started to approach him, intending to lift the pillows.

"Don't!" André warned. "You're only wearing a mask, Rachel. You mustn't touch me unless you're wearing full protective clothing."

With an enormous effort of willpower he managed to prop himself up. As soon as he had done so he fixed her with a penetrating stare.

"I didn't ask you to go through all this for a social chat, Rachel, pleasant though such an experience invariably is," he said.

Rachel took a deep breath.

"I've come to listen, André. I don't know if you realised at the time, but last time we spoke I deliberately chose not to listen. I didn't want my loyalty towards you to interfere with my loyalty towards François Dupont."

"So what has changed?" André asked.

For a long time there was silence.

"You're dying, André. That's what has changed."

He rolled his eyes to heaven.

"The things a man has to do to make a girl listen to him," he said.

The humour failed. In fact it made her feel angry. She remembered Flannery and Flannery's three little girls.

"Tell me what you've got to say, André. And then, if I may, I'll go."

André raised his emaciated arm and indicated a pile of papers in the corner of the room.

"Over there. Read that lot."

She fetched the sheaf of papers and sat down again. They were handwritten, as if even the humble typewriter was technologically too advanced for this semi-nomadic 'free community'.

"Your research?" she asked.

André's face cracked into a smile.

"Yours actually. If you remember, it was you who put me onto this project in the first place."

Rachel laid the bundle of papers on the floor and picked up the first sheet, reading fast but with total concentration. It took her over an hour to finish. When she had done so, she gathered the papers together and placed them back on the table where she had found them.

"It's not conclusive," she said slowly, a strangely confused look on her face. "Nothing whatsoever in that lot is conclusive."

123

Again André smiled his pathetic smile.

"Sorry boss. I ran out of time."

She looked back at the sheaf of papers lying where she had placed it. It couldn't be like he was saying. It just wasn't possible.

André could see the distress written all over her face.

"Why don't you go then, Rachel? You've done your duty. You've heard me out. Now you can go back to your comfortable flat in New Vienna with a clean conscience."

Rachel rose slowly to her feet, intent upon walking out as he had suggested. But however hard she tried she could not take her eyes off the pile of papers she had just read, sitting just where she had placed them on the table in the corner of the room. They seemed to taunt her, to challenge her to seek out the truth, however unpalatable that truth might be.

She sat down again.

"And you? How sure are you? In your own mind?" she asked numbly.

Once again, the strange choking sound came out of André's mouth.

"I never was a gambling man, Rachel. There isn't any concrete proof, is there? You know me too well to expect me to run with a story like this without any proof."

Rachel looked at him sharply.

"You ran to the Americans, André."

"I only ran with what I knew for sure. Nothing more, nothing less. But as you probably know, the soothing words of François Dupont appear to have convinced Goldberger that the Danish story was correct and that I'm just another frustrated dissident with a grudge."

"Which you are," she pointed out.

The slight movement of André's shrunken head indicated he took her point.

"Of course. So why don't you go?"

Again Rachel tried to rise, but this time she didn't even get on her feet.

"I can't, André. You know that. Not having read that stuff. Not till I know."

She could almost feel André relaxing as he lay on the bed.

"That's all I'm asking, Rachel. I can't finish this work, and anyway I've exhausted nearly all the sources I can approach from the outside. But you're on the inside, you might be able to find something out that will tell you whether I'm right or I'm wrong. Just look into it, Rachel, that's all I want."

Rachel's head was beginning to spin. For the past two years she had held François Dupont in awe. She had loved him, respected him, helped him in what she had earnestly believed to be his quest to save Europe from total disaster.

So how exactly was she now expected to come to terms with André Rostropov's extraordinary assertion that the same François Dupont was personally responsible for a disease which had already wiped out over a third of the world's population?

* * * * * *

She sat alone on the bed and read the papers through again for the fifth or sixth time. André might be dying, but the disease did not seem to have impaired his impressive logical faculties. Every statement was qualified, every lingering doubt made clear, every unsubstantiated assertion laid bare. But despite the continual hedging, the frequent qualifications, the freely accepted gaps in the reasoning, the document she was reading was a terrifying and ferocious indictment of François Dupont.

André began the case against him with a painstaking demolition of the Danish story. It had been compiled in conjunction with Bjorn and several other dissident scientists in related fields, and proved beyond reasonable doubt that the research undertaken at the Danish laboratory could not possibly have resulted in the development of a mutant agent with the characteristics of the White Death. Most of the evidence had come directly from scientists who had worked at the Danish plant, nearly all of whom had subsequently caught the disease and died.

It was this story, the most well-substantiated part of the whole document, which André had taken to the Americans. But he had deliberately concealed from Goldberger the rest of the material in order to set a trap for Dupont, a trap which would help establish whether the hunch which had been worrying André for many months was well founded.

Goldberger had unwittingly played his part according to plan and had immediately informed Dupont of the accusations André had made. The critical test was then to see how the European President would react in the face of this new information. Predictably, he had promised Goldberger that he would investigate the earlier European Commission report prepared while Vintner was still President to see if it was true. At that time, he could legitimately have disclaimed responsibility for the earlier report and declared the Danish story to be a bigoted Green Party fraud.

But Dupont had failed the test set for him. His own scientists had produced yet another report that flew directly in the face of the evidence André and his colleagues had assembled with the help of the scientists from the Danish plant. Reluctantly, Rachel had to admit that the evidence of a cover-up by François Dupont was virtually unassailable if the technical material in André's report was true.

But why would Dupont go to such apparent lengths to conceal the falsity of the Danish report? What did he have to gain from such a cover-up? These were the next questions to which André referred in his report. But when he moved on to these issues he himself admitted that the evidence was far more circumstantial.

André made no secret of the fact that he started from an assumption of Dupont's guilt. He openly accepted that he didn't like the man and believed him to be thoroughly evil. That had been the basis of his original warning to Rachel several years before not to trust him. According to André, this presumption of evil, the 'stench' of evil as André called it, had originally been based on nothing more than an anguished childhood in Brezhnev's Russia coupled with a mature adult life in pursuit of truth in human affairs.

So feeding the Danish story to the Americans had been as much André's test of himself as a test of François Dupont. In the best scientific tradition, he had tried to falsify his own presumption of Dupont's guilt. He had tried to prove himself wrong, but instead had only succeeded in reinforcing his growing conviction that all was not as it seemed.

Having critically examined his own feelings, André turned to Dupont's. He tried to approach the problem laterally, taking as his starting point a seemingly absurd hypothesis, the hypothesis that Dupont had tried to conceal information about the origin of the White Death simply because he himself was in some way responsible for it.

Wearily, Rachel laid the report down on the table and lay back on the bed. As André had no doubt known when he had persuaded her to come to see him, the hypothesis once raised could not be easily dismissed. However hard you tried to dislodge it from its perch, it remained doggedly in position.

André had attempted a difficult task, an objective character analysis of a man he clearly detested. Together with some of his colleagues in the underground, he had pieced together a detailed life history of François Dupont that stretched to some two hundred pages. Much of the material had come from publicly available sources, but they had not confined themselves to such evidence.

The most perceptive section about Dupont concerned his child-hood. Agents of the underground had visited Epillion. They had spoken with many people in the village who had known Dupont's parents during his early life. A number of these people had apparently formed the opinion that Dupont's young mother had been mentally unstable, and a few had even been convinced that she had taken her own life. In his usual manner, André had heavily qualified this section of his findings, repeatedly reminding the reader that it would be unwise to place too much reliance on idle village gossip concerning events so many years distant in time.

Rachel shuddered as she remembered her conversation with Claude Maurisseur and his eye-witness account of Dupont's mother's death. At the time she had not read any particular significance into what she had understood as the unbearable grief of a recently-bereaved young mother. But in the context of the hypothesis postulated by André, she could not help but wonder whether his mother's mental disorder had been permanent.

André's analysis of Dupont's childhood did not stop at Epillion, however. Eye-witness accounts substantiated the impression Rachel had already formed that the time he had subsequently spent in the children's home had been an unhappy one. Until fairly late in adolescence, Dupont had been a lonely boy, suffering from acute asthma compounded with a marked propensity to stammer.

Shortly before going to university, however, the report noted a striking change in Dupont's character, a rapid transition from the underdog to the leader. Those who had grown up with him remembered how the stammering had disappeared, to be replaced by a dis-arming charm that always seemed to diffuse conflict while at the same time securing Dupont's point of view.

His natural leadership qualities now apparent, Dupont had gone on to develop what André described as the 'killer instinct'. In his early life as a television journalist, the young reporter had not been afraid to assert his right to control events as well as report on them. It was only one small step from there to the European Presidency he had so successfully grasped when the opportunity arose.

Having established to his own satisfaction that Dupont had the ruthless personality profile capable of trying to control events through manipulating in some way the disease, André turned to two outstand-ing questions, why and how?

As far as the why was concerned, André pointed to Dupont's meteoric rise to a position of absolute power as a direct consequence of the White Death. He argued cogently that someone with a pathological obsession with power such as François Dupont would stop at nothing in order to achieve his goals.

But it was on the 'how' question that André had so far drawn a complete blank. Dupont himself had no scientific training and it was difficult to see how he could personally have engineered the disease. André's explanation of this point was, however, at least half-way convincing. Itemising in detail numerous occasions when Dupont had used his power in the media to gain influence over others, he postulated that at some stage Dupont had gained a position of influence over certain elements of the scientific community who had agreed to co-operate with him in his bid for power.

Rachel finished reading the report and wearily laid it down on the floor of the hut. Through a chink in the wooden boards over the windows she could see it was already dark outside. Somewhere out there in the night, the formidable security apparatus of François Dupont's Greater Europe would already be searching for her, scouring the moors with the most sophisticated surveillance equipment.

Part of her, a powerful part, still wanted to ignore the document beside her as an absurd compilation of crude circumstantial evidence and embittered innuendo spun around a ridiculous central hypothesis. André might hate Dupont but she didn't. For two years she had lived with him and loved him, knowing his tenderness as well as his strength, and she found it hard to accept that the Dupont she knew would have been capable of the terrible, almost unthinkable, crime that André had suggested.

She dearly wished she was a woman like so many others, able to trust her instinctive feelings about someone without question. But she knew deep down that she was not like other women, that however much she still loved François Dupont, she would not be able to sleep at night until she had conclusively proved to herself that André Rostropov was wrong.

A wave of exhaustion seemed to overcome her. She lay back on the bed, relishing the warmth from the log fire. And then, suddenly, she remembered the first time she had ever made love to François Dupont, she remembered the unexpected way he had picked her up and pushed her roughly against the picture window of their flat, she remembered the tremendous power of his thrusts within her, she remembered her own feelings of elation and ecstasy. She remembered all the exhilaration and joy she had felt on that occasion.

But she also remembered his words as he had knelt exhausted on the floor beside her after they had finished, staring out into the pale night sky. 'One day I believe you will know me for what I really am, Rachel. And I hope ... I pray ... that the beauty of your love for me will withstand the terrible pain that knowledge will surely bring."

* * * * * *

Somebody was shaking her roughly by the shoulders.

"Wake up! You must wake up!"

She opened her eyes. A tall young Scandinavian was looking down at her anxiously.

"Get up and follow me. We've got to clear out of here fast!"

She sat up.

"Why? What's happened?"

"Security police. They could be here in less than a quarter of an hour."

Rachel looked at her watch. It was only six-thirty in the morning.

"But you can't move all these people in fifteen minutes."

Bjorn looked away.

"They're not coming. Only us, Mrs McNie. Only you and I."

"But what about the others?"

Bjorn was impatiently stuffing André's handwritten manuscript into a small knapsack.

"Like you said, you can't move a whole community in fifteen minutes. They'll be picked up."

Rachel stared at him in horror.

"But you can't let them get André."

Bjorn had finished with the manuscript and was rapidly pushing some food from a cupboard into the knapsack.

"They won't get André," he announced bluntly.

"Why not? I thought you said it was just you and I going."

Bjorn stopped what he was doing and rounded on her.

"André and I had discussed all this before," he said. "With the drugs at their disposal, he knew they'd find out everything if they caught him. So when he heard they were coming, he told me to finish it for him."

Rachel looked at him in abject disbelief.

"He's dead?" she said numbly. "André's dead?"

Bjorn ignored her remark, hurriedly finishing the packing. But then suddenly he stopped and turned to face her again, his ashen face studying her intently.

"I forgot to say before, Mrs McNie. But if you want to, you can stay here and be rescued."

Rachel stared at him in surprise.

"Are you serious?"

"It was André's dying wish."

She hesitated, but only for a second.

"Do you have your revolver with you?"

Bjorn pulled it from his pocket.

"I'll come with you," she said. "But as your hostage, you understand. Not of my own free will."

The Swede swiftly returned the revolver to his pocket.

"Naturally, Mrs McNie," he said, throwing her her coat and pushing open the door. Outside, the hut in which she had been sleeping was surrounded on all sides by the towering heather-clad granite mountains of the Central Highlands. Nearby, ancient stone huts with impromptu wooden roofs were arranged on either side of a small stream. The rest of the community must have been cowering within the huts, for the place appeared completely devoid of human life."

"What now?" she asked.

Bjorn had already started running towards a dark pine forest some way away from the settlement.

"Follow me," he called over his shoulder, "and don't stop until you get to the trees."

Rachel raced along behind him as fast as she could. But Bjorn had already been in the forest for some time when she finally arrived.

"Look!" he said, pointing back towards the tiny huts.

From four directions helicopter gunships were moving in fast in what was clearly a thoroughly planned operation. As they swept down to land in a ring around the settlement, uniformed soldiers jumped clear and took up defensive positions around the primitive houses, crouching down low as they awaited the order to move in.

Bjorn laughed bitterly.

"Fools," he muttered. "They must think we're heavily armed."

Rachel glanced at him.

"Shouldn't we be off?" she asked. "It won't be long before they've worked out I'm not there."

Bjorn nodded and started tramping away from the beleaguered settlement, leading her deeper and deeper into the forest. It was almost pitch dark amongst the trees, but Bjorn seemed to know where he was going.

They walked in silence for a while.

"The trouble is," he said eventually, answering her unasked question, "that as soon as they work out you're not with them, they'll immediately seal off all the roads into the area before starting a land search."

As he was speaking, Rachel tripped over a low branch and fell to the ground. Bjorn came back to her and extended his arm to help her up.

"In your contingency planning," she said drily, "I expect you thought of that."

"Yes," he said, "we did."

For a long time they moved on in silence until at last they reached a clearing where the trees had only recently been felled. Leading into it from the far side was a rough forest track. At first sight the clearing appeared completely deserted, strewn with the kind of debris left behind when foresters have finished their work. But on closer examination Rachel could see a vehicle concealed beneath the undergrowth.

Bjorn started pulling the branches away, his muscular arms heaving logs which would have taken several normal men to shift.

"Move some of the smaller stuff, will you?" he called. "I shouldn't think it'll take them that long to work out that Margaret is not in fact you."

Rachel took hold of a smaller branch and gave it a tug.

"Who's Margaret?"

"Before the troubles began she was a stage actress. She'll fool them for a while, but some time or other one of them will think to check properly."

Rachel fell silent and carried on moving the branches. Soon the vehicle began to emerge more clearly.

"Where the hell did you get this?" she said, looking in some surprise at a small military jeep.

"Nicked it ages ago," he said. "We've been saving it up for a rainy day."

He threw the last branches to one side and climbed up into the driver's seat, grabbing hold of a large plastic bag full of clothes.

"Here," he said, throwing her a uniform, "put this lot on and sling your old stuff away."

They both changed into the uniforms, hiding their old clothes carefully beneath the undergrowth, and then climbed into the cab. Bjorn started the engine and steered the jeep cautiously down the rough forest track.

"Think it'll work at a road block?" Rachel asked sceptically.

Bjorn pointed at a little grey box mounted to the dashboard.

"Ever seen one of those?" he asked.

"What is it?"

"It receives and transmits vehicle communication codes. Nobody's going to challenge us with one of these on board."

"Surely the codes didn't come with the jeep."

Bjorn laughed.

"No way. They change them every day quite unpredictably." He pulled a little floppy disk from the pocket of his jacket and inserted it into a slot in the grey box.

"I'm impressed," Rachel said quietly.

Again Bjorn laughed.

"It's a technological age. How long do you really think free communities like ours would survive if we just wandered around eating berries?"

"But this is sophisticated hardware," she said. "You must have people working on the inside to get hold of this."

The smile vanished from Bjorn's face.

"I can't tell you that, yet, can I? After all, I don't even know whose side you're on."

Rachel looked away. On the seat behind her, André's last testament lay safely inside Bjorn's knapsack, still taunting her as it had done the previous evening. But before doing anything she needed time to think, to sort out the information from the disinformation, to reconcile in her own mind exactly how much of André's extraordinary story deserved to be taken seriously.

"I don't know if André told you," she said, "but before all this ... before the 'troubles' as I think you called them ... he and I were quite close. I trusted André and I trusted his judgement. And now he's made these terrible accusations about a man who's very close to me. I can't decide whose side I'm on until I've had a chance to think."

"I suppose that's all it's reasonable to ask," he said. "But you should know that I was André's closest associate in the underground. I think I know just about everything he knew about the White Death, far more than he did on the technical side. So you must feel free to ask me anything you want to know that isn't covered in the report."

Rachel's thoughts returned to the previous evening and her conversation with André. There had been several points in the report about which she had wanted to question André. But André, alas, was no longer in a position to answer.

"Did you help compile the technical evidence refuting the official version of the disease's origin?" she asked.

"Yes," Bjorn replied, swerving the jeep hard to the right to avoid an enormous pothole in the road. "The poor scientists I spoke to are nearly all dead now. All except one mysteriously died at the time Dupont's report was being prepared for the Americans and the one who survived has now changed his account completely in a way that corroborates Dupont's version. But according to our original eye-witness accounts, although various types of similar infective agents could just conceivably have been developed at the Danish plant, the White Death was not one of them. And anyone who says anything different is wrong. It's as simple as that."

Rachel watched Bjorn's face as he drove. In some ways he was rather like a younger version of André. It was easy to see why they had been friends.

"It's a big step from a cover-up to genocide," she observed.

"We never said we had proof against Dupont. We simply said he had a case to answer."

Rachel laughed inwardly at the thought of somebody putting François Dupont in the dock. One of the reasons she was sitting in the jeep now was that she knew perfectly well he'd come up with a totally convincing explanation if she went back and challenged him. He was that sort of man.

"Just suppose you're right," she said, "just suppose he did get hold of a germ warfare bug and release it. What difference would it make now?"

Suddenly, without any warning, Bjorn slammed on the brakes. The jeep skidded to a halt.

"Why the bloody hell do you think we've got you here?" he snapped angrily.

His question stopped her dead in her tracks. Now that she thought about it, the answer wasn't totally obvious.

Bjorn calmed down a bit and switched off the engine.

"Sorry," he said, "that wasn't fair. I was just thinking of André lying there on that bed just now while I shoved a revolver down his throat and pulled the trigger. For a second it made me lose my cool."

"I suppose if you convince me you're right I can give you information about François. Or maybe you even want me to kill him."

Bjorn shook his head.

"I'm afraid we need much more than that. The White Death is a genetic mutation. So far, every scientist who's tried – and plenty have – has failed to make any headway against it. But if we can only find out more about its origins we might be able to make some progress towards finding a vaccine, or at the very least some kind of treatment."

"So you want me to use my connections with Dupont to find out where the disease originated."

Bjorn slowly nodded his head.

"I know it won't be easy, but we calculated that you're our best chance – possibly our only chance."

He started the engine again and they continued to drive. For a long time, Rachel sat in silence. Bjorn was talking about François Dupont as if he were a psychopath; a scheming evil man capable of destroying millions of people simply in order to satisfy an insane lust for power. And he didn't just think it for no reason, he had a substantial body of convincing and coherent evidence pointing in exactly that direction. But unlike Bjorn and André, she knew François Dupont personally. She didn't just know his public face, she also knew his private face.

And she knew, as nobody else could possibly know, that the François Dupont in Bjorn's imagination was simply not the same man as the François Dupont she had come to love so very much.

DEVON, ENGLAND, NOVEMBER 2006

They had left the jeep far behind, somewhere in a remote lay-by near the Scottish border, and had switched twice to other cars. Their latest vehicle was a pale blue Citroën, a special low-energy electric version capable of a magnificent top speed of just over fifty miles an hour. After an interminable drive along motorways left half empty by the massively subsidised rail network of Dupont's Europe, they finally arrived at a small but prosperous stone-walled farm tucked away in the softly folding countryside of south Devon.

Bjorn swung the car into the ramshackle farmyard, scattering terrified chickens to either side, before bringing it to a halt in an ancient stone barn piled high with winter fodder. He clambered out and held the car door open for Rachel.

"We're here," he said, carefully grabbing the knapsack and leading the way through the farmyard towards a small barn that appeared to have been converted into a holiday cottage.

"The farmer and his wife are expecting us," he said, pushing open the door and leading her inside.

The interior of the cottage was immaculate, small bunches of freshly-cut autumn flowers decorating the quaint old furniture. The uneven stone walls of the converted barn were hung with a series of watercolours of eighteenth-century rural life, while the tiny living room was dominated by a log fire blazing in a fireplace which seemed quite out of proportion with the rest of the room.

Rachel peered through the living room window at the main farm building on the far side of the yard.

"Do the owners know who I am?"

"No," Bjorn replied, "but they won't try to find out."

Despite her attempt to stay alert, the warmth was beginning to make her feel tired. She sat down in one of the armchairs and numbly watched the pattern thrown up by the flames."

"I'd never supposed you were so well-organised."

Bjorn stood by the fire and warmed his hands.

"Like I said before, we have to be. The free communities need a network of these contact points with the rest of society in order to operate at all."

She glanced through the window at the farmhouse.

"So the farmer isn't one of the living dead, then?"

Bjorn smiled.

"No," he said. "Actually he's the chairman of one of the newly-elected regional councils. In public, he and his wife are amongst François Dupont's staunchest supporters in this area."

Rachel winced. Recently, she had found herself wincing every time the name of François Dupont was mentioned. It reminded her of the dilemma in which she found herself.

"Are we safe here?" she asked.

"I think so," Bjorn replied. "Safe enough to give you the time you said you wanted."

Rachel studied the flames leaping up into the fireplace. Unlike the flames in the artificial gas fire in her old home with Tom, they created a continually changing pattern. In some ways they were like Dupont himself, exciting precisely because they were in a state of continual flux.

"I'm inclined to accept André's evidence on the cover-up," she said at last. "The only way it could be false would be if André had invented the whole thing. Once I allowed myself to be convinced that he'd done precisely that, but now I've seen him again with my own eyes I know that's not the case. André may have been many things, but he was never dishonest."

Bjorn remained silent. He knew perfectly well she was talking largely to herself.

"But what I'm having trouble with is the rest of it. There's something about the rest of the story that doesn't hang together properly. It's difficult to be precise but I suppose it's François himself. I just don't see how he's capable of such a thing."

135

Bjoırn sat down in a chair opposite her and eyed her intently.

"You mean from your personal knowledge of him."

Rachel returned his gaze.

"Let me be frank with you about François Dupont," she said. "I share entirely your view of him as tough, effective, decisive, intolerant of fools and somewhat self-opinionated, although I don't necessarily regard all of these things as negative qualities. But I do not accept, I do not think I will ever be able to accept, that he is either evil or insane."

"So do you have an alternative explanation? I'll be all too pleased if you can think of a better way of accounting for the facts."

"Tell me," she said, "don't you have any leads on the White Death? Any information at all that might be useful?"

Bjorn was thoughtfully inspecting his fingernails.

"Did André ever tell you how we met?" he asked.

"No."

"It was a little while before the coup which brought Vintner to power, shortly after you asked him to start looking into the Green Party's accusations. He came to visit me at the Stockholm Institute where I worked and asked me exactly the same question as you did just now. Somebody had apparently told him that I was the equivalent of a sniffer dog when it came to these matters.

"I'd already been investigating the White Death for over a year when he came, trying to get hold of some kind of clue. I was beginning to make some progress, or at least I thought I was. The obvious starting point in any quest was the military research institutes, and I had been granted free access by the military to both the relevant scientists and the classified documents. But I'd systematically worked through all the laboratories and drawn a blank. The disease didn't appear to come from any of the research programmes then being undertaken. Of course that didn't mean it wasn't the military. But if it was, it was part of the military research machine that nobody was telling me about.

"André and I decided to work together, with him handling the political aspects and me the scientific material. I suggested he start by investigating the movements of the published scientists I thought might have been capable of developing something like this. It was a tough job to expect André to do and it involved a great deal of painstaking research, but eventually he came up with a possible lead."

Bjorn hesitated.

"I don't suppose Dupont ever mentioned somebody by the name of Victor Stein, did he?" he asked.

Rachel shook her head.

"Nope," she replied. "Never."

Bjorn shrugged his shoulders.

"Too much to hope, I suppose," he muttered. "Stein had been working for a number of years at a leading military research institute developing reversible infective agents with military applications. He was highly regarded by his employers, a well-paid military scientist with a young family to support. Then one day, about seven years ago, he handed in his notice. Four weeks later, he vanished without trace.

"The military weren't too pleased, of course. They like to keep tabs on former employees who've had access to sensitive information. But military intelligence couldn't find him, and nor could André."

"I suppose he might have gone to work for a foreign government," Rachel suggested.

Bjorn caught her gaze and held it.

"He might have done," he observed drily. "Or he might have gone to work for François Dupont."

Again Rachel flinched. It still seemed absurd. But having accepted the reality of the cover-up, the logical possibility was hard to reject.

"What else do you know about this man Stein?" she asked. "Did you find any connection with François?"

"We know quite a lot, but we couldn't find anything very exciting about him. His wife had died a few years before he resigned, leaving him with a kid to bring up by himself, and in between the kid and the housework most of his free time was used up. In short, he was just like most of us scientists in our private lives: boring as hell."

"One vanishing scientist in the right discipline," Rachel murmured. "It's not much to go on, is it?"

Bjorn looked at her forlornly and shrugged his shoulders.

"No," he said, "I guess it isn't."

For a long time a sombre silence filled the room.

"Do you have a family?" Rachel asked at last.

"No, thank Christ. Before the troubles I was married to my work."

"And what happened to your work after the coup?"

He scowled.

"Some bureaucrats from New Vienna started asking questions about what we were doing at the Institute. They talked a lot about priorities, about rationalisation, about making the best possible use of the available funding..."

"You mean they closed you down."

"Yes. They pulled all the money out of the research project and

137

it collapsed."

"So what did you do? Personally, I mean. How did you become one of the living ... I mean, how did you come to join a free community?"

"Same as André. I was scared out of my mind."

"I thought André was a political."

"He was, I suppose. But even politicals can be frightened, you know."

"Were you scared because the Institute had been closed?"

"Of course. It was obvious they didn't want any more probing done, and it was an open secret that I didn't believe any of this Danish rubbish that the Green Party were pumping out. So it seemed likely that they would want me and others like me out of the way. And now they had a perfect method of doing it at their disposal."

She looked at him in amazement.

"You don't seriously mean ..."

"The blood tests. Of course I do. Jesus Christ, Rachel, living with François Dupont sure has made you naive, hasn't it? Just how the hell do you think they get rid of undesirables in this lovely continent of ours these days. Look at Manfred Leitner. Look at Luigi Rossetti. Look at Olav Horstramm. Look at Roger Smith. All leading experts in the White Death, just as I was. And like me, all of them knew enough to protect themselves effectively from infection from the time the first cases came to light. The only difference was they weren't as scared as me, they stayed at their desks in the new Europe. And all of them are now dead, having been picked up with positive blood tests at the very first screening."

He looked aggressively at Rachel. But she wasn't even listening to him any more. For in her mind she could hear the sound of Tom's cello, its soft echoing melody calling to her from his distant Spanish exile as he comforted her children.

And suddenly, sickeningly, she began to realise the full extent to which she might have been wrong about François Dupont.

* * * * * *

Bjorn had been gone for several days, leaving her alone in her peaceful rural retreat while he pursued his enquiries. From her bedroom window, she could see for miles across a wide valley, its broad expanse carpeted with grassy meadows dotted with sheep. The sheep at least were a comfort to her as she waited, their periodic bleating a constant reminder of her tranquil childhood years, soothing nerves which were growing increasingly ragged as the long empty hours passed.

Her daily life offered little to relieve the monotony. From time to time she had seen the farmer and his wife as they moved about the farm busying themselves with their daily affairs, but they made no attempt to return her gaze or even to glance in the direction of her place of safety. Every morning, however, she would find a cardboard box laden high with provisions waiting for her on the front doorstep, together with a good supply of the day's local and European newspapers.

The television news was full of her disappearance and the massive search that had been launched across the continent to trace her. If the authorities had any idea that her disappearance was at least partially voluntary, they showed no public sign of being aware of it; according to the media, she was simply the unwilling victim of a vicious terrorist attack.

The ancient clock on the living room mantelpiece ticked quietly as she tried to make sense of her conflicting thoughts and emotions about François Dupont. There was still so much that didn't make sense, so much conjecture that could have been based on little more than a combination of coincidences. Perhaps, when Bjorn Haverstamp finally returned, she would know enough to decide. But in the meantime she had no choice but to try and put the love she felt for François Dupont on pause, to withhold judgement on his guilt or innocence until such time as she had sufficient information on which to reach a fair verdict.

Suspending her emotions sounded straightforward enough, but as the days and hours ticked by the strain was gradually beginning to tell. Increasingly, she found herself pacing around the little house, rather like a tiger confined in a cage too small, trying through the repeated movements of her body to relieve the tension she felt within. Every now and then she would look longingly outside, dearly wishing she could walk across the open fields in the hazy autumn sunshine to clear her head, but she knew full well that these were foolish thoughts. Her face was too well known, the risk of discovery too high.

She was just about to switch on the television to catch the latest news bulletin when she heard the sound of a car driving into the farmyard. A few minutes later, Bjorn stepped purposefully through the front door and into the lounge.

"Hi," he said, eyeing her cautiously to see if any change had come over her while he had been away.

She looked at him, the tension becoming unbearable.

139

"Well?" she said.

"Like I told you, he's dead," he replied bluntly.

Rachel could already feel her heart sinking.

"Are you sure?"

Bjorn looked at her for a moment before replying.

"It was your test, wasn't it?" he asked.

She nodded. Like André before her, she had set a test – a controlled test – to try and establish whether Dupont was guilty or innocent.

"Just tell me, Bjorn," she said, her eyes pleading with him. "It's been hell just sitting here."

"His Harley Street office is under new management. I went in and pretended to be an old patient of Sir Francis'. The receptionist told me his practice had closed shortly after the date you spoke to him and that he had left no forwarding address. The neighbours at his old Belgravia address told me he had been found positive and been taken away by the health police. One of them had actually seen him being carted off – apparently he made quite a fuss, continually bleating on about how important he was and how he was sure there must be some mistake."

Rachel looked at Bjorn in despair. He rose and came towards her, and she could almost touch the overwhelming sense of pity he felt for her as he took her hands in his.

"I'm afraid there's more. I happen to have an old friend in that data collection centre in Warsaw, the one you say Sir Francis was plugged into the day you saw him. She was a junior statistical officer from my old Institute in Sweden. When I joined the underground she agreed to help me later on if ever I needed it. We've sort of kept in touch with each other over the months, although ever since she got the job in Warsaw we've been pretty careful, and I've never yet asked her to filch me any information before. But this time I decided to use her.

"It was a long shot but it came off. Apparently she works in just the right place, in the computer centre, and so she has had access to all the routine records flowing in from the testing programme throughout Europe ever since it began. Without really being sure of why, she has been quietly ferreting away back-up copies of the main data-files just in case they would be useful one day. So I asked her to run over the files just before and just after your interview with Sir Francis Morley and compare them in the way you indicated."

Bjorn watched Rachel carefully, sensing the devastating effect the news he carried would surely have on her.

"I'm afraid they were changed, Rachel. The records were adjusted within two days of your encounter in Harley Street."

As he spoke, Rachel could feel her head beginning to spin.

"So he was right," she said blankly. "Forty-seven was the correct number after all."

Bjorn nodded slowly.

"I'm sorry," he said simply.

But already Rachel could feel the debilitating numbness she had felt for several days beginning to clear. For she had set the test herself, and now there could no longer be any doubt. As she had known at the time, it was in any event highly improbable that she could have been one of only forty-seven people in Europe who had avoided catching the disease despite having repeated unprotected intercourse with a known carrier. But the deliberate change in the computer records subsequent to her meeting with Sir Francis confirmed the worst fears that had been eating away at her mind throughout the hours she had sat alone awaiting Bjorn's return.

There was no doubt that Dupont had had the power to alter the records. There was equally no doubt that Tom and the children had stood in his way when he wanted to win her for himself. And now she simply had no choice but to accept the painful fact that the man with whom she had been living for the past two years had deliberately dispatched her family into a grim internal exile from which they would never be able to escape.

But when she reflected on her own emotions as she sat and watched the logs crackling ferociously in the grate, she could still not help but be surprised just how rapidly the intense love she had once felt for François Dupont could dissolve into a deep feeling of ice cold hatred.

* * * * * *

"I can't do it, Bjorn. I simply can't do it."

Bjorn watched her wearily as she busied herself in the tiny kitchen and dearly wished that he could allow her to hide away. She was like a frightened animal, boxed into a corner from which she knew there could be no escape. For Rachel McNie was simply too rational, and he knew full well it would only be a matter of time before she accepted the inevitable.

"All right, then, tell me another way?" he said quietly.

The clattering of pots and pans became more feverish. "I'm not saying it's not a sensible thing to do, but I just don't think I can pull it off. You don't know him like I do. He'll see straight through it."

She was lying, of course. In reality she didn't want to do it, but he had to admit she was right when she said it wouldn't be easy.

Bjorn adopted the most soothing voice he could muster.

"Look Rachel, all I'm asking is that you try. If you don't think it's going to work out after you've given it a try then we'll get you out again. That I promise you."

Rachel picked up a large cucumber and started slicing it into tiny pieces with a long sharp knife. If she had had Dupont in the room, the look on her face suggested that the knife would have been used for other purposes.

Suddenly, Rachel laid down the knife and looked at Bjorn with pleading eyes.

"I just don't understand how I can have been so wrong about him, Bjorn. I've been living with him for two years, for Christ's sake. I've talked to him about what I believed to be his most intimate thoughts. I've gazed into his eyes. I've kissed him. I've made love to him. And all the time I was doing it I didn't know he was a . . ."

"A mass murderer," Bjorn finished softly.

"Yes," she said, picking up the knife and continuing to slice the cucumber.

"But you've told me yourself there was an impenetrable side to him, a side you didn't see."

She didn't reply. She didn't want to admit to Bjorn, she almost didn't want to admit to herself, that it had been precisely that impenetrable side of François Dupont which she had found most attractive.

The aggression she felt faded as quickly as it had arisen, only to be replaced by an almost inconsolable sense of loss.

"I can't do any cooking now," she said quietly, laying down the knife on the side and walking through to the lounge. Bjorn followed quietly behind.

"Is it really the only way, Bjorn?" she asked, standing with her back to the fire and facing him.

He nodded.

"O.K. But how do I do it? I can't just breeze in one day and ask him, can I?"

"No, Rachel, I don't suppose you can. But you did say that you felt he was getting ever more intimate with you. Maybe you can encourage him to talk. Or maybe you can establish some link with our disappearing research scientist by the name of Victor Stein?"

Rachel looked up.

"The honest truth is, Bjorn, that I've never really understood why François was so keen to win me for himself. Now that I know he was prepared to go to the extreme lengths of sending my family away I'm even more puzzled. What the hell does he see in me?"

Bjorn smiled.

"Are you fishing for a compliment, Rachel?" he asked.

"It's no compliment. Something about me has made me a desirable companion to a man who's going to reduce Genghis Khan and Adolf Hitler to also-rans. Surely you can see it's a disturbing thought?"

Bjorn looked at her solemnly for a long time.

"Don't take this amiss, Rachel, but I'm no mass murderer and I could find you a desirable woman. The fact that Dupont was drawn to you does not transfer even the tiniest part of his guilt onto you."

Rachel looked at him glumly. Dupont was gone, Tom was locked away on the far side of the continent. She longed to crawl away, back to the wild empty moors of her youth. But that, she knew, could never be. From somewhere deep within herself, she would have to find the courage to act.

LONDON, ENGLAND, NOVEMBER 2006

"O.K., Rachel, let's run over it one more time."

Bjorn stuffed the revolver into his jacket pocket and sat down on the bed. As he spoke, Rachel continued pacing nervously up and down the dingy rear bedroom of the London flat to which they had moved the previous day from their Devon retreat. The fading wall-paper was peeling, exposing crumbling plaster which filled the tiny room with the faint smell of rot. Apart from a small single bar electric fire and a wooden chair, the only furniture in the room was an old cast-iron bed with a decaying mattress thrown on top.

"I've been locked in this room since I was picked up," she said. "I don't know where it is because when I've been alone I've been chained to the bed so I can't reach the window and when I've been with someone I've had to wear a blindfold at all times so that I can't see my interrogator."

"Tell me about the interrogations."

"There were two people, a man and a women. They were trying to find out information about your plans, anything I might have overheard, any papers I might have seen."

"What were the interrogation sessions like?"

"It depended on who was doing the interrogating. Until today it was generally the man. He was softly spoken, with a faint German

143

or Scandinavian accent. He tried to reason with me, to persuade me to make life easy for myself. He seemed to know André Rostropov, whom he said was dead, and I think he may have been trying to persuade me to give information voluntarily. He told me absurd stories about how you were crazy for power and how you had released the disease in order to achieve your goal of European domination."

Bjorn stood up and grabbed her arm.

"It's essential you get that bit right, Rachel. You can judge how to do it better than I, but with your tone of voice, with your body language or simply with your intellect you must intimate to him that even if the story were true you would stay loyal to him. But under no circumstances must you let him think you believed the stories you heard."

Rachel nodded and Bjorn released her arm. She could tell that he was feeling as uncomfortable as she was at the thought of what they both knew was soon to come.

"After a few weeks I sensed the man was giving up hope of gaining my co-operation voluntarily," Rachel continued nervously. "He started threatening me, obliquely at first but with increasing irritation. He said that if I carried on refusing to accept what they were saying and refusing to help them, he would not be able to prevent the woman from taking over the interrogation."

"What did you tell him?"

"Quite a lot. I was playing for time because I was frightened of what the woman would do to me."

"What happened then?"

"Two days ago the woman came to the room. After a while she started screaming at the man, telling him that I was Dupont's slut and that I knew far more than I was letting on. She said he had two more days to get something worthwhile out of me or she would take over. Then she stormed out of the room and slammed the door.

"After that the man started pleading with me to tell him everything I knew. He seemed convinced I knew something about the disease which I wasn't admitting. I denied everything. I told him that even if you had invented the bloody disease Europe was still a better place for it because of the things you had done . . ."

"Go easy on that bit, Rachel. You could easily overdo it if you're not careful."

She swung to face him and tried to smile.

"I know," she replied. "I'll do my best."

Bjorn nodded. From his pocket he produced a small spray containing a woman's scent and sprayed a little around the room.

"I know that," he said softly, bracing himself inwardly for the ordeal ahead.

Rachel stopped pacing and looked out through the grubby net curtains at the litter-strewn inner-city street that lay two stories below.

For a long time there was silence.

"Are you ready?" she asked softly.

He came and stood beside her.

"Are you sure?" he said "Are you absolutely sure?"

Rachel turned and looked at him.

"Was André sure?"

Bjorn met her gaze.

"Yes," he replied, no hesitation in his voice. "It was me that wasn't sure, not André. But this is different, I would never have asked you to do this. I'm still not sure it's absolutely necessary."

"You don't know Dupont like I do. He's never had grounds to doubt me before, but I know that he can be incredibly suspicious when he has a mind to be. He knows André was a friend of mine years ago, he knows I tried to trace him after he went running to the Americans, and if once he starts thinking I'm not on his side there's no telling where it'll stop."

Bjorn pulled her gently towards him.

"Logically, I know that's a good enough reason in itself for this, Rachel. But there's another reason too, isn't there? Don't you think I've got a right to hear it from you."

She remained sullenly silent for several minutes.

"Tell me, Bjorn, how many people have died of the White Death?"

He hesitated.

"Globally. Several billion perhaps. Several billion more are already infected."

Rachel could feel her whole body convulsing with self-hatred. She had allowed herself to love and comfort a man who had brought so much unspeakable suffering to the world? She had let him kiss her, she had let him hold and cherish her, she had let him caress and penetrate her. And all the time she had enjoyed what he was doing. Now, at last, she had an opportunity to purge at least some tiny fraction of the shame she felt within her soul.

"Several billion people," she repeated, her voice almost inaudible. "They're my other reason, Bjorn. And now for Christ's sake let's get on with it before I lose my nerve."

Bjorn nodded grimly as Rachel lay on the bed. Then he started strapping her legs and arms to the iron bedposts. When he had finished he looked down at her pleadingly, as if to persuade her to draw back from the ordeal she had herself proposed.

Rachel looked up into his soft and kindly eyes.

"I know you're a good man, Bjorn," she said, "but you must do what is necessary just as I must endure what is necessary."

Her eyes closed as if to indicate that he should begin.

She could hear the rip of material as Bjorn tore off a strip of the dirty sheet that lay strewn across the bed and securely bound her mouth so that she could not scream. Then, without another word, she could feel rough hands tearing away her clothing, exposing her naked on the bed. And then, seconds later, the pain began.

She pulled desperately at the straps which held her down, not daring to open her eyes lest Bjorn see that her courage had failed her and stop his awful work. And suddenly she remembered the first night she had made love to Dupont, she remembered how she had feared he would push her backwards through the glass and out into the moonlit sky high above Vienna.

And then the glass did break. Dupont was holding her in his arms and they were falling down to earth together, hurtling past the black and silent office block towards the pavement far below and certain death. She tried to pull away, at least to die alone and not within his evil clutches, but his powerful arms would not release her. He gripped her ever more tightly, silently pleading with her not to let him die alone. And slowly, to her horror, she began to realise that she was no longer resisting him. She was holding him too, clutching his shaking body with her arms, kissing his forehead in one last futile gesture of love before eternal darkness engulfed them both.

NEW VIENNA, AUSTRIA, THREE DAYS LATER

She was awoken by a respectful knock on the bedroom door.

"Come in!" she called, propping herself up in bed and trying to collect her thoughts as fast as possible.

The door swung open and Justine Medoc entered, carrying with her a small tray bearing a cup of tea and a plate laden with an enormous piece of apple strudel.

"I've brought you some of my home made strudel," Justine said, her voice distinctly more deferential than it had ever been before.

Rachel smiled at the young girl and allowed her to lay the tray on her lap.

"How are you this afternoon?" Justine asked.

"Much better, thank you. The aching has eased now."

Justine smiled affectionately and turned to leave.

"Don't go," Rachel called after her.

Justine returned to the bedside and sat down at the end of the bed.

"We've hardly had a chance to speak since I got back. Why don't you tell me what's been going on since I've been away?"

Justine rolled her eyes to heaven.

"You've no idea. He's been impossible to live with. Moping about from morning till night. At times he could hardly bear to perform his public functions."

Rachel looked at her glumly. From the moment she had returned to New Vienna and set eyes on François Dupont the hatred she had felt for him during her incarceration in Devon had been fading fast. Now she was merely perplexed, angry with herself that she could not remain more resolute.

"Are you pregnant yet?" Rachel asked.

Justine laughed.

"Some chance. Oh, it's not that I didn't get him to try, but he just couldn't do the business. He said he was missing you too much."

Again Rachel flinched. Since her return from captivity she had been relieved that the injuries she had asked Bjorn to inflict on her had been sufficient to dissuade Dupont from making any physical advances. But she was recovering fast and it would not be long before she would have to endure his caresses once again.

She started munching her way through the strudel.

"Mmm, it's good. I didn't know you could make strudel."

Justine smiled.

"I picked it up from somewhere once."

Rachel eyed her carefully.

"I'm bored lying here, Justine. If you've got the time, why don't you tell me something about your childhood. I mean, what did you do when you weren't peeking at François through the ceiling."

Justine laughed.

"I was a funny little kid, I suppose," she said. "I never felt I fitted in anywhere properly. Certainly not at school. I suppose it didn't help that my father kept moving house, so every time I started making some friends we'd move to a new country."

"Your father? Were your parents divorced, then?"

"No. My Mum died when I was about seven years old. I can only barely remember her."

"And your father moved around with his work."

147

"Yes. When I was a teenager he wanted to pack me off to a boarding school, but I threw a paddy so he let me stay with him."

"You don't often talk about your father, Justine. You should invite him to stay sometime."

The young girl looked away.

"Didn't you know?" she mumbled.

Rachel looked at her and shook her head.

"My father's dead. He's been dead for over two years now."

Rachel swallowed hard.

"I'm sorry," she murmured apologetically. "I didn't know."

Justine tossed her hair away.

"It doesn't matter, Rachel. Really it doesn't. Forget it."

Rachel placed another piece of strudel in her mouth. It was probably too much to hope that Justine would say that she had met François Dupont while he was round for dinner fixing up a grand scheme of European domination with her dad. So she decided to try another track.

"Justine, have you ever heard of someone called Victor Stein?"

Once again, the younger girl flicked her hair away from her eyes.

"Victor Stein? No. Why do you ask?"

"Because while I was in captivity they kept asking me about a man called Victor Stein. Some sort of scientist. They seemed convinced François knew him but I've never heard him mention the name."

Justine shook her head decisively.

"Nope. Never. Have you asked François?"

"Not yet. I forgot to mention it last night."

Justine looked at her thoughtfully.

"Rachel, François told me about the stories they were telling you in captivity. All about how they said he had invented the disease in order to create a political climate in which he could grab power. You didn't believe all that rubbish, did you?"

"No!" Rachel answered, slightly too quickly. "I told them it was utterly ridiculous."

The previous evening, shortly after her return, she had carefully studied François's face as she had confronted him with the accusations André had levelled at him. Somewhat to her surprise, he had not flinched. Instead, he had rolled his eyes upwards and smiled his impenetrable smile, muttering something about the pathetic state of the underground that they should have to sink to such depths. Then, without further comment, he had carried on talking about something else as if she had not spoken. It was exactly the response she had not been expecting, and it seemed to offer absolutely no opportunity of returning to the subject later without arousing his suspicions. So she had not yet mentioned Victor Stein's name in Dupont's presence.

"Rachel?" Justine asked, cutting across her thoughts. "What would you have done if it had been true? I mean, what if they'd convinced you that François really was guilty of something horrible like that?"

"That's rather a silly question, don't you think? Of course he didn't invent the White Death. Why should he?"

"Well, I don't know. Maybe to get power, like they said."

"I know François enjoys being the boss, but that seems a bit extreme, doesn't it?"

Although Rachel hated admitting it, Justine's frank question had caught her off guard.

Justine laughed.

"I'm not saying he did invent it, Rachel. I'm just curious to know how far your obvious love for him would stretch."

Rachel hesitated. There was just a chance that any answer she gave would filter back to Dupont himself.

"I don't really know what I'd do," she said thoughtfully. "But I know enough about François to know that if he'd done such a thing he'd have done it with good motives in mind and not just out of vulgar self-interest."

"Good motives for genocide?"

Rachel laughed.

"Precisely. And that's why it's a stupid question. That's why I told them they were daft . . ."

A stabbing pain between her legs suddenly took her breath away.

"Rachel? What's happened?" Justine cried, rising from the bed.

The pain subsided as quickly as it had arisen.

"Oh, nothing. Sometimes I get a twinge, that's all."

Justine looked at her with sympathy.

"They didn't much like being called daft, did they?" she said.

Rachel winced at the memory of the pain.

"No, they didn't. But I'd rather not talk about it if you don't mind."

For a few moments there was silence. Then, from the adjoining living room, a faint chime announced the impending arrival of the lift. A few seconds later Dupont himself entered the room, the strange mixture of anxiety and relief with which he had greeted her the previous day still written on his face. He threw a smile towards Justine and approached Rachel.

"How are you, my love?" he asked softly, bending low over the bed to kiss her on the cheek.

Rachel returned the kiss.

"Much better, thanks. You're back early."

"Cancelled some meetings. You always said I must delegate more. So today I celebrated your return by taking your advice."

Despite strenuous efforts not to, Rachel could not help but feel pleased to see the man. Three days previously she had managed to convince herself that she loathed him beyond recovery, yet now she was back with him she could already sense him tugging her gently but persistently back into his orbit.

He seemed to be in a good mood. She was just trying to risk bringing up the subject of her interrogators' accusations again when to her surprise Justine saved her the trouble.

"Tell me, François," Justine asked, "have you ever heard of a man called Victor Stein?"

Shocked by the directness of the question, Rachel carried on sipping her tea whilst watching Dupont intently. For a moment he seemed lost in thought.

"Yes," he said at last. "As it happens I have."

Rachel tried not to show the astonishment she felt.

"Wasn't he that scientist who vanished from a military research establishment in Germany some seven or eight years ago?" he asked.

Rachel felt obliged to intervene.

"I didn't mention it last night, darling, but my captors kept on going on about someone called Victor Stein. They said you had some sort of link with him and that it was he who had helped you develop the White Death. "

Dupont looked at her with a slightly annoyed expression.

"Oh. It's that again, is it? Well, if it was true that I had Victor Stein in my pocket then I suppose I might at least have had the means at my disposal, if not as yet the motive."

"Why? Rachel asked. "Who is he?"

"An expert in biological warfare. Worked for N.A.T.O. for many years. A pretty clever boy by the sound of it. Then he just vanished into thin air. Some people in the military were more than a trifle embarrassed by the whole thing, which is how I came to hear about it."

"Somebody told you?"

"Yes. They've a bitchy lot in the military. One senior officer in military intelligence wanted to embarrass another one who'd been given responsibility for clearing up the Stein business so he came up with the bright idea of giving me a ring. I was almost tempted to run a programme on it but I couldn't fit it into the schedules."

Rachel took another sip of tea.

"But you investigated it yourself?" she asked casually.

Dupont flicked her a vaguely irritated glance.

"You seem very interested in all this, Rachel," he said, his tone matching his look.

This time, at least, Rachel had a prepared response. She glared at him accusingly.

"If you'd had some bitch sticking electrodes up you and shouting the name Victor Stein in your ear at the same time you'd be a trifle curious too, darling."

The anger vanished instantly from Dupont's face.

"I'm sorry, that was unforgivable of me," he said gently, leaning forward and kissing her on the cheek. But he didn't continue talking, he just sat still for a long time, as if he was thinking very hard.

"I wonder . . ." he said eventually. "I wonder if they're right."

For nearly a minute he sat silently on the bed, deep in thought.

"You remember that stuff Goldberger told us," he said at last, addressing Rachel. "You know, all that business about how the Danish story of the White Death's origins was untrue."

Rachel could feel her mouth going dry. She nodded.

"Well, you know I told them our research had confirmed the findings of the original investigation."

"You told me that too," Rachel observed.

Dupont grinned.

"Well, it wasn't. Like I said, the whole thing was a pack of lies put together by the Green Party freaks. The White Death couldn't possibly have originated in that Danish plant."

"No?" Rachel whispered.

"When we interviewed the surviving scientists who'd worked there it soon became apparent that the infective agent could not have come from those laboratories."

Rachel could feel her head spinning. Dupont wasn't supposed to be saying these things, he was supposed to be denying them.

"So why did you lie to the Americans?," she protested. "Why didn't you tell them the truth?"

Dupont looked at her askance.

"Think about it," he said drily. "Lionel Goldberger was trying to score points off me, trying to discredit Europe in general and me in particular. That's why your old chum Rostropov tipped them off in the first place, isn't it? Anyway, it would have been political folly to allow a politician like Lionel Goldberger to claim the credit for discovering the truth about a thing like that, since whatever anyone said it would have looked as though we in Europe had been involved in some sort of murky underhand cover-up. So I decided to cover-up our cover-up, if you follow my meaning."

As Rachel listened to him, she followed his meaning all too well. Because if she chose to believe what he was now saying, a good half of André's carefully assembled case against him would collapse into nothing.

"Hang on a minute, François. I still don't see why you lied to me about your reply to the Americans."

Dupont adopted his most pathetically hang-dog expression.

"Sorry about that," he said.

"But why did you do it? I thought we spoke the truth to one another."

"I really am terribly sorry," he repeated.

Normally when he went coy on her like this she found it appealing. Today it made her angry.

"Why?"

His face became serious.

"Because of your old friendship with André Rostropov. I didn't want to hurt you any more, that's all."

Rachel shook her head.

"Why should the truth have hurt me so much?"

"I knew you were upset when you discovered that he had joined the living dead. But later, when you became convinced he was a political, out to destabilise our regime, it seemed to make you accept an unpalatable truth better. If I had told you that all his stories were true it would have stirred it all up again for you, wouldn't it? It would have made you feel rotten again."

Rachel stared at him in horror. As usual, he was right. It would have made her feel bad.

"I'm not a child, François," she muttered.

Once again, he hung his head sheepishly, lowering his eyes to the floor.

"How many times does a chap have to say sorry?" he said.

Suddenly Rachel remembered the reasoning that had gone through her mind just before the helicopter gunships had arrived to rescue her in Scotland. She had stayed with Bjorn precisely because she had feared this sort of thing happening, precisely because she had feared that if she went back to Dupont he would persuade her with clever arguments and weaselly words that André's case against him was ill-founded, or at the very least not proven. Now it was beginning to seem as if she had been right to be fearful.

152

"O.K. François," she said, resolutely determined to get to the truth, "I'll forgive you this time. But I want to know right now what other things you've lied to me about. I don't want to keep stumbling across other of your thoughtful lies every time we talk."

He looked at her solemnly.

"Everything?" he asked gently. "Even if it is painful for you."

She nodded. Dupont flicked a glance at Justine and she quietly rose and left the room. When they were alone he moved closer to her on the bed.

"How can a man ever be totally honest with a woman?" he asked.

"I thought you were being honest with me until just now," Rachel lied.

"For example, would it not be hurtful if I told you that I found Justine sexually attractive."

Rachel gulped.

"I'm not stupid," she said. "Justine's a lot younger than I am?"

"But would these words not hurt you?"

Rachel looked at him intently.

"If you were so worried about hurting my feelings, why did you move her in here with us?"

"You know the answer to that. Because I wanted her to bear me a child that you clearly did not wish to bear for me. Although it was a trifle unusual, I thought moving her in with us was the kindest and most honest thing I could do in the circumstances. I do not see that our experiences since she has been here have proved me to be wrong."

"And your assertion when I first knew you that you did not want another child was another lie?" Rachel asked.

Dupont nodded.

"Another lie," he admitted. "But I hope you will at least allow that my motives were not remiss."

He was looking at her with those big baleful eyes of his, pleading as he had pleaded so many times before for her understanding and approval.

"And what about my family?" she blurted out suddenly. "Were Tom and my three children another of your little deceits?"

She couldn't be sure, but she thought she might have seen him flinch.

"What do you mean by that?" he said, rapidly regaining his self-control.

"My captors told me some terrible things while I was with them," Rachel continued. "For example they told me that my family did not really have positive blood tests. They told me that you had fixed the tests so that you could win me for yourself."

Dupont did not speak. He rose from the bed and walked across the room towards the window. Pushing a small recessed button to open the curtains, he gazed out moodily towards the city far below.

"And what was their evidence for these accusations?" he asked.

"The way you fiddled the records in Warsaw."

Dupont turned to face her.

"I did not 'fiddle' any records," he said slowly. "I corrected the records."

She stared at him in disbelief.

Dupont met her gaze accusingly.

"I thought as much," he muttered. "It is not me who has been lying, but rather you. How dare you sit there and accuse me of deceit when you lie a thousand times more than I do. You have been bewitched by the lies you have been fed by Rostropov and his cronies. You have believed every last one of their stories and accusations. And then you have the nerve to come back here and start telling me how much you have missed me and how you did not believe a word they told you."

Rachel looked at him in horror. She didn't know what to do, what to say.

Aggressively he took a step towards her.

"Admit it!" he shouted.

The anguish in his tortured face was unmistakable. She tried to steady herself, to retain some semblance of self-control, but to no avail.

"What's happened to my family, François?" she cried out, tears forming in her eyes. "For God's sake tell me what's happened to my family. I don't know who to believe any more."

The burning anger inside Dupont seemed to subside.

"After you heard of your family's disappearance, you secretly went to see Sir Francis Morley in his Harley Street consulting rooms. Right?"

"Yes," Rachel whimpered, no longer caring that he knew.

"Straight after your visit he came to see me. He told me all about what had transpired that morning."

"But why? I thought he was scared of you."

Dupont tried to smile, but it turned into a twisted grimace.

"He was. In point of fact he was more scared of me than he was of you. That is why he came to see me. He told me how surprised he had been that the records suggested such a low probability of your avoiding infection. He suggested a thorough and immediate check through the raw data files for internal consistency."

Rachel suddenly remembered the look of surprise on Sir Francis' face as he had checked and rechecked the data on his computer screen.

"You mean there really was an error!"

Dupont nodded.

"Yes. These things happen in a complex operation like that. It was easily corrected."

"So my family are carriers then. There's no mistake."

Dupont shook his head sadly.

"I'm afraid not," he said softly.

She looked at him with a confused expression. He lowered himself sadly onto the bed beside her.

"I have always known you loved me, Rachel. Do you not remember the day we spoke in the cathedral at St Stephan's?"

She nodded.

"If you had not loved me then you would not have reacted in the way that you did."

She looked into his eyes and knew he spoke the truth.

"I had no need to push your family into a camp in order to win your affections since it would only have been a matter of time before you would have come running to me anyway. Poor Tom, he is a very sweet man, a very kind man, but I know full well you never really loved him."

As he spoke, Rachel could feel all trace of internal resistance collapsing. The evidence so painstakingly compiled by André and Bjorn to establish Dupont's guilt was at the very least open to innocent explanation, and now as she looked at Dupont she could sense how utterly absurd their wild theorising had been. She should have trusted her instinct all along, she should have known that a man like François Dupont could never be the evil psychopath they had supposed.

But despite her growing conviction that André and Bjorn had reached the wrong conclusion, she tried hard to retain her powers of judgement, to recall in detail those parts of their argument that Dupont had not yet refuted.

"There are still some things I don't understand," she said. "For one thing, it seems to me that it is necessary to trace the source of the infective agent involved in the White Death in order to stand a chance of isolating the cure."

Dupont smiled.

"Those, I imagine, are the words of Bjorn Haverstamp, the man responsible for interrogating you, or should I say persuading you?"

He knew so much already, Rachel could see little point in further deceit. It would only serve to make him angry again.

"Yes. How did you know?"

"It was an anonymous telephone call to the police that enabled them to trace you. The officer who received the call said that the man who phoned spoke English with a faint Scandinavian accent. And anyway, Bjorn Haverstamp is one of the few scientists with a good understanding of the White Death who is known to be in the underground."

"He said knowledge of the source of the White Death would make a treatment easier to find. Are you saying he was lying?"

"No," he said. "Probably he was not lying. That is why I was so interested in the suggestion that Victor Stein may have been responsible for its development. But it would have been helpful if instead of hiding away in the underground your Haverstamp man could have come forward with this suggestion somewhat earlier."

Rachel suddenly remembered something Bjorn had told her, but before she had been able to formulate a question Dupont had taken hold of her arm.

"I would allow no other living soul in Europe to interrogate and cross-examine me in this way, Rachel. Remember that whilst we speak, my love."

Rachel fell silent.

"Do you wish me to stop?" she asked coldly.

His face softened.

"No," he said. "You have been away from me for three weeks and you have listened to many accusations made against me by my enemies. So I will try to answer whatever questions you may have in order to try and prove my innocence of the heinous crimes of which I stand accused."

"Tell me why you closed the Stockholm Research Institute where Bjorn Haverstamp worked?"

"It wasn't closed. Its funding was cut."

"Don't play games with me, François. I'm not in the mood."

"I closed it because its work was finished. It was absurd to have scientists with sound knowledge of the White Death spread out all over Europe. Better to concentrate them all in one place, at the multibillion eurofranc Research Laboratory I ordered to be constructed right here in the heart of New Vienna. But oh no, your Haverstamp man wasn't interested in that. Perhaps he had already fallen under the influence of André Rostropov."

"He had," Rachel observed drily, "but what about the other scientists. I can't remember their names, but he reeled off a great long list of scientists who had contracted the White Death."

Dupont smiled aggressively.

"And why were you surprised at that?"

"He said they would know how to avoid catching the disease."

Dupont's savage smile turned into a cynical laugh.

"That's something I've always noticed about scientists. They're so insufferably proud of their own ability not to get into trouble. I think they think of themselves as a superior species, quite separate from the rest of us poor ordinary mortals. Were they depriving you of your sleep while you were in their hands? Is that why you appear to have completely lost the ability to think for yourself?"

The remark struck home. Perhaps she had allowed herself to be persuaded too easily. And now that he mentioned it, it wasn't particularly surprising that scientists investigating an infective agent of unknown properties should have contracted the disease. She resolved to me more careful with her remarks in future.

"So you didn't know that Bjorn Haverstamp suspected Victor Stein of having developed the infective agent behind the White Death?"

Dupont shook his head.

"No, but as I say, it is an intriguing idea. We should try to trace him if we can. I will put the secret police onto it first thing tomorrow morning. Perhaps we can trace him."

A germ of an idea was formulating in Rachel's mind. A crazy idea, perhaps, but an idea that nevertheless might be useful.

"Will you meet him?" she said bluntly.

Dupont looked at her with a perplexed expression.

"Who? Stein?"

"No. Bjorn Haverstamp. Maybe you could persuade him, François. Maybe if he met you face to face he would see you must be innocent. He's a good scientist and nobody's fool. Maybe you could start to work together against the White Death, rather than against each other."

"Will he agree to meet me?"

"I don't know. All I can do is ask him."

"Does this mean I have been found not guilty," Dupont asked.

Rachel looked at him.

"Perhaps," she said. "But first I would like to see you persuade Bjorn."

Dupont met her gaze for several seconds.

"Very well," he said eventually. "If he agrees and it can be done without undue security risk, then I will agree to meet him."

Rachel could feel a sense of relief washing over her. For if there was to be a trial, and it did indeed appear that one had already commenced, then now at least she would not have to stand in judgement alone.

Dupont looked down at her cautiously.

"May I stay with you tonight?" he asked uncertainly. "In the light of what we have said I will understand if you find my presence repulsive."

By way of answer she pulled the cover back. Silently removing his clothes, he climbed beneath the enormous continental quilt. Their eyes met.

"Will you promise me just one thing, my love," he said softly.

She nodded, allowing him to draw her head onto his chest.

"I have already surmised that it was you who asked Haverstamp to injure you so as to trick me into believing you were being held against your will. Yet it must have been so very hard for you to endure such pain. Promise me now that you will never allow such a terrible thing to happen again."

Rachel could still feel the dull aching between her legs where she had invited Bjorn to electrocute her. Everything had seemed so clear at the time, the difficult path she must travel straight and true. But now, apart from the ache, she could feel nothing but an unbearable guilt that she had been so unfaithful to the man she loved. Yet despite her unfaithfulness he had forgiven her, he was holding her to him and reassuring her. And despite herself, she could feel all remnants of doubt about his conduct dissolving rapidly into nothing.

"I love you François," she murmured, and as the tears began to flow uncontrollably down her cheeks and onto the broad expanse of his chest, she gradually became aware of the infinite relief flowing through his body as he gripped her tightly in his arms.

* * * * * *

She stumbled and fell, grazing her knee and cursing the arrangements upon which Bjorn had insisted for their meeting. Around her and above her, the jagged rocky outcrops of the limestone Alps seemed to mock her insignificance as she clambered up the path, laughing at her petty concerns as if they were of no importance whatsoever when compared to their own unimaginable lifespans.

Far, far, below she could see the car which had brought her to the start of the path, a tiny blue fleck standing in a deserted lay-by beside the lake. From the car she had trudged up alone through a sweet-smelling pine forest that clung with grim tenacity to the sides

158

of the mountain range until eventually she had emerged above the tree-line into the rocky Alpine pasture through which she was now passing. High above her, an eagle soared, its eyes scanning the mountainside for prey. Somewhere, no doubt, the bird would have spotted Bjorn's lonely figure as he lay in wait for her high above.

Her heart was beginning to ache, a combination of strenuous exercise and altitude, and she wondered whether this bizarre journey represented some kind of punishment Bjorn had decided to inflict on her for the betrayal he must have felt she had inflicted on him.

She had written to him shortly after her conversation with Dupont, passing the letter to him indirectly in the way they had arranged during their stay together in Devon. In the letter, she had explained to him openly everything that had happened since her return to New Vienna and asked him to agree to a meeting with Dupont in order to try and resolve their differences.

Three days later a reply had arrived, transmitted from a Post Office in a remote Alpine village. In the letter, Bjorn had refused to consider a meeting with Dupont unless Rachel first agreed to meet him alone. Then he had specified exactly when and how she should come to the meeting. The arrangements, he had clearly stated in his letter to her, were not negotiable.

Rachel had discussed her actions in advance with Dupont, but he had not interfered with her plans in any way, and had agreed instantly to her request that he make no attempt to use the security forces to apprehend Bjorn during the course of their meeting.

"Over here!" a voice called urgently.

She turned. Some distance away to one side, climbing out from behind a huge boulder lying at the base of a jagged rock-face, she could just make out Bjorn's tall figure. Gratefully, she clambered over the rocks towards him.

"I was beginning to think you were going to make me climb right to the top," she muttered as he helped her clamber up to join him.

Bjorn didn't reply. He looked nervously around as if to reassure himself that she was alone.

Rachel looked at him with annoyance.

"There's no point in all this, you know," she said. "If François wanted to get you he'd do it all right. This stupid mountain wouldn't stop him."

"Maybe," he said, pulling a revolver out of his pocket. "But at least up here I'll see them coming."

Rachel eyed the revolver suspiciously but said nothing. It had already occurred to her several times that in the light of her betrayal

159

Bjorn might just decide to kidnap her for real this time.

"I tell you he's not going to," she said bluntly.

Bjorn looked at her for a few seconds and then sat down beside her on the rock. But he kept the revolver on his lap.

Rachel tried to smile.

"Well, here we are," she said, deciding not to risk any more ill-chosen remarks about the venue of their meeting.

Bjorn turned to her.

"Was your letter straight?" he asked.

"What do you mean?" she replied.

"Forget it," he muttered. "I can see for myself that it was."

Rachel decided to get directly to the point.

"He's got a pretty good defence together for himself. I'd like you to hear it."

Bjorn shrugged.

"I'm listening."

"I'd like you to hear it from him."

Bjorn turned and looked at her with an expression of contempt.

"Does it sound better when he says it?" he said sarcastically.

Rachel ignored the implication of his words.

"You should meet him." she said. "He's not like you think he is. That's the main thing wrong with your version of reality."

The contempt had not yet disappeared from his face.

"You're hardly an unbiased judge of that, are you?" he said.

"I know that. But that's exactly why I want you to come, you idiot," she responded angrily, suddenly taking exception to the manner in which he was addressing her.

The bluntness of her remark seemed to stop Bjorn in his tracks.

"I suppose you've got a point there," he said with a forlorn expression.

Rachel smiled.

"I sometimes think André was more of a scientist than you are, Bjorn," she said.

Bjorn looked at her with a puzzled expression.

"He had a more dispassionate approach than you, less . . . emotional."

"That's what he said when he was cross, too," he said wryly.

Rachel laid her hand on his arm.

"So will you agree," she said.

Bjorn looked out thoughtfully at the view. For a long time he said nothing.

"First," he said eventually, "I will listen to the arguments he has put from you. Only then will I decide."

She had hoped the situation would not arise. For despite her earlier words she held within her a secret dread that it really was only Dupont's physical presence that made his arguments seem so convincing. But Bjorn had left her with no choice, so she proceeded to recount in detail the explanation Dupont had given her. For most of the time Bjorn listened in silence, only occasionally interjecting to ask for clarification of one point or another.

When at last her arguments were exhausted Bjorn remained silent for a long time, gazing down as the lengthening shadows of the mountain peaks slowly moved across the valley floor beneath them. He almost looked as if he were day-dreaming, not thinking about what she had said at all.

Rachel glanced apprehensively at the sun as it sank lower and lower towards the horizon.

"I've got to go, Bjorn. Soon it'll get dark up here."

He shook himself out of his reverie.

"It's not proven either way, is it, Rachel?"

His words were like a knife cutting through her. He gazed at her intently.

"I'm sorry, Rachel, but those arguments he presented to you are no more than a possible alternative explanation of what has occurred. They do nothing to actually disprove André's account of events. So now we are faced with two plausible contrasting versions of reality, that's all."

She looked at him with growing horror. Why was it that she was so confident of Dupont's innocence when she was with him, but as soon as she left his side all the doubts within her seemed to climb out from their secret hiding places and assault her senses? For Bjorn was absolutely right, of course. Dupont had presented her with absolutely nothing that disproved the accusation of genocide André had levelled against him, he had merely provided an innocent explanation of his conduct to set against André's guilty one. And Bjorn was absolutely right to remain suspicious.

As she had climbed the mountain to meet him she had been sure that she would clamber back down the path to the waiting car with the same conviction that Dupont was innocent. Yet now the nagging doubt had returned to haunt her once again.

Suddenly she turned to Bjorn, deliberately allowing him to see the anguish she felt within.

"Meet him, damn you," she pleaded. "I tell you I don't think he's capable of it. Logically I accept what you're saying about the evidence, but whenever I'm in his presence I just don't believe he is capable of doing the things André says he did. There's a quality about François Dupont I can't put my finger on. It's why I love him and it's why I trust him. Maybe – just maybe – if you meet him face to face you'll see what I mean and you'll see why he cannot be guilty of these evil actions."

Bjorn looked at her, still paralysed by indecision, almost as if he himself were frightened that entering the presence of François Dupont would dissolve his own powers of reasoning as it appeared to dissolve hers.

Far away in the west, the giant red globe of the sun touched the very highest of the mountain peaks, and as it did so a chill wind seemed to strike suddenly at the rock on which they sat.

"For God's sake, Bjorn," Rachel whimpered, "don't make me go back there and stand in judgement on him all alone."

The indecision seemed to pass from Bjorn's face. Tenderly he drew her towards him.

"I'll come," he whispered softly. "For you, Rachel, I'll come."

* * * * * *

For five long hours the two men had remained hidden away behind the solid oak doors of the Presidential office at the Chiemsee château. No interruptions. No mealbreaks. No walks on the lawn. Not even a hurried cup of coffee.

Throughout this time, Rachel had sat alone in the small ante-room, staring numbly through the window at the formal gardens beyond and only occasionally daring to glance nervously at the huge double doors. For despite her earnest protestations Bjorn and Dupont had both independently insisted on excluding her from their meeting.

She had travelled down with the President from New Vienna early that morning, leaving only shortly after the sun had risen. Throughout the dawn flight to the military airstrip near the island and the ensuing helicopter transfer he had been unusually silent, responding monosyllabically to her periodic attempts to lighten the atmosphere between them. And although she had been responsible for the impending meeting that was so obviously the cause of his disquiet, it still pained her to see him troubled in this way. For despite all her attempts to maintain her distance, she recognised now that she was firmly back on François Dupont's side in this gargantuan struggle to lay claim to the truth.

But she was still fearful about the meeting taking place behind the oak doors. For in truth she had come to value and respect Bjorn

162

Haverstamp almost as much as she had valued and respected André Rostropov in years gone by. Bjorn was a thinker, a man who represented the very best of the rational European thought that had dominated European life since the Renaissance. And however much Rachel might admire the decisiveness and strength that made François Dupont the perfect leader for a continent in mortal danger, she still hoped that the values and attitudes embodied in Bjorn would not forever be extinguished in the emerging new order.

Bjorn had arrived at the château in mid morning, coming alone as he had promised in a small motor boat from the far south of the lake. Under normal circumstances, the troops responsible for perimeter security would have apprehended him immediately, but they had been warned of his impending arrival and had allowed him to approach the island without hindrance.

Rachel had gone down alone to the water's edge to greet him, to reassure him once again that his personal safety was not under threat whilst within the grasp of François Dupont. But her attempts to reassure him had been as futile as they had been with Dupont earlier, and he had merely nodded politely to her remarks as they had walked towards the house.

Suddenly, one of the two oak doors burst open and Dupont emerged, his superficially restrained appearance concealing a look of unmistakable triumph.

"Will you not join us, my love?" he asked, his face beaming as he held the door for her to pass.

Rachel arose apprehensively and entered the Presidential office. Bjorn rose to his feet as she joined them and tried to force a smile, but she could see from the expression on his face that he had been right to dread a face-to-face encounter with a man she could already see was an erstwhile adversary.

Dupont stepped over to his desk and pressed a button.

"Some coffee and cake, please, Frau Grodzinski," he said brightly into the tiny camera concealed in the pencil rack, and then his eye fell upon the fine old clock upon the mantelpiece.

"Goodness me, is that the time?" he asked. "I thought we had been talking for less than two hours."

Still Bjorn had said nothing, and every time Rachel attempted to meet his gaze he looked away.

"Well?" she said abruptly.

Dupont looked at her and smiled broadly.

"I'm sorry, my love. I hadn't realised you had been sitting outside for over five hours. This was unforgivable of us."

Sometimes he gave the appearance of being incredibly obtuse. But it was only an appearance.

"I'm not grumbling about the length of time I was waiting outside," she said gruffly. "Having set this meeting up and then having been excluded by your mutual request, I would now like to be informed of its outcome."

Dupont looked at her in amazement, but before he could reply, Bjorn stepped abruptly forward.

"May I speak with her alone, please?" he asked quietly.

Cautiously, Dupont flicked a glance in his direction.

"Of course," he muttered. "Call me when you are ready."

He withdrew quietly and closed the door behind him, leaving her alone with the younger man. As soon as he was gone, Bjorn slumped down into a small sofa near the window and momentarily closed his eyes. When he opened them again, his face had cleared somewhat, almost as if Dupont's physical removal from the room had allowed him space to think properly again.

"You were right about François Dupont," he said with a weak attempt at a smile.

"In what way?" Rachel asked.

"He's persuasive. Very persuasive."

"And did he persuade you?"

Bjorn looked up at her and shrugged.

"When we were up on that mountain, you asked me not to let you stand in judgement on him alone. It implied a trial. Well, today he has had a trial of sorts. For the last five hours I have cross-questioned your François Dupont in immense detail. I have tried every imaginable method of wrongfooting him, of forcing him to contradict himself on some essential point so as to disprove his version of events. And you will probably be relieved to know that I have failed to convince myself that he is lying."

She looked at him silently for a moment.

"And the truth?" she asked.

Bjorn smiled.

"Ah," he said, "the truth is an altogether tougher nut to crack. From a strictly scientific point of view, I suppose I must remain an agnostic on the question of the truth."

"What the hell's that supposed to mean?" she asked.

Again he looked at her.

"I'm afraid we still have two functioning hypotheses on the table, Rachel." He jerked his head towards the anti-room where Dupont was waiting. "For Christ's sake, even he accepts that."

She looked at Bjorn in amazement.

"Does he?"

"Yes. He was generous enough to say as much. I must say, he's more of an intellectual than I'd given him credit for."

Rachel sat down wearily on the sofa beside Bjorn.

"What are you going to do, then?" she asked.

Again the look of defeat passed across his face.

"In centuries past, many agnostics joined the priesthood. As I say, I'm left with a conflict between two versions of reality that might on the available evidence be compatible with the truth. Unless new material comes to light, I have to accept that fact. Yet in the interim I have to act. It is my duty as a human being to act. Painful though it is for me as a trained scientist to say so, I have to find another way of choosing between the two versions."

He stopped talking for a moment and looked sadly at Rachel.

"You won't like my method of choosing," he said presently.

Rachel said nothing. But from her face it was clear that she had already surmised the answer.

"I have spent a great deal of time with you under fairly extreme circumstances," he continued. "Despite the fact that we started on different sides of a seemingly insurmountable divide, I have come to respect your opinions and your general approach to life greatly. From the very outset – and despite your deep personal attachment to François Dupont – you were prepared to listen to André's version of reality with an open mind, to analyse the evidence in a dispassionate way. You were even prepared to forgo the chance of escape in order to win time to think freely. In short, you are a woman of great rationality and in no way the poodle of François Dupont that André Rostropov believed you had become. Yet you always resisted André's version of events, you always suspected Dupont to be innocent. You did that on the basis of . . ."

Rachel laughed cynically.

"Intuition?" she said cynically. "So you will decide how to act on the basis of my intuition?"

Bjorn nodded.

"I said you wouldn't like it," he said bluntly.

For several minutes they sat together in silence. Before the meeting between Bjorn and Dupont, she had hoped and prayed that Dupont would win her friend around. But not like this. Not by falling back on her gut feeling that he was not the evil man André had supposed. The whole idea of the meeting had been to share the burden of responsibility, not transfer it all back onto her shoulders.

She looked at him with pleading eyes.

"But now you've met him, talked to him for so long, don't you share my intuition at all?"

Bjorn looked at her intently for several moments before replying.

"Frankly, Rachel," he said softly. "François Dupont leaves me cold."

* * * * * *

She could feel his weight almost crushing her as his body heaved back and forth above her, his face hidden from view beneath her shoulders. Since her return from captivity there had been a new urgency about Dupont as he made love to her, an intensity that was reflected not just by the frequency of their lovemaking but also by its nature. It was almost as if their physical relationship was building up towards some kind of new crescendo, although what would follow the inevitable climax was as yet far from clear.

In truth Rachel had never really understood the connection between François Dupont and sex. For eighteen months, during the early phase of their relationship, he had made no move towards her, respecting absolutely what he believed to be her desire to maintain a platonic relationship. Then, after she had been reduced to begging him to touch her, they had begun their physical relationship against the huge plate-glass window in the living room and she had first glimpsed the true power of his feelings towards her. That night had been a watershed, but since then a calmer period had ensued, a period in which the manner of their sexual conduct had become almost normal, a valued release from the tensions of government that daily lay upon his shoulders. It had been a happy time for them both.

Oddly enough, Justine Medoc's sudden and unexpected arrival on the scene had not really disturbed the equilibrium. Periodically Dupont had slept with the younger girl, especially during the days in the month when she was capable of becoming pregnant, but he had made no secret of this with Rachel. And always he had returned to her bed afterwards, preferring to sleep by her side than with Justine.

But Rachel's kidnapping had changed everything again. It was as if the fear was back, the carefully concealed yet unmistakable fear that seemed so often to consume Dupont when he was in Rachel's company. It was clear that her disappearance had stirred up once again his morbid fears of losing her, fears compounded by his realisation that she had nearly joined the ranks of his enemies. And as the overbearing fear increased, so his embraces became more feverish, until Rachel began to feel that she might suffocate under the sheer

166

intensity of his emotion.

The thrusting slowed and Dupont's breathing gradually eased, but he stayed on top of her and his weight if anything became more difficult to bear. She endured it silently for several minutes, but then, fearing he might actually fall asleep, she gently moved her body beneath him.

"François," she murmured softly, "you're crushing me."

He lifted himself up and lay beside her, his eyes meeting hers. The urgency might be gone, but the strength of feeling remained.

"Stay with me," he said quietly.

She smiled.

"I'm not going anywhere," she said. His eyes looked at her suspiciously. "Never again," she added.

"I didn't fully convince him, you know?" Dupont murmured, turning onto his back and staring disconsolately at the ceiling.

Rachel lifted her head and laid it on his chest.

"He's working for you now," she murmured. "That's enough, isn't it?"

Dupont shrugged.

"I don't give a damn what Bjorn Haverstamp thinks," he muttered. "It's you I care about. The only reason I wanted to convince him is so I'd convince you."

Rachel lifted her head and looked down into his anguished face.

"I never really doubted you, François," she said calmly. "Deep down inside, I never really doubted your good intentions. I had no choice but to address the facts André and Bjorn presented to me, but now you have shown yourself to be innocent there really isn't a problem, is there?"

Dupont said nothing. It was obvious that there still was a problem, at least for him, but nothing she could say or do was going to take it away. She decided to change the subject.

"I was talking to Justine," she said quietly.

Dupont looked at her irritably but said nothing.

"You ought really to go to her tomorrow," she added. "It's her time, you know."

Dupont looked as though he was going to say something sarcastic, but then he appeared to change his mind.

"Very well," he said, "if you wish it."

Rachel smiled. Normally she would have made a gibe at his remark, but tonight she could see that he was in no mood for humour of any description.

"Will you at least be happy when she becomes pregnant?" she

asked, hoping at least that the thought of impending fatherhood would cheer him up.

"Yes," he said morosely, turning away from her and lying on his side.

Rachel looked at him sharply. There was something about the way he had replied that made her sure he was lying. Something about the tone of his voice. But the thought was absurd.

If intercourse had failed to improve his spirits, conversation about his future fatherhood was proving equally ineffective. She decided to try politics, a subject on which he usually thrived.

"Are you worried about the Federation meeting next week?" she asked gently. "Are you worried because you'll have to talk face-to-face with Lionel Goldberger again."

The medicine worked exactly as planned. Dupont sat up in bed and grinned.

"Dear old Lionel?" he said with glee. "I'm not worried about him. Frankly, darling, President Lionel Goldberger is no match for François Dupont. Not even, as he would say it, in the same ball park. I would have thought you could have judged that from our last encounter. He's so incredibly vain, he doesn't even realise when somebody's pulled the wool over his eyes."

"Like me," Rachel muttered.

As soon as she had uttered the words she regretted them, but Dupont's mood must really have improved dramatically because he flashed a smile of such disarming charm that she could not help but smile back.

"Do you think the Federation meeting will achieve anything?" she said. "I mean, do you think it will achieve anything other than high-sounding communiqués and first rate photo opportunities."

Dupont grinned.

"Don't forget your precious referendum, my love," he said. "High-sounding communiqués and excellent photo opportunities are very important to a man about to embark on a democratic career."

Rachel's referendum plan was still proceeding apace and had been fixed for two months time. It could hardly be described as a return to genuine democracy, of course, since Dupont's media machine was heavily biased in the direction of a pro-Dupont vote, but it was perhaps better than nothing.

"Did you ever commission that opinion poll you were talking about a little while back?" she asked.

Dupont nodded.

"I did," he said drily, "but frankly I don't believe the results."

Rachel looked at him with curiosity.

"They show me with eighty percent support," he explained, attempting unsuccessfully to hide the elation he clearly felt.

"François the Great Protector," Rachel murmured, repeating one of the more poetic phrases used by some of Dupont's more iconoclastic supporters to describe the leader of Greater Europe.

"I think they were too scared to answer honestly," Dupont said quietly.

Despite herself, Rachel remembered the stories she had heard in the underground about the tactics used by the secret police to repress opposition and curtail dissent.

"Are they right to be scared?" she said quietly.

He looked at her with an odd expression.

"If I win, I have no intention of persecuting those who vote for my removal, if that is what you mean."

"And if you lose? I don't think for a minute you will lose, François, but what would you do if you did."

Dupont said nothing for several moments.

"I will organise free elections next year in which I will not stand. I am not indispensable for the rest of eternity. Soon I will be free to retire."

Again, his words puzzled her. Dupont was not yet fifty years old.

"You're a strange man, François. Sometimes I think you're hungry for power, yet now you talk of retirement as if it is a thought you relish."

Again, she regretted her words as soon as she had spoken them. From his face, she could see that the black mood which had settled over him immediately after their lovemaking was returning fast. He lay back on the bed and stared moodily at the ceiling.

"To tell you the honest truth, Rachel, I'm not sure a man like me deserves the luxury of retirement," he said softly, yawning and closing his eyes. "Perhaps a man like me deserves a crueler fate."

* * * * * *

Dupont lay sound asleep beside her, his body rising and falling in an even motion as he breathed. Rachel lay beside him and watched his sleeping form, having long given up her own futile attempts to drift into sleep. However hard she tried, Dupont's last remark before falling asleep had upset her, and she had tossed and turned beside him for many hours trying to make sense of yet another of his incomprehensible utterances.

She finally gave up trying to sleep and rose stealthily from the bed. Walking through to the darkened living room, she touched a panel and the huge curtains swept aside to reveal the panoramic view of New Vienna. Far away in the east, over the flatlands of the Hungarian plains, the pale sky gave the first clue of the approaching dawn.

At this hour of the morning there was a silence in the air, an almost tangible silence that permeated every corner of the room. It was as if the whole world were asleep, husbanding its energies for the senseless struggle of another long day ahead. In the room she had just left, even François Dupont slept. Only she was still awake.

The silence began to become oppressive. She wandered over to the large desk in the corner of the room, sitting down and intending to write a letter to her children. As if to compose herself, she gazed for several moments at the little cluster of four photographs neatly arranged in one corner of the desk, one each of Tom and the three children. Her husband had sent them to her only a few weeks before, and the sight of them brought back poignant memories of her earlier life.

There was little point in sinking yet further into melancholy. She picked up a pen and pulled out a sheet of paper from the drawer. But then, before she had written a single word, a strange thought suddenly came upon her, a thought prompted by the sight of the group of photographs sitting on the desk. For however hard she tried, she could not recall a single occasion on which she had ever seen a childhood photograph of François Dupont.

She put down the pen and double-checked her memory. She had seen photographs of Dupont as a young journalist, earlier photographs of Dupont as a university student, but never once a photograph of Dupont as a child. Nor, come to think of it, had she seen any photographs of Dupont's parents or any other members of his family. For some reason, it had never occurred to her to ask him to show her his old photograph album.

"Johann!" she ordered, curiosity getting the better of her.

A clatter followed by a whirr followed by a gentle thud announced the arrival of the household servant.

"Check household inventory files for the location of the photograph album containing François's old photographs."

"Files do not contain such an item," announced the machine after a respectful pause.

She looked at Johann with a bemused expression.

"Re-check, analysing internally all personal record books in the flat."

The machine pretended to re-check.

170

"There is no item in the flat that could contain such photographic records, Rachel."

Suddenly Rachel was cross with herself that she had not asked him about it earlier. Everybody had old photos lying about. It seemed almost offensive that there were none in the entire flat. And the fact that she had been frustrated in her initial desire to see them only made her want to see them all the more.

"Research main data banks for photographs of François Dupont as a child and display," she commanded.

The television set in the opposite corner of the room hummed into life.

"Shall I display in chronological order?"

Rachel nodded silently.

Nothing happened.

"Yes," she said irritably, remembering the stupid machine only responded to voice commands.

A picture appeared of a boy of about five wearing short grey pants and a pressed white shirt. The boy looked tense and frightened, and she suspected that the photograph had been taken by officials at about the time he had been despatched to the orphanage.

"Next!" she commanded.

The five-year old disappeared and was replaced by a timid boy of about ten. Another official photograph, she suspected, and once again the face was filled with an anxiety that Rachel had herself glimpsed so many times in the adult Dupont during the course of their relationship.

"Next!"

The rather pale and spindly pre-adolescent became a healthy looking lad of some fifteen years of age. But more striking than the physical changes were the eyes. The cowering frightened look had vanished almost completely, and the other François Dupont, the strong confident François Dupont the world and come to know, was staring at her from the television screen.

"Next!"

A pause. The television screen went dead.

"Photographic record only contains three elements," Johann reported calmly.

She looked at it and frowned. François Dupont had been around for a while, and not just as President either. It seemed almost inconceivable that only three childhood photographs had found their way into the central computer records.

"There must be some other photographs in existence. Try his father and mother."

The machine whirred.

"No photographs exist," it stated.

Rachel thought for a moment. The fact that no photos had ever been filed of François's mother and father was perhaps a little surprising in view of his public prominence over the years. But there was one other place where she could be fairly sure of finding a photograph of Dupont.

"Prior to the Treaty of Brussels, did the French government maintain official photographs of children attending state orphanages?"

A clatter.

"Yes, Rachel," came the response. "Group photographs were filed annually in every year since 1953."

"Remind me of the name of the orphanage François attended after the age of five?"

"Our Lady of Grace, in the village of Rosillion."

"O.K. Johann, let's have the group photographs of the Our Lady of Grace for the years from 1960 to 1975. In chronological order again please."

Rachel turned to the blank television screen and waited. For several moments, nothing happened.

"Begin!" she ordered.

"No records exist for Our Lady of Grace," the machine reported.

"But I thought you said they did?" Rachel snapped back.

Again the hesitation. She had noticed before that computers weren't very good at handling situations when they had made general statements and were then forced to contradict themselves.

"Correction to earlier statement," the machine announced, putting on its most formal and machine-like voice as if by way of apology. "Photographic records do not exist for all French orphanages during this period. They exist only for most French orphanages."

Rachel looked at the machine suspiciously.

"And not for Our Lady of Grace?"

"No."

"Why not?"

"I have no information."

The machine was flustered, that much was clear. They were designed to behave like friendly little people, not to come out with stupid bureaucratic lines like 'I have no information'.

Rachel shook her head and stood up, walking towards the window and looking down at the early morning traffic in the city street below. It might only be a machine, but after living with it for so long she

172

felt she knew its little mannerisms pretty well. Yet the theory formulating in her mind to explain its current confusion was not one she particularly wished to entertain. She tiptoed nervously towards the bedroom door and peeked through at the silent sleeping figure of François Dupont. She knew she had no right to be thinking what she was thinking, no right to start double-crossing him again having promised him only hours before how she had pushed all her doubts aside.

She eased the bedroom door silently closed and returned to the machine.

"Photographic records are missing from how many French orphanages during this period?" she asked.

Silence.

"I have no information."

She thought for a moment. It couldn't be a press ban, the central computer knew full well that Johann was the President's personal terminal. And then an idea suddenly occurred to her.

"Are you sure, Johann?" she whispered slowly and deliberately.

A long pause.

"I have no information."

She stared at the machine for several minutes in utter horror, wishing with all her soul that she had not asked her final question. But she had asked it, and now she could not unask it. Poor innocent Johann had answered her deliberate request to repeat itself using exactly the same words as it had used originally. Yet she knew it was programmed to invariably answer in different words so as not to appear rude to its owner. It was a crude and simple mistake, but it confirmed her worst fears.

* * * * * *

If Dupont wasn't enjoying his meal there was certainly no outward sign of it.

"More meat, anyone?" he asked optimistically, stirring the huge bowl of beef bourguignon in the centre of the circular mahogany dining table with a large wooden ladle and looking expectantly at his three companions.

"Not for me," Justine said, flicking her hair to one side and smiling sweetly at him.

Rachel glanced apprehensively towards Bjorn, who was sitting morosely opposite Dupont, his eyes lowered.

"I shouldn't think any of us do, darling. You gave us such generous portions the first time round," she murmured.

Bjorn roused himself from his reverie and looked up.

"None for me thanks," he added.

Dupont ladled himself another portion.

"I hope you don't mind if I do then," he said, sitting down heavily in his chair and continuing to eat.

Rachel looked at him gratefully as he steadily munched his way through his second plateful. At least it prevented him from talking.

Justine looked at Bjorn with a puzzled expression.

"You were that guy who came over to help us from the underground, weren't you?" she asked.

Bjorn's misery, which had been growing ever since he had stepped into the room, became even more pronounced.

"Yes," he muttered. "That's me."

Dupont stopped eating and looked at her sourly.

"Why don't you zip your lips, Justine," he said with a dry smile. "I am extremely grateful for the valuable contribution Dr Haverstamp has brought to the work of the clinic. If there was a time when we did not quite see eye to eye, that time has long since passed."

Suitably reprimanded, Justine allowed her hair to fall once again over her eyes and began picking silently at the half-eaten bowl of lettuce beside her plate.

The diplomatic requirements of the meal temporarily claiming precedence over its gastronomic appeal, Dupont looked up at Bjorn.

"I have heard that you are making some progress at the clinic, Dr Haverstamp," he commented approvingly. "It seems it was a good decision to put you at its head."

Bjorn grunted.

"A little perhaps," he said, "But we are still scratching at the surface. Until we identify the original sequence pattern that led to the D.N.A. transformation we will not make a major breakthrough."

Rachel looked sadly at Bjorn. After their initial meeting, Dupont had astounded everyone by appointing him as Director of the lavishly equipped clinic established in New Vienna to investigate the White Death. From being an outcast and an outlaw, he had been instantly transformed into the most influential scientist in Europe. Yet the change did not appear to have brought him any great happiness.

"I'm sorry," Dupont said apologetically. "You'll have to explain that to me in simple language."

Bjorn looked up at the President.

"It means that if we understood more about the series of genetic mutations that have led to the creation of the White Death we would be more likely to be able to develop an effective treatment for it.

An analogy would be a man trying to find his way out of a highly complex maze. Without any clues to help him, he might keep going up blind alleys and take many years to find the way out. But if someone had left a piece of string showing the route it would be a great deal quicker."

Dupont met Bjorn's questioning gaze head on.

"The alternative hypothesis?" he murmured.

At his words Bjorn looked away with an embarrassed frown.

"Don't be stupid, François," Rachel interjected. "Bjorn's words implied no such thing. It is merely a statement of scientific fact."

Dupont raised his hands as if in self-defence.

"But of course, my love," he said. "It was only my little jest." He looked across at Bjorn. "Did you not tell Rachel that I had accepted in full the theoretical plausibility of your alternative hypothesis?"

Bjorn nodded but said nothing.

"It is a standing joke between Dr Haverstamp and I, Rachel," Dupont continued. "My guilt is not proven, but then neither is my innocence. And if I am indeed guilty, and know the terrible secret of this disease, then it stands to reason that I could make the life of our hypothetical man trapped in a maze considerably easier."

If Bjorn found the joke funny, there was nothing on his face to indicate the fact.

Johann clattered noisily into the room.

"Are you aware that it is already three o'clock," it said respectfully to Dupont.

He glanced down at his watch.

"My goodness me," he announced, scooping up the last few pieces of beef from his plate and stuffing them into his mouth. "As I explained earlier you must excuse me. I must attend a meeting on next year's financial statement which promises little other than excruciating boredom."

He rose from his seat and moved towards the lift.

"You at least will be having a much more enjoyable time," he said wistfully. "It is English apple crumble and cream for desert."

Two minutes later he was gone, leaving an awkward silence in his wake.

"Would you like me to serve the apple crumble?" Johann asked politely.

Rachel glanced apprehensively at Justine.

"Are you hungry, Justine?" she asked.

The girl was still smarting from Dupont's earlier rebuff, sitting

175

with her eyes lost from view beneath her fringe. She shrugged her shoulders.

"Not particularly," she muttered, rising to her feet. "In fact, if you'll excuse me I think I'll go and rest for a while."

Bjorn rose politely as she departed. Then he resumed his place and looked at Rachel with a tired expression.

"Are we going to eat some, then?" he said, as if the idea of some apple crumble with cream was the first pleasant thought that had crossed his mind all day.

"Why don't we have some later," she said casually, "after we've had a walk in the garden?"

Bjorn looked disappointed.

"I'd rather have some straight away," he said. "To tell you the truth, I couldn't really relax with my food while he was here. I'm still hungry."

Rachel rose to her feet and glowered at him.

"Nevertheless, Bjorn, a walk in the garden would definitely do you good."

This time he got the message. Rising solemnly to his feet, he followed her quietly out into the garden. They walked in silence until they came to the low railing that was all that divided the roof garden from a sheer drop of fifty-five stories to the busy city street below.

Bjorn looked nervously over the edge and involuntarily took a step backwards.

"Do we really have to stand here, Rachel?"

"Just at the moment," she said drily, "it's the safest place I can think of."

Bjorn looked sideways at her.

"What the hell does that mean?" he asked.

"I don't really know. But something's happened. Something I have to talk to you about. That's why I arranged with François for you to come round today."

A look of panic was rapidly spreading over Bjorn's face.

"I really think we can talk freely here," she said. "His own flat is the last place in Europe he would be likely to have bugged, with the possible exception of the garden of his own flat."

Bjorn nodded silently, but she could tell from his face that despite his apprehension her words had transformed his spirits. The old flame was back in his eyes.

"What's happened?" he asked.

"When you and André were doing your study of François, did you ever come across any photographs of him as a child?"

Bjorn thought for a moment.

"I think so," he said. "I can't really remember."

"Think back, Bjorn. I think it might be important."

"Yes," he said slowly. "There were a few. But they didn't seem terribly important to us. We were more interested in the interviews we had with people who'd known him then. I told you that before. Why is it so important?"

"A few nights ago I couldn't sleep. It suddenly occurred to me that I'd never seen any of François's childhood photographs. You know, the kind we all have ferreted away in a cupboard somewhere."

Bjorn glanced at her with a frown.

"And he doesn't have any?"

"No. At least, not here in the flat."

Bjorn shrugged.

"Come on, Rachel. I agree it's a bit odd, but there's so much that's odd about François Dupont that one more abnormality doesn't seem particularly surprising to me. And he did live in a children's home."

"But that's not all, Bjorn. I was curious. Not suspicious, you understand. Just curious. So I asked Johann to check the central computer files and dig out some old photos for me. It could only locate three."

Bjorn eyed her apprehensively.

"Three?" he repeated.

Rachel nodded.

"That struck me as more than odd, it struck me as downright weird. So I asked Johann to pull me up some group shots of François's old orphanage. The computer had previously informed me quite dogmatically that the French government kept meticulous records of that kind which were automatically transformed into microfiche and stored in the central data banks."

Bjorn stared at her.

"Suppressed?" he asked.

She nodded.

"All the photographic records relating to the orphanage have been removed."

"But can you be sure they were deliberately suppressed?" Bjorn asked. "Maybe they were just mislaid. Come on, Rachel, it was all a very long time ago."

Rachel turned to face him.

"That's a state-of-the-art seventh series household computer in there, Bjorn. Programmed to behave with impeccable courtesy and never use the same words twice when asked to repeat itself. But when

I challenged it, it did just that."

Bjorn tried to look casual, almost as if he were fearful that Justine or some electronic eye were observing them. But the attempt failed.

"So someone has introduced a block into the computer on that line of enquiry and accidentally screwed up the courtesy programme," he said softly, and the look in his eyes told her the next question he was going to ask without him having to speak the words.

"Yes," she said flatly. "It could only have been done by François himself."

Bjorn thought hard for several minutes.

"Does he know you've been prying?" he said at last.

Rachel shrugged despairingly, remembering the humiliating way he had surmised that she had asked Bjorn to torture her.

"How should I know? I don't seem to be able to do anything without him knowing about it ten minutes before it happens."

A slight breeze had picked up, bringing with it a hint of snow from the distant Alpine range away to the west.

Bjorn started to shiver.

"So why do you think he's done it, Rachel?"

Again she shrugged.

"Christ knows. Maybe like you say it's simple paranoia. Fear of people prying into an unhappy past, even if the person doing the prying is one who has access to his personal terminal."

"But you don't think that, do you?" he asked.

For a long time she was silent. Then, wearily, reluctantly, she shook her head.

"There's something there we haven't understood, Bjorn. I'm certain of it. Something's not straight. And the key lies in the Our Lady of Grace Orphanage."

* * * * * *

The guilt was the worst part of it. Whichever way she ran, whichever crazy explanation of reality she adopted, she was continually confronted by an ever-growing, all-consuming sense of guilt.

She still loved him, of that there could never again be any doubt. Whatever the as yet undiscovered secrets of his life, she felt sufficiently confident of her own emotions to know that she would stay by his side to the end, however bitter that end might be. Yet despite herself, despite her earnest promises to him after he had discovered her last betrayal, she had betrayed him again. It made it hard to look him in the face when they were alone together.

In truth she had told Bjorn of her fears before she had had time to think. It had been a reflex reaction, she had allowed it to be a reflex reaction, when she had arranged for him to come to lunch so that she could ask him to use his contacts in the underground to investigate once again the circumstances of Dupont's dark and lonely childhood in the French Alpine orphanage.

The limousine in which she was sitting swept regally onwards through the pleasant southern suburbs of New Vienna towards the low foothills of the Alps and she tried hard to think of other things, to escape both the guilt and the need to reconcile and explain her own actions to herself. But the very mundanity of the surroundings, the prim rows of neatly whitewashed houses with their carefully tended gardens, prevented her from doing so.

There was the stench of tragedy in the air, of that she was becoming increasingly certain. And if she was right, it was a tragedy so unspeakably horrible that the human mind could not fully comprehend its true dimensions.

Much to Rachel's relief, a sharp turn to the right brought all chance for further contemplation to an end as the car swept through a pair of high gates and on into the grounds of Bjorn's clinic. Once it had been a modern civilian hospital, but now the wards and lobbies had been transformed at vast public expense into what was indisputably the largest medical research establishment in the world.

The car drew gently to a halt and Bjorn came down the steps at the main entrance to greet her. As soon as she had stepped out into the bright winter sunshine, he shook her formally by the hand.

"Thanks for coming," he said. "It's good to have the opportunity to show you around at last."

The words were intended for public consumption, but as he spoke it was hard not to notice the tension in his voice.

Together they started climbing the stairs and entered the main building, Rachel's personal security contingent holding respectfully back but always remaining well within earshot.

For about an hour they exchanged pleasantries with staff as they toured the buildings, for this was the first formal visit of the President's consort to the clinic and therefore an important occasion for the entire staff.

Despite its change of use, the building in which they found themselves retained the feel of a hospital. The long central corridor running down the spine of the building, with its white painted walls and sharply resonant echo, bustled with serious-faced men and women in white coats busying themselves about their affairs. Most of the wards running off the central corridor had been converted into laboratories or offices, and every now and then Bjorn would steer Rachel into one or other of these areas to show her some particularly sophisticated piece of medical hardware or to introduce her to one of his more important professional assistants.

"I can see you're spending a lot of money," she asked as they entered yet another laboratory, "but are you making any progress?"

Bjorn looked at her, surprised at what he took as a veiled reference to their earlier conversation. But then he realised that she was referring to the disease.

"As a matter of fact we are," he said bluntly.

Rachel stopped.

"Real progress?"

Bjorn nodded.

"Yes. A great deal of real progress. Almost a breakthrough, you might say."

"You found some string, then?"

He looked at her blankly.

"String?"

"I was thinking of your maze."

Bjorn nodded.

"A lucky break, perhaps. Even a man in a maze sometimes has a lucky break."

Bjorn flicked a glance at the security personnel.

"I'll tell you about it if you like," Bjorn continued, "but I'm afraid it's got to be in confidence." He pushed open a door to a small empty office to one side of them and stepped inside. "Let's go in here, this one's not in use at the moment."

The most senior of the five security staff appointed to look after Rachel's welfare stepped smartly forward, politely obstructing her passage into the room.

"Yes, Luigi?" Rachel asked.

"I do not recollect this room being security cleared for private discussions, Mrs McNie," he said softly, a worried frown on his face.

Rachel knew he had his orders, orders that had been considerably tightened up since the Scottish fiasco. Security staff were to be present at all times unless the room had been thoroughly checked beforehand. Generally speaking, it was a sensible rule.

Bjorn was looking at her anxiously.

She puffed herself up imperiously.

"Don't be silly, Luigi," she muttered gruffly, sweeping past him and closing the door in his astonished face.

For several seconds they both looked back at the door, half expecting Luigi to follow them in. But the door remained closed.

"What's he going to do now, Rachel?"

She watched the door suspiciously.

"Nothing, I hope. At worst, he'll phone his boss in the Commission building for instructions. That'll take a few minutes.

Bjorn was already sitting down at the desk and roughly pulling some papers out of his briefcase.

"I think we can talk in here," he continued. "I was pretty certain the main conference rooms would be bugged by security, but not a glorified broom cupboard like this place."

Rachel looked at him apprehensively. They might have got every room covered in a building of this importance, but then they simply had to speak somewhere.

Bjorn picked up a brown paper envelope and fingered it thoughtfully for a few moments.

"Have a look at this," he said at last, handing it to her.

Rachel sat down at the empty table and carefully opened the envelope. Inside, going slightly yellow with age, was an old newspaper, a faded copy of a local French weekly.

"Page sixteen," Bjorn added softly.

There was something about the tone of his voice that made her wince. A sense of relief, perhaps, if not a sense of triumph.

She lay the newspaper carefully on the table and turned to page sixteen.

"The sports page?" she murmured, searching the page for something of significance.

"Don't read it, look at the photo in the bottom left hand corner," Bjorn said impatiently, throwing an anxious glance in the direction of the door.

The tiny photograph was not easy to see, a result of the antiquated printing technique. It showed a group of four boys aged around fourteen or fifteen years. Wearing nothing but their swimming costumes, they stood with wet hair in a close group, one of their number clutching a small piece of paper with illegible writing on it which he was proudly displaying for the camera.

Rachel peered carefully at the image before her, lifting up the newspaper to have a better look.

"François?" she murmured, but even as she asked the question she knew the answer. For despite the poor quality of the reproduction and the long passage of years since the camera had done its simple work, there could be no mistaking that disarming mixture of keen, clear intellect and dark underlying passion which was the hallmark of the man she loved.

She glanced at the brief caption to the photograph. "Local boys win relay race!" Nothing of great significance there, nothing which could explain the triumphal tone she had detected earlier in Bjorn's voice.

The young scientist was fidgeting nervously opposite her, still apprehensive that the security guards would enter. And as soon as she had lifted her eyes from the newspaper to meet his, the words he had been holding back since the beginning of their conversation began to pour forth.

"You were right about the orphanage holding the key," he said, speaking softly but rapidly, "but it wasn't easy to find. Since André was down there the whole area has been turned into an enormous Care Centre, and you know what that means. So we tried to track down the three people we'd traced before when we were looking into Dupont's childhood. But they've all gone too."

Again Bjorn glanced nervously at the door.

"Trying the local press was a long shot. The offices of the local paper lay inside the sealed zone, but it had once belonged to a larger regional chain which had a central records office outside the new Care Centre, a records office with back copies of all the old newspapers carefully ferreted away together with a helpful old lady to help you find your way around."

"Surely it had all been transferred to microfiche?" Rachel interjected.

"Of course it had been. Maybe they'd kept this place open for sentimental reasons, or perhaps to keep the local history society sweet. Anyway, if my people weren't suspicious enough already they soon became more so, because it turned out they weren't the only people nosing around in the records for that period. Several weeks back the old lady had a visit from somebody else claiming to be doing research into the early life of François Dupont."

Rachel looked up at him sharply.

"Security police?" she asked.

Bjorn shrugged.

"My guess is they had instructions to use the computer's automatic search programme to track down all the issues in which certain key names appeared. As I'm sure you know, the computer could scan the entire text of twenty years' back issues in microseconds and tell the user the exact location of each reference. Anyway, by the time we arrived on the scene, a number of issues were missing from both the microfiche and the hard copy records.

Involuntarily, Rachel's eyes moved back to the caption on the photograph: "Local boys win relay race!"

"Yes," Bjorn continued, watching her eyes, "they missed this one because the caption is so vague. It doesn't use any of the critical words that might have been checked. We only found it at all because I remembered you telling me what a good swimmer he was and suggested a thorough search of the sports pages."

Rachel looked at the picture thoughtfully for a few moments before laying it back on the table.

"So what's this prove?" she asked.

Bjorn flicked yet another nervous glance in the direction of the door.

"Christ, Rachel, don't you see. It's not François Dupont who's the interesting one in that photograph. It's the plump little boy with the close cropped hair on the far left of the group."

Picking up the paper once again, she stared for several seconds at the photograph, trying unsuccessfully to place the blurred adolescent face of Dupont's team-mate. Her eyes rose uncertainly to meet Bjorn's.

"You don't recognise him, do you, Rachel?" Bjorn murmured softly.

She shook her head.

He pulled another photograph out of his bag and handed it to her. It was a formal close-up of a rather unhappy-looking young man in his early twenties. She carefully compared his image with the boy in the picture.

"It's him all right," she said at last. "There's no doubt about it."

Again the look of triumph flashed across Bjorn's face.

"François's fellow swimmer," he said slowly, intent on making sure she understood the full significance of his words, "is no other than the illusive Victor Stein."

She stared helplessly at the tiny photograph, trying to force the image to change, to turn the group of teenage swimmers into the innocent journalistic snap it had once been. But the longer she studied it, the more times she checked and cross-checked the image in the newspaper with the likeness of Victor Stein as a young man, the more she began to realise that there was no further escape. The alternative hypothesis was no longer the alternative hypothesis. It had become the truth.

"I'm sorry," Bjorn muttered.

She looked at him blankly.

"How come you didn't know this already?" she asked at last.

He shrugged.

"André might have been good, but he wasn't infallible. It might seem obvious after the event, but he had no reason to suspect a childhood link." He gestured towards the photograph. "Look at them, Rachel, they're only kids."

Rachel shrugged. Mentally, her question had only been a holding tactic, a way of avoiding the awkward question of what to do with the new information now it had become available. But Luigi was only a footstep away on the other side of a door, perhaps bracing himself at this very moment to interrupt their private conversation on the orders of the Commission Security Chief or even Dupont himself. There was no time to waste on idle musings.

"What do you want to do, Bjorn?" she said limply, no longer trusting herself to have an opinion.

Bjorn carefully replaced the photographs in the brown paper bag before allowing his eyes to rise and meet hers.

"Absolutely nothing," he said quietly.

She looked at him in astonishment.

"I wasn't lying when I told you I was making progress in finding a vaccine, Rachel," he continued, the excited tone in his voice hard to conceal. "We've been running the specifications of the disease through a new computer programme that's been developed here at the clinic. To be honest with you, even I don't really understand all the ins and outs of it, but I think we're making real headway. Give me a month of uninterrupted work with the massive resources of this clinic behind me and I tell you there's a fifty-fifty chance we'll have cracked it."

Rachel closed her eyes, forcing herself to concentrate, to retain her sense of reason and delay the inevitable crisis that she knew would soon overwhelm her.

"Any attempt at disclosure to the Americans would be foolish at this critical stage," Bjorn continued. "It could so easily backfire and result in my removal from the clinic or, indeed, the cancellation of the whole research programme. Better to wait a few weeks and see if I can finish the job."

"And then?" Rachel asked.

He hesitated.

"Surely you know the answer to that question," he said at last, his voice lowered and his eyes averted.

Rachel's head sank slowly down onto her arms. Bjorn was right. She did know the answer. The very second he had the vaccine safely in his hands he would run to Lionel Goldberger and the Americans.

But this time there would be no further need to spin Dupont along. With the Americans safely in tow and able to transmit details of the case against Dupont across the continent from their vast array of communications satellites, the President of Europe's hold on power would quickly evaporate. His immense popularity would wane, the morale of the security forces would crumble, the military would turn their backs on him. And the very best he would be able to hope for would be that the inevitable lynching when it came would be swift and relatively pain-free.

A thought occurred to her and she lifted her head.

"And what if I tell him?" she asked softly. "You know I love him, don't you?"

This time he met her gaze.

"I know you won't," he said bluntly, the emotion he felt showing for the first time since their conversation had begun. "But I'm not stupid, Rachel. For all I know he might be listening to our every word. But if he makes a move against either me or the clinic then the salient facts of both our research here and the evidence against him will immediately be made available to the Americans. He might slow down the progress we're making towards a vaccine, he might be able to ensure that he sends a few more million people to their deaths before the vaccine comes on stream, but either way he's finished."

This time it was Rachel who looked away. The sanity of Bjorn's triumphal declaration of Dupont's impending fate was entirely rational. It was she who had the problem.

Bjorn checked himself.

"Sorry, Rachel," he said. "I didn't mean to put it quite like that."

She took no notice.

"And what if you fail? You said yourself there was only a fifty-fifty chance."

Bjorn carefully lifted the brown paper bag from the table and replaced it in his briefcase.

"If I fail," he said slowly, "then it's back to square one, isn't it? Before we only guessed at the link with Stein. Now we know. Somehow or other, you're going to have to persuade François Dupont to tell you exactly where we can find him."

* * * * * *

He slept beside her in the bed, his breathing steady, the look of quiet tranquility on his face mocking the sense of agitation she felt within her. She remembered André during his last hours in the remote Scottish hill settlement, his deathly white features a cruel shadow of the handsome upright man he had once been. But she knew that André was merely an image, a concrete representation of a far greater tragedy, a tragedy that had befallen the whole of Mankind as billions had fallen victim to the terrible scourge of the White Death and billions more had suffered the silent private agonies of bereavement.

But there were no longer any innocent explanations, only a riddle as yet unresolved. For the clear establishment of a childhood link between François Dupont and Victor Stein simply could not be rationalised away, since the link between Dupont and a scientist capable of developing the White Death had always been the crucial evidence André had unsuccessfully sought in his quest to prove the grim charges he had made against his enemy.

Moreover, all the evidence pointed to a brutal cover-up, as the President had used his absolute authority to suppress all the evidence of their shared childhood. Stein's disappearance from the military had occurred many years before, and Dupont must originally have reasoned that no one in their wildest imaginings would ever have postulated a connection between the two men.

Rachel smiled wryly to herself as she recalled it was she who had originally let André Rostropov loose on the subject. But Dupont had not reckoned on either André's thoroughness or his obsessive paranoia, and it was only when she had herself alerted him to André's carefully constructed hypothesis about a possible link with an obscure military scientist that he had felt it necessary to act. So all traces of the orphanage had been obliterated, the buildings themselves incorporated into a new Care Centre and the remaining people who had been unlucky enough to share Dupont's childhood liquidated. Nearly, very nearly, he had succeeded in covering his tracks.

Carefully, intently, she studied Dupont's face, the face that was the cause of the emotional conflict within her. For if the salient facts of his conduct were now gradually becoming clear, the central riddle still remained unresolved. The man beside her was guilty of sending several billion human beings to their deaths, an act of genocide unparalleled in human history. Yet as he slept his face was strangely untroubled, almost as if he were at peace with himself. And therein, she knew, lay the riddle it was her private duty to solve.

Her own emotions swirled backwards and forwards. She remembered Tom, she remembered her children, she remembered the normality of her earlier life. She had not asked for all that to be taken away from her, she had not asked to be thrust into this bizarre relationship with François Dupont. But now that she was with him she knew she could not leave him, she simply could not walk away from the inevitable final act of a tragedy of which she was now an integral part.

She wondered if Eva Brown, Adolf Hitler's faithful mistress, had ever lain in bed in the quiet of the night and felt as she did now. Had she ever woken up to this particular nightmare and been forced to choose? Had she realised too late that the man she loved was guilty of hideous crimes and yet been powerless to prevent herself from loving him with all her soul? A tiny vial of poison had finally resolved her riddle, and now Rachel wondered if a similar fate awaited her.

But it was indeed a strange kind of love she felt for François Dupont, a strange kind of love that motivated her actions. For overtly, she was once again a part of the underground, conspiring with Bjorn Haverstamp to bring an end to Dupont's absolute grip on the levers of European power and in the process free the world from the clutches of the White Death. Her realisation of the terrible crime he had committed permitted no alternative course of action.

The guilt she felt arose not from her actions, which had been urged upon her by Bjorn, but rather from her emotions. For she knew she should hate and despise the man who had brought so much suffering to herself and to the world, she should feel repulsion at the very sight of him, she should desire nothing more than to take a knife whilst he slept and thrust it deep into his heart, twisting and turning the blade ever deeper into his body in a futile attempt to purge the evil from his soul and assuage her own terrible guilt at having loved and supported him.

But she didn't feel any of these things about François Dupont. She simply knew she loved him with all her heart and being.

Realising that sleep was not going to ease her mental anguish, she slipped quietly out of bed, tiptoeing through to the kitchen. Johann was resting quietly in the corner, plugged into the electrical socket in the corner of the room recharging itself for the day's work ahead. As she entered, it shook itself out of its slumbers with a polite little clatter, disconnected itself from the wall and shuffled respectfully towards the centre of the room.

"Hallo, Rachel," it said softly, aware that a human visitor was unusual at this hour of the night and programmed to respond in a suitably sympathetic tone. "Can I help you with something?"

Rachel looked down at the little robot and for once found herself almost envying it.

"Johann?" she asked, sitting down on a stool so as to be closer to its height.

"Yes, Rachel."

"Johann, do you ever worry?"

187

The polite clatter continued significantly longer than usual.

"I am not sure how to interpret your question, Rachel?" it answered, the puzzled tone disconcertingly human.

Rachel smiled wryly.

"Oh, forget it, Johann," she murmured, wondering whether it might after all have been a mistake to have it reprogrammed to respond to a human name. At the time it had seemed a good move, a sensible way of getting her relationship with Justine Medoc off to a good start.

She rose from the stool and turned towards the living room door, intending to sit by the picture window for a while and see if the panoramic view would do more to clear her brain than a conversation with a mobile computer terminal. But before she had gone three paces she stopped dead in her tracks and turned to stare at Johann once again.

"My God!" she whispered softly, amazed at the absurd idea to which her train of thought had led.

For a long time she stood stock still, and then she quietly left the room.

* * * * * *

Dupont was busying himself straightening his tie in front of the bedroom mirror, having failed to get it quite right on several previous attempts.

"When I was a kid," he muttered, "they used to sell a kind of tie that was already made up. All you had to do was hook it on to the shirt collar."

Rachel sat on the side of the bed and watched him struggle. After a night without sleep she should by rights have felt tired, but strangely enough she felt wide awake.

"Do you want me to help?" she asked.

Without a word, he ripped off the tie and turned to her with a disarming smile.

"Thanks," he said, handing her the offending object.

A few moments later the tie was correctly in place, but Dupont made no attempt to draw away. Instead, he drew her gently towards him.

"I really don't know what I'd do without you," he murmured softly, lowering his head and kissing her brow.

Her eyes rose slowly to meet his gaze.

"Much the same as you've done with me, perhaps," she replied.

For a while he said nothing.

"I think not," he said presently, drawing slowly away from her and lifting the jacket of his suit from the back of a nearby chair.

Rachel swallowed hard.

"Will you be back late tonight?" she asked.

He nodded.

"I fear so. Are you going out?"

"I don't know. I haven't decided yet."

Dupont frowned.

"You will keep Luigi informed of your plans, won't you, my love? he murmured. "After the scare you gave him at the clinic, word has reached me that he has become rather fearful of the unexpected."

His words came as a shock. It was the first time he had commented upon her unscheduled meeting with Bjorn the previous day.

"I'm sorry about that," she mumbled.

Dupont turned to her with a smile.

"You're not betraying me again, are you?" he said.

She looked away, pretending to start applying some make-up that lay conveniently on the dressing table. She was ninety-nine percent certain his remark had been in jest, but only ninety-nine percent.

"Don't be ridiculous," she muttered, "there's no reason why I shouldn't have been talking to Haverstamp."

"It's not the fact that you were talking privately to Haverstamp that I'm objecting to. It's the fact that no security check had taken place."

"All right, François," she said, deciding not to pursue the topic, "I promise I'll speak to Luigi as soon as I've decided what I'm doing."

A final glance in the mirror having convinced Dupont that the state of his attire was appropriate to his forthcoming appointments, he turned to Rachel and kissed her once again, this time on the lips.

"It's only because I care," he said quietly, and without waiting for a response he turned brusquely on his heels and strode out of the room.

For a moment Rachel remained seated, staring numbly at the door through which he had departed. Then, when the sound of the lift door closing had assured her that the coast was clear, she rose purposefully from her chair and walked the short distance down the hall to the room where Justine slept.

Pausing only for an instant to collect her wits, she pushed open the door without knocking and crept into the young girl's bedroom.

Justine was fast asleep, sprawled diagonally across a spacious double bed, her naked body only half concealed beneath a single white sheet. Rachel crept stealthily across the room and knelt down on the floor beside her face, carefully and systematically comparing the girl's features with the image seared onto her memory the previous day.

"Justine," she murmured softly, touching her gently on the shoulder.

The girl awoke with a start.

"Rachel?" she said blankly, sitting up in bed and rubbing her eyes. "What's up?"

"I've got to talk to you, Justine. We might not have much time."

Justine flicked her hair away from her eyes and looked at her apprehensively.

"What do you mean we haven't got much time?"

Rachel took a deep breath and met Justine's enquiring eyes full on. "Because I think your father's life might be at risk, that's why."

The moment she had uttered the words she knew she had guessed correctly. The confused yet fearful expression on Justine's face was enough to confirm the truth.

"What do you mean?" she mumbled blankly. "My father's already dead. I told you that."

Rachel held her gaze, refusing to allow the eyes to escape.

"You may perhaps be right, although I think we are still in time."

This time the fear in the young girl's face was unmistakable. But still she resisted.

"What are you talking about, Rachel?"

The game began to pall.

"I'm talking about Victor Stein."

Her defences were palpably crumbling.

"Victor Stein," she repeated numbly.

"Justine, we're wasting valuable time. I know your father is Victor Stein. I know about the White Death. I know about pretty well everything."

At her words the last vestiges of resistance crumbled away.

"How?" Justine asked blankly. "How do you know?"

"It doesn't matter how I know. But the main thing is we have to act now."

Justine glanced nervously at the door, as if she was half expecting Dupont to enter.

"But surely François has dealt with it. He can stop them getting at my father."

Rachel stared at the young girl. She knew a great deal about Dupont's actions, that much was clear, but despite everything she seemed to retain an air of almost adolescent innocence.

"No Justine," she said, "you don't understand. I'm not talking about some resistance plot. It is François himself who will give the orders for your father to be killed."

Justine froze, trying to find some mental approach to words that made no sense.

"I'm sorry, Justine," she continued, "but I think François is losing his mind completely. He wants Stein dead because he knows too much. He told me that. He's got scared. He's already destroyed the orphanage, everything and everyone that could have linked him with your father and the disease. The very moment Stein's role in the project is over, he's going to kill him too."

She allowed the full force of her words to sink in.

"Everyone and everything?" Justine mouthed.

Slowly, deliberately, Rachel nodded her head.

"I loved François, you know that. I've shared a great deal with him. Until now, I've always trusted him. I didn't think that power would change him. But gradually, almost imperceptibly, I can see he's becoming corrupted by it. He's like Joseph Stalin in the last years of his life. He's starting to devour his closest allies because they are the only people who can possibly threaten his position."

Justine was staring out of the window.

"It's no easier for me than for you," Rachel added.

Justine turned towards her, her face white with fear.

"You don't really think he'd ..." she began, but her words trailed away.

Rachel laid an arm gently on her shoulder.

"After your father's dead it won't be long before he removes you. And after that, I think, his thoughts will start to turn to me."

Justine lay in the bed and stared blankly ahead of her. And then, just as Rachel had hoped she would, she started to talk.

"I knew he never loved me. But I've wanted him from the moment I first set eyes on him as a child. He used to come and talk to my father when I was a kid. Always he came alone, always I was reminded to say nothing of his visits, and always they would go into my father's study and hide themselves away for hours on end while they spoke. He was so full of mystery, this man I saw so often on television, this man who seemed to have a hidden life in the heart of my home.

"After a while I knew I wanted to possess this secret visitor, to displace my father as his confidant, to enter the closed room and feel his body and his mind close to mine. Part of me always hoped the feeling would die as I grew older, but as the years slipped by I slowly began to understand that they wouldn't. I looked at the boys in our local community and tried hard to be interested in them, knowing my dream to be absurd. I hoped I could shake myself free. But I couldn't. He had become too important to me."

Justine stopped short and looked at Rachel with pleading eyes.

"You understand it, don't you? That's why we get on all right together, isn't it? You understand how it is to be in love with François Dupont."

Rachel said nothing.

"Then one day, when I was about fifteen years old, I found out about what they were plotting together in the secret room. I told you about how I used to spy on his bedroom. Well, I used the same trick to spy on my father's study, drilling a little hole in the ceiling so I could overhear them speaking from the attic. It was then that I discovered everything they were planning together . . ."

As she spoke, Rachel was listening intently to every word, hoping to get the answers she wanted. It was tempting to ask Justine to explain things, to fill in the critical missing details about Dupont's conduct that were as yet unexplained. But the only reason Justine was talking at all was because she had accepted Rachel's earlier confident assertion that she knew everything already. A single question, a single casual request for further elaboration, and she risked giving rise to a dangerous suspicion in the young girl's mind that she had been tricked into divulging the truth.

"My knowledge gave me power," Justine continued, "but I didn't use it. I was patient, confident I would be able to win François for myself when I was ready. I had decided I wanted to be his wife, to share his destiny and raise his children. That was my dream and it was a dream I intended to make into reality."

Rachel smiled wryly.

"Some people would have called it blackmail, Justine. You simply blackmailed him, didn't you?"

Sadly, Justine nodded her head.

"It didn't work out as I had planned. François was always very friendly towards me. I thought . . . I hoped . . . that when I grew up he would come to me of his own free choice. That was why I waited. That was why I said nothing about the knowledge I possessed."

"And then I came along and spoiled your dream," Rachel added.

Justine flicked her hair away from her eyes.

"Yes," she said numbly, but without bitterness. "Shortly after I discovered the truth François stopped visiting my father completely. With the White Death at large, they must have decided it was too dangerous for them to meet any more. For years, I didn't see him once except on television."

"But you could have blackmailed him then, Justine. I don't understand why you waited so long."

"I didn't want to blackmail him, I wanted him to love me. Only later, when I realised that he was helplessly consumed with love for you, did I decide to settle for second best. I knew I was safe, I knew my father had a vice-like hold over him, and I decided to use the knowledge I possessed to force him to take me seriously."

"He certainly did that," Rachel said. "He even agreed to father a child for you against his wishes."

Justine looked away, a lost sad look haunting her face.

"I know he doesn't really want one, but he'll be pleased one day ..." Again, her words trailed slowly away, a rapidly fading relic of a crumbling dream.

"Are you sure about my father?" she asked.

"His role is soon over. The moment it is, your father will surely die."

Justine rose morosely from the bed and walked over to the window, staring down into the street far below almost as if she were watching for Dupont's return.

"I always thought he was loyal to my father," she whispered. "Without my father's work, none of this could have happened."

Rachel moved closer to her.

"I'm sorry, Justine," she murmured softly, "but I can only tell you what François has told me of his plans."

"But what can we do? From what you say, we're all in the same boat. Everyone who knows is in the same boat."

"But not very many people do know, do they, Justine? André Rostropov guessed at it but he's already dead. Dupont has pretty well convinced Bjorn Haverstamp that he had nothing to do with the White Death. It's only your father, you and I. We're the only ones left."

A look of despair was passing across Justine's face.

"Where is your father now?" Rachel asked, risking a question which had to be asked.

"In a small house not far from Vienna. On the plains just to the east of the Neusiedlersee. He's lived there under an assumed identity ever since this business began. Officially, he's a junior employee of the research institute investigating the White Death."

Rachel flinched. Once you knew it, it was blindingly obvious. But she had been right to be wary of asking Justine questions.

"I thought you knew all this?" Justine asked suspiciously.

"Of course I did," Rachel replied, thinking as fast as she could, "I just didn't know exactly where he was, that's all."

To Rachel's immense relief, the young girl seemed to accept her explanation at face value.

"I've never been there, of course, but he lives in a little village called Neustein. Quite near to the old Hungarian frontier."

"Neustein," Rachel repeated slowly. "And his name? What was your father's name in his new identity?"

This time, somewhat to her Rachel's surprise, Justine didn't flinch.

"Hallenbaum. Fritz Hallenbaum."

Rachel nodded silently, and without a further word started edging towards the small videophone terminal set into the dressing table. It was approximately three metres from the dressing table to the bedroom door, and the bedroom door had a key on the inside. The timing would have to be perfect.

"Why don't you put some clothes on, Justine," she suggested. "We can't do anything with you naked, can we?"

Justine nodded and moved towards the built-in wardrobe on the far side of the room, the side furthest away from both the dressing table and the door. Her head disappeared inside. As soon as she felt it was safe to do so, Rachel allowed her fingers to slide quietly behind the videophone terminal until she had clearly grasped the power cable. But no sooner had she done so than Justine's head reappeared and the young girl swung to face her.

"What shall I ..." she began, but her words faded away as she saw the grim expression on Rachel's face.

Without further delay Rachel tugged violently at the videophone cable, ripping it free of the terminal. Then, before Justine had had a chance to react, she sprang to the door, ripped the key from the keyhole and dived out of the room, locking the door securely from the outside and pulling out the key.

It took just a few seconds before Justine started to scream, but when she did scream it was a scream of intense terror, as she realised that she had betrayed both the men she loved. But Rachel didn't flinch. She watched the door calmly for a few moments, half expecting her to start shouting for help, but the scream seemed to subside into little more than a whimper.

"What on earth is going on?"

Rachel swung round at the sound of the voice.

"Johann!" she exclaimed, realising that the commotion had caused the little machine to come clattering along the corridor to investigate the crisis.

Justine must have heard the machine's words.

"Johann, unlock the door," she called through the door.

Rachel stared in horror at the tiny robot. In her haste she had completely forgotten that it could unlock all the doors in the flat using its own set of keys.

Already the machine was extracting its keys and extending its tiny arm towards the lock.

"Don't!" Rachel ordered.

Johann stopped.

"I'm sorry," it said politely, "but I wonder if you would be kind enough to clarify my instructions."

Contradictory advice from Justine and Rachel did nothing to help resolve the machine's uncertainty.

Several further requests for clarification, always carefully phrased using different words, produced the same clash of wills.

Eventually Johann stopped clattering. Instead, it stood stock still, something it hardly ever did when in human company. Rachel eyed it suspiciously, wondering what it was going to do next.

"I am receiving absurdly contradictory instructions," it stated in a rather disgruntled tone. "Before proceeding further, I will therefore seek clarification from the President."

It fell silent.

Rachel looked at the machine in panic. Perhaps, already, it was contacting Dupont's secretarial computer with an urgent request for him to be contacted. But then she had a good idea.

"Turn off your ears," she instructed, her voice carefully lowered to prevent Justine from hearing.

Obediently, the machine disconnected its hearing function, a standard privacy feature in advanced household computers. The feature was designed for people who didn't like the idea of a computer listening to their most intimate conversations, but now it had an altogether different application.

The machine appeared to have obeyed, because a decorative surface panel drew back to reveal a small screen and a keyboard.

Justine was still screaming at Johann to release her, but now to no avail.

"There is no need to disturb the President," Rachel typed swiftly onto the keyboard. "Your instructions have become clear. Leave the door locked and go to the living room to await further instructions."

"Thank you," the machine replied apologetically, its voice circuits still functional. "Logically inconsistent instructions are very difficult for me to obey."

The screaming through the door was becoming tedious.

"You can save your breath, Justine," she called through the closed door. "I've disconnected your videophone terminal and I've switched off Johann's listening circuits. There's no way you can get out and there's no way you can contact anyone."

Justine fell silent. But it was a strangely pathetic silence. Rachel checked herself.

"I don't mean you any harm, Justine," she called more gently. "Really I don't."

She turned and walked briskly through to the living room, carefully closing the interconnecting doors so as to prevent Justine overhearing her. Then she seated herself comfortably next to Johann's keyboard and began to type.

The first instruction she gave via the keyboard was to establish videophone contact with her father in Scotland, breathing a sigh of relief that the security service had insisted on dragging him at last into the twenty-first century after the kidnapping incident.

A few moments later his wizened yet still alert face appeared on the screen.

"Hallo, father," she said, trying to find the right words to explain herself.

"Hallo, darling," he said with a smile. "I have to admit it's nice to see you, even if it does have to be through one of these ridiculous boxes."

It was good to see his face. Good to see a face she knew she could trust, whatever happened to the rest of the world.

"Listen carefully, father," she said. "Something important has happened and I want your help. There's no one else I can trust?"

"No one?" her father repeated, his face growing serious.

"You can write this down if you like," she said, knowing that Dupont could easily recall the videophone conversation if he wished.

"I don't need to write anything down," her father insisted. "Just get on with it, girl."

Rachel nodded.

"Victor Stein is Fritz Hallenbaum from Neustein. He is a junior employee of the White Death Research Institute in Vienna. Got it?"

Her father repeated the words. Then he looked sharply at her. "And what do you wish me to do with these words I have remembered, Rachel?"

"Nothing, I hope. Nothing unless anything happens to me. But if something does happen, if you don't hear from me by tomorrow evening at eight o'clock, then make sure the information gets to the Director of the White Death Research Institute in Vienna and to the American Government. I don't care how you do it, but make sure you use several different routes as a precaution."

"I see." he said slowly. "And can I involve other people? People

I trust?"

He was thinking the same as she was thinking. If anything happened to his daughter, then something was likely to happen to him.

Rachel smiled grimly and nodded.

"Sadly, father, I think you must. But I'll leave it to you how you do so. But it's equally important the message only gets through if you don't hear anything from me."

Her father nodded.

"I'll do what you ask," he said, "and I won't ask for any explanation. But promise me one thing, Rachel."

She smiled.

"I know, father," she said, remembering the advice he had always given to her as a child. "If you can't be good, be careful."

He looked at her thoughtfully.

"Until tomorrow evening, then," he said at last.

She smiled at him again and nodded, swiftly pressing the button to break the connection.

"Would you like to make another call?" Johann asked.

"Yes," Rachel tapped in swiftly. "Connect me with Professor Bjorn Haverstamp at the White Death Research Institute."

Several minutes later Bjorn's face appeared on the screen, the triumphal expression she had seen the previous day if anything even more pronounced.

"Any more progress?" Rachel asked, trying to make her voice sound as casual as possible.

Bjorn opened his mouth as if to say something but then he seemed to check himself.

"A little," he said non-committally.

She nodded.

"Bjorn," she said, "do you have a scientist working for you by the name of Fritz Hallenbaum?"

Bjorn hesitated for a moment, but then he shook his head.

"I can't place him right now," he said at last. "But there are several thousand scientists here. I don't know all of them personally. If you hang on a minute I'll check."

"Thanks, Bjorn," she said. "But don't let him know you're doing so."

He nodded and disappeared from the screen. Rachel sat back anxiously and waited. She knew full well she was taking a risk by asking Bjorn, but she just had to cross-check that the information Justine had given her was true.

A few minutes later Bjorn's face returned to the screen.

197

"You're right," he said, "a man called Fritz Hallenbaum does work here. He's a junior employee in the computer analysis section."

"Is he at work today?" she asked.

"Hang on?" Bjorn said, and again he disappeared.

"No," he said when he returned. "I've checked with his department head. Actually she's a bit miffed with him because he's not turned up at work for the last two days. And he hasn't phoned in with any explanation."

"Thanks, Bjorn," she said with a reassuring smile.

She flicked a switch and the screen went blank. Then she rose thoughtfully from her chair and started pacing up and down the room. Below her, through the panoramic window, she could see the world proceeding with its affairs, blissfully impervious of the unfolding drama in the Presidential apartment on the top storey of the Commission building. She gazed into the distance, recalling the many experiences she had shared with Dupont while the world below had undergone such profound changes.

Her thoughts were interrupted by a gentle clatter as Johann prepared itself to make an announcement.

"There is a call for you, Rachel?"

She turned abruptly.

"From whom?" she asked.

Only when nothing happened did she remember she had disconnected the hearing circuits. She walked over to Johann and tapped in the question.

"Professor Bjorn Haverstamp."

Seconds later Bjorn was back on the screen.

"Rachel," he said. "I've got some news for you on Dr Fritz Hallenbaum. Bad news, I'm afraid."

She looked at him sharply.

"I got personnel to check out the reason for his unexplained absence. He's security cleared, after all, and he knows he's supposed to phone in if he can't get to work. Anyway, they tried ringing him at home but couldn't get through. So then they gave the local police station a ring and asked them to check his house."

He paused, his eyes probing hers.

"I'm afraid he's dead," he said at last.

She looked at him in horror. Victor Stein dead. There had to be a mistake.

"Apparently the local police were just about to phone us when we got through to them," Bjorn continued, answering her unspoken question. "Early this morning they had a call from one of his neigh-

198

bours complaining about an unpleasant smell emanating from an open window. When an officer went round to investigate he found Hallenbaum's body swinging from a light socket in the middle of the living room. According to the doctor's report, he's been dead for several days."

Rachel looked blankly at Bjorn.

"Can you tell me who he was?" he asked eventually, unable to restrain his curiosity any longer.

Rachel continued staring at him for a few moments, but she was scarcely listening to his words.

"No one important," she muttered, forcing herself to speak. "Thanks for letting me know."

She flicked the switch and watched Bjorn fade from the screen. Alone again, anger and fear jostled for supremacy in her mind as she tried to unravel the full implications of Victor Stein's violent demise. Slowly, mechanically, she raised her hand to Johann's keyboard, intent upon instructing it to summon Dupont immediately to her presence, but then she allowed her arm to drop back passively to her side.

François Dupont would return soon enough when night fell. And in the meantime, while she waited, she could prepare herself for what she knew was going to be the most difficult encounter of her entire life.

* * * * * *

She glanced at the clock hanging high on the wall above the map of Dupont's vast European empire. It was already midnight, long past the hour when she had been expecting his return. Her eye travelled slowly round the room, the room which was full of so many memories of her life together with Dupont. In the corner was the desk, the solid, majesterial desk where they had sat together and planned some of the reforms that had transformed European society in the years of his rule. Whatever else he may have done, those reforms were not the work of an evil or crazy man bent on personal aggrandisement whatever the cost. For, ironically, Europe was in so many ways a far better place than it had been before the coming of the White Death. The slow slide towards environmental degradation that had characterised the latter half of the twentieth century and the first few years of the twenty-first had been sharply reversed, as Dupont's total control of the levers of power had brought the great corporate institutions, both public and private, under watchful control. Yet Dupont had been careful never to allow the constructive nature of competition and individual initiative to be undermined in his new European order. Unlike his twentieth century predecessors as totalitarian leaders, he had firmly resisted excessive growth in the power of the state as a tool for implementing his personal plans. Rachel knew full well from the times when she had seen him wrestle with the intractable issues that had confronted him that it had been a difficult struggle, but yet a struggle he had won, to combine the strategic central direction of power with a flowering of individual initiative at all levels of European life.

The proof of his undoubted success lay in his popularity with the people over whom he ruled. For while cynics might have argued that it was his tight control over the media which was responsible for his popularity, Rachel knew enough history to be sure that a powerful despot could only ever force people into a kind of numbed and silent acquiescence, never create the genuine popular enthusiasm which was obvious whenever François Dupont appeared in a public forum. It was a popularity that she had been sure would withstand the test of the referendum she had advocated, the referendum for which Dupont was now actively preparing, the referendum which she now knew would never take place.

Her eye swung onwards, past the desk and towards the giant plate glass window where they had first made love. Now, at last, the meaning of his words to her that night were beginning to make sense, words that expressed his inexplicable hidden fear that she would reject him if she knew the truth. Over and over again she had sensed that fear, the fear that told of a man deeply afraid to face life – or was it perhaps death – alone and unloved.

A soft humming from the direction of the lift shaft brought her reverie to an abrupt end. She rose to her feet and turned to face the door of the lift, afraid lest her courage should fail her in the encounter to come if she remained seated. For several moments nothing happened, but then the door slid slowly open.

The moment he saw her expression his face became ashen.

"You know everything?" he said slowly, stepping from the lift and meeting her gaze.

Slowly, she nodded her head, not really caring that he already knew.

"And for how long have you known?"

"For certain, since I spoke to Bjorn Haverstamp at the clinic. It was Haverstamp who found out about you and Stein."

"Stein is dead," Dupont murmured, and somewhat to her surprise she could see a look of deep loss pass across his face.

"I know," she said quietly. But the look of loss angered her. "I thought you had killed him just as you killed the others. What's one more when five billion have already died."

Dupont said nothing. Instead, he walked slowly across the room, past where she was standing, and gazed out through the window at the moonlit night beyond.

"I'm sorry you found out like this," he said. "I always meant to tell you myself. But I was always so afraid . . ."

"Of what?"

"Afraid of what I realise now I should not have been afraid of."

He turned to face her, and she could see the gratitude in his eyes.

"Afraid that you would reject me," he continued, "that you would cease to love me when you knew the truth."

His remark caused her to flinch. Of course she should have stopped loving him. There were five billion reasons why she should have stopped loving him.

For a long time she said nothing. And then, her voice scarcely more than a whisper, she asked the question she had waited for so long to ask.

"Why? Why have you done all this?"

He fixed her with his eyes.

"A cull. A tightly controlled cull that is now very near to completion."

She looked at him incredulously.

"A cull? But a cull is what you do to animals, not to people."

He raised his eyebrows.

"A cull is what you do to a species that is heading for extinction because it can neither control the rate at which it is reproducing itself nor the rate at which it is destroying the natural habitat upon which it depends. Usually though not always these two phenomenon are closely linked. A cull then becomes necessary to prevent the species destroying itself completely."

"And you believed this was happening to Mankind?"

"Not just I. Many people far wiser than I had warned of the dangers to the planet's support systems from our burgeoning global population. Once it was thought to be merely a problem of deepening poverty, but more recently the threat to our environment has become more prominent. So as you see, the problem has been staring us in the face for many decades, it is just that no one had the courage to deal with it."

"But . . ."

Dupont smiled wryly.

"I know your objections," he said, "and you know me well enough after all these months to know that I have agonised long and hard about every single one of them."

Despite herself, Rachel could feel her legs beginning to give way beneath her. She really should have known better than to expect Dupont to appear repentant for his actions once confronted by them: it was always in precisely these situations that he appeared at his most majesterial. She slumped back onto the sofa behind her.

"Tell me the complete truth, François, not the garbled edited versions you have told me in the past to appease my frail human sensibilities."

Dupont sat down on the sofa beside her. And as he did so he looked tired, as though he was just coming to the end of a long and tiring day's work.

"As you surmised, I first met Victor Stein at the orphanage. We were both about thirteen years old, and as soon as we met we knew that destiny would draw us together, although in a more immediate sense it was our mutual love of swimming which cemented our relationship. Victor's background was very similar to my own, orphaned at the age of six through the suicide of his parents. It brought us together, two lonely frightened children in an institution that tried but failed to provide the love we needed. At the time, of course, we had no thoughts of the plan we later set in train. That only came much, much later.

"After we left the orphanage Victor went to university to study the biological sciences. He was fascinated by the developing art of genetic science, by the possibility that our species might be able to develop the capacity to manipulate life itself. It was a dream of which he never lost sight, although its manifestation took a direction in which he could not in his wildest imaginings have envisaged."

"As soon as he had finished studying he was approached by the military and began his career in one of their biological warfare research institutes. It was around that time that we started to become cautious about allowing our friendship to be public knowledge. To some extent it wasn't hard, since even as children we had carefully hidden the warmth we felt for each other from our fellows for fear of becoming objects of derision. But now that Victor had a sensitive job in the military and I was beginning to attract some attention as an aggressive young journalist under a rising star, we felt it might be prudent to play down the links.

"But Victor was unhappy working for the military. They had the funding for the kind of research in which he was interested, but he always felt their underlying purpose was one of senseless violence. The research was aimed at human beings as enemies, rather than at human beings as cherished treasures to be improved upon and enhanced. But he carried on working for them, hoping that one day his work would be put to more constructive use.

"Throughout this period, I was becoming increasingly depressed about the failings of my fellow men, perhaps because I was spending too much time studying the failings of the individuals they freely selected as their leaders. At the same time, I was becoming interested in the broader patterns of human development, watching with growing horror as Mankind seemed to be heading into a kind of giant Malthusian trap. World population was on the rampage; in 1975 the four billion mark was breached, by 1987 five billion, by 1997 six billion. Already by the early 1990s, United Nations estimates for world population in 2025 ranged between eight and a half and nine and a half billion people. Such growth rates were untenable in view of the limited nature of global resources. Mankind, exuburant yet over-confident Mankind, was heading rapidly for a fall.

"But the research that began to emerge during the last decade of the twentieth century suggested far worse consequences than a continuation and exacerbation of the grinding poverty to which most of the world's population had always been subject. It suggested the growing possibility of total global catastrophe, a collapse from which there would be no recovery. Forecast after forecast showed the planet's life support systems breaking down under the sheer strain of its spiralling population . . ."

He hesitated and glanced in Rachel's direction, as if to check whether it was necessary to provide more detail in order to substantiate the thrust of his argument. She tried desperately to think of a challenge, to argue against facts of which she and other thinking people had been well aware for many decades. But she could find no flaw with his diagnosis of the world's problems at the beginning of the twenty-first century. Everybody knew that global population had been growing at an unsustainable rate for decades, everybody knew that the environmental demands of so many people clamouring for a decent living standard on our tiny underresourced planet were likely to lead to disaster. But it wasn't the diagnosis for the world's problems she was unsure about, it was the treatment adopted by Dupont to deal with them.

"I know what you're thinking," he continued. "I could have done nothing, I could have left well alone and allowed 'nature' to take its course, whatever that may have been. Malthus never required conscious human intervention to control the population. War, famine and natural disease were enough."

Speechless, she nodded.

"Don't you see, Rachel, it's like I said at the beginning. It's why a conscious cull was needed. If you don't cull, you take an acute risk of losing the lot, of standing by and watching the whole species eradicate itself. I am convinced that is the road down which we were travelling. And travelling at an increasingly alarming speed.

"It was clear to me that the world had become segmented from an economic point of view. On the one hand we had the rich areas – Europe, America, the Pacific fringe. High and apparently sustainable incomes had brought with them stable populations and technologies that allowed the small numbers of people lucky enough to live in these areas to anticipate steadily rising living standards. But even within these relatively insignificant areas, our soaring material demands were imposing unsustainable environmental costs. Within the rich areas, however, it was still possible to turn the other way, to live life for today and ignore the planet our children and grandchildren would one day inherit.

"But we in the world's rich zones were living under a false sense of security. For the dice were slowly being stacked against us by the burgeoning mass of the world's poor. It was they, not us, who were likely to have the last laugh. For they were not going to tolerate for ever the widening disparities in living standards between rich and poor. Not only would the pressure of economic migration become increasingly difficult to resist, but eventually the increasingly mobile technologies of mass destruction, developed by the rich for their own internal struggles, would have fallen into the hands of the poor. Eventually, even the richest of the world's inhabitants would have been forced to wake up to the dire state into which the planet had fallen."

Dupont stopped and smiled at her.

"You will have some questions, I expect?" he murmured. "I am painting a very broad picture which does not do justice to the complexity of the issues involved."

"I can perhaps accept that what you say was a likely outcome, François. Many other people would accept it too, I suspect. But how could you be certain that Mankind would self-destruct without your intervention? Certain enough to justify the terrible carnage for which you are plainly responsible."

Slowly, thoughtfully, Dupont nodded his head in agreement with her words.

"Imagine you are a doctor," he said. "You have a patient before you who is seriously ill. You are ninety-five percent sure that if you do not remove the patient's legs immediately he will die. What will you do?"

Rachel met his gaze head on.

"I might ask for a second opinion."

He smiled.

"I did. I asked for far more than that. I spend nearly ten years asking questions. Agreement about the catastrophic effects of population growth amongst scientists was almost universal."

Angrily, Rachel rose to her feet. The conversation was too calm to be civilised; they were talking about genocide.

"You know damn well that's not what I mean."

Dupont eyed her with annoyance.

"Do sit down, Rachel," he said drily. "My clinical manner disturbs you, but you will see soon enough before this night is through that it is merely a thin facade allowing logic to clear the dangerous clouds of emotion that constitute both our species' greatest strength and its greatest weakness."

The sheer savagery with which he uttered these last words caught her completely off guard. She sat down again.

"But you were right when you said that I failed to answer your question fully," Dupont continued, his voice once more calm and controlled. "You meant that I should have taken a second opinion before administering so potent and unpleasant a cure for the world's ills as the White Death."

Dupont lay his head back on the sofa and watched her intently.

"O.K.," he said softly, "suppose I had asked for someone to share the responsibility with me. Suppose for example that I had asked you."

She looked at him with horror.

"I have asked for your advice on other matters. Why not on this? So answer me, Rachel, what would you have said?"

She said nothing for the simple reason that she did not know what to say. A look of triumph spread across Dupont's face as he watched her struggle.

"There you are, you hesitate. You do not instantly denounce the logic in what I have done, you countenance it, you try to weigh up the pros and cons. Already it has become acceptable to you."

"I didn't say that."

Dupont laughed.

"It doesn't matter, Rachel, the issue is academic. You know perfectly well that Victor and I couldn't have called an international conference to discuss what we were proposing. We would both have been locked up in a top security lunatic asylum. We had the means to administer the cure, we were prepared to take the responsibility upon our shoulders and our shoulders alone. You could say that we had the courage to act where others only talked."

The triumphal expression with which he said these words passed rapidly from his face.

"But you asked me for the whole story, Rachel, and now you should listen to it. As you will see in due course, it is important that you listen to it."

Again as before, the finality of his words surprised her. But she asked for no explanation.

"It was Victor who gave me the inspiration for the plan. He told me of an infective agent he had been painstakingly developing for the military. It was a reversible infective agent of complex origins, designed to be released into enemy populations to cause panic, whilst the vaccine would be held in reserve to use as a bargaining counter, or, if necessary, to protect the users from possible infection. In short, a highly effective piece of weaponry.

"Victor had developed this agent largely on his own and had told nobody the full extent to which he had succeeded. He had always trusted my judgement, and now he asked me for my advice. It was then that our joint vision emerged to use the agent, not in anger as part of a war between nations, but rather as part of a larger struggle to save Mankind from itself."

"So it was you who helped Stein to go underground?"

Dupont nodded.

"It wasn't hard. Then as now I was well-connected. Very well-connected. Victor had done the essential scientific work already, the important thing was to prevent knowledge of the infective agent or the vaccine from leaking out."

A thought suddenly occurred to Rachel.

"But Victor Stein is dead, François. What will happen if Bjorn fails to discover it independently from his own research? How will you stop your cull?"

Dupont laughed cynically.

"Your friend Haverstamp thinks he is a very clever young man, but he is not quite as clever as he thinks. With my help Victor had assumed the identity of a junior scientist in the computer department of the Institute, close enough to the centre to keep me informed of what was going on on a technical level but not close enough to draw excessive attention to himself. So don't you see, Rachel my love, it was Victor himself, at my instigation, who set in train the scientific events that will inevitably lead Haverstamp to think he has discovered the vaccine. That was all essential to our plan."

Rachel looked at him wide-eyed.

"And with his work complete Victor Stein . . ."

Dupont nodded sadly, and again she glimpsed the sense of loss.

". . . took his own life," he finished. "Victor was a great man, a quiet man perhaps, but a great thinker and a great humanitarian nevertheless."

Dupont must have felt the silence that ensued oppressive, because he rose slowly to his feet and stood once again by the window, gazing out sadly into the night.

"So now I am alone," he said softly. "With Victor gone, I carry the guilt for my actions alone."

Rachel rose silently to her feet and came to stand by his side.

"Tell me the truth about Tom and my children?" she asked, her voice no more than a whisper.

He did not turn to face her.

"They are safe," he said. "They were treated with the vaccine before they went to the Care Centre. They were never in any danger from the White Death."

She watched his lonely face and suddenly realised the full extent to which she was important to him. She had always supposed he would have carried on without her, that their love was independent of the man himself, but now she saw with complete clarity that he had simply had no choice but to claim her for himself in order to help him through the critical years of his life. Suddenly, Dupont swung to face her, and she could see that the emotion he felt was becoming increasingly hard to restrain.

"To love with logic and not with sentiment is a hard thing indeed, my dearest Rachel," he whispered, taking her shoulders in his hands. "You are the only person I have met besides myself who is capable of such a thing. I sensed it always in you, and now I know it for certain. I needed your love, I did not believe I could continue without your love, and that is why I took you away from your family. And you would be wrong if you did not believe that my actions in so doing have added very considerably to the guilt of which I have just spoken."

Deep within herself, Rachel sensed that he was already speaking of the past. Soon, very soon perhaps, she would be reunited with her family.

"But why do you speak of guilt, François?" she asked gently. "If you believed your actions to be right, why do you now feel such guilt?''

He smiled.

"Do you really think I am so heartless I cannot conceive of the human suffering that has happened because my mother failed to smash me against the rocks beside her so many years ago? Do you really think that my logic allows me to become so crassly insensitive to the suffering I have caused to happen. It is one thing to believe I was right to do what I did, quite another to do so with no feeling of guilt. But it is a guilt I shall soon enough assuage."

"And when will Bjorn Haverstamp find the vaccine?" she asked.

Dupont shrugged.

"Soon, I hope. Not yet, but soon. The carnage has gone on long enough. It is high time it was stopped so that the reconstruction phase can begin."

"But the moment he does, you're finished. He'll run straight to the Americans when he has it in his hands."

As if by a huge effort of willpower, Dupont forced himself back from his sombre reverie. Once again, perhaps for the last time, he was the masterful leader of all he surveyed.

"You must listen to what I have to say now very carefully, Rachel, and then you too must play your part in my plans.

His expression frightened her but she said nothing.

"Who knows about my role as the originator of the White Death?"

Rachel thought for a moment.

"Bjorn Haverstamp, Justine Medoc and me. Other people may have vague suspicions, but no one else knows the full story. We have been very careful to conceal the truth."

"Good," Dupont continued, "it is then exactly as I thought. It is not too late to spare the world the truth."

Rachel could feel the fear rising within her.

"Stop talking in riddles, François. When Haverstamp has the truth he will tell the world. You can't stop him. You have to run, because for all your quiet reason you'll be lynched when people find out what you've done."

He looked at her thoughtfully.

"I will not be lynched," he said, "because I will already be dead. I thought you had understood that."

He had spoken in his usual calm manner, almost as if he were announcing his plans for the following year's tax rates rather than his imminent suicide.

"But ..." she began.

He brushed her sentiment aside.

"Do you really think that after what I have done I could settle down into a quiet retirement, even if such a thing were possible?"

She should have argued back, she should have tried to persuade him to run and hide with her, to make a fresh start behind a new identity in some far off place on the far side of the world. He was a clever man and she was a clever woman. Despite everything, they would have stood a chance.

"No," she said, allowing her eyes to meet his gaze, "I don't suppose you could."

Dupont enfolded her gently in his arms.

"There was a time when I dreamt it might have been possible," he murmured. "Despite everything, I have always dreamt of building a normal life, a life as other people lead, a life in which I could have lived out my days with you in tranquility. But it was always an illusion. A man such as I cannot lead such a life. And anyway, now my lifeless corpse will be the minimum price Haverstamp will accept in exchange for his silence. Of that, at least, I am sure."

Rachel looked at him with a confused expression.

"His silence?"

Dupont nodded.

"With a vaccine on stream and Victor and I dead, there will be no need to tell the world the truth. It will only hamper the work of reconstruction by many years. A disease is such an anonymous enemy, an enemy from which every part of the globe has suffered. But imagine what the effect will be if the world should learn that the disease was deliberately released by Europeans, Europeans who sat out the whole tragic episode with an absolute minimum of inconvenience and destruction. It will enhance and electrify the hatred between North and South precisely at a time when there should be a coming together."

Rachel could feel his arms tightly embracing her as he spoke, his words holding a vision for a future he would never see.

"The world will soon recover from the White Death. Global population is now reduced to less than one half of its previous level, but the other economic resources on which we depend – both natural resources and capital infrastructure – are still by and large intact. With the passing of the White Death, nutrition levels will rapidly rise, living standards will soar across the globe, and as they do people will freely choose to reduce the numbers of children they bear, just as they did in the richer parts of the world in the twentieth century. Soon the world will be a place of plenty, not just for those lucky enough to live in the rich countries but for everyone . . ."

His words trailed away and she could feel him shudder.

"Will he remain silent?" Dupont asked, his voice showing nothing of his emotions.

"I think Bjorn hates you, François. He does not tell me so but I think he does."

"When I am dead, call him immediately. He will need to see my body as proof that I am gone. Only then must you try to persuade him, not for my sake, but for the sake of the world."

"And what of Justine?" Rachel asked quietly. "What will you do with her? This morning, after you left, I tricked her into telling me everything she knew and then locked her in her bedroom. She doesn't even know her father is dead."

Dupont flicked a glance in the direction of the young girl's room. "Poor, dear Justine," he murmured. "She could have been the love of so many sensible young men. But no, she had to choose me."

"And blackmailed you?"

Dupont laughed.

"She thought so, I think. But I knew she would never have dared to use the knowledge she possessed. It would only have served to bring about her father's death. My reasons were different, for Justine never realised the strength of my feelings towards her father, my gratitude for the companionship he had brought to me in my youth. I freely chose to humour his daughter, Rachel, even to the extent of allowing her to bear me a child."

"Something she will never now do," Rachel added.

Dupont smiled.

"Maybe that is for the best. Like my mother before me, I am not sure how many Duponts the world can tolerate. Perhaps it is for the best that I leave no heir."

"Will you speak to her, François?"

Slowly he released her from his embrace.

"If you wish," he said grimly, and strode off down the corridor towards her room.

It was a long time before he returned, but when he did she could hear from far away the sound of Justine's plaintive sobs in the room he had left behind. Dupont glanced at Rachel and strode over to the window. For many minutes he said nothing, gazing out listlessly into the pale night sky. Far away in the east, the dawn was drawing close.

"I think it is time," he said at last.

Rachel looked at the man standing before her and felt the almost superhuman strength within him. It was as if she was standing in the presence of a new Christ, a man sent to rescue the world from the folly of its own sins. By rights she should have felt a terror at the approaching death of the man she loved so deeply, but instead she felt only a sense of awe. She wondered if Mary had felt the same strangely calm emotion before the cross on that dark and distant Friday nearly two thousand years before.

"How?" she whispered.

He walked into the kitchen and returned with a glass of water. Then he put his arm deep into his pocket and produced a small opaque sealed packet.

"When I was a little boy growing up in the Alps," he said slowly, "we often went into the woods with one of the housemasters to collect mushrooms. There were many different kinds you could eat, and I became quite an expert on them. But these I have never yet tasted."

He produced the tiny fungi from the packet and held them thoughtfully in his hand.

Rachel stared in horror at the innocent-looking plants, a slow fear creeping through her soul that she would not be equal to the task before her, a fear that she would start screaming at him to stop, to hold back from the quick fateful movement that would bring his life to an end.

"Will it be quick?" she asked.

He smiled.

"I believe there are others which are quicker. But you must know that this is a choice I have made of my own free will. It is my own private way of atoning for the indescribable suffering I have caused. But it would still be best, perhaps, if we were to say our farewells now."

She held her hand out towards his arm and touched it. Tears of emotion, so long held back, were forming in her eyes.

"I will always love you, François," she murmured softly. "I will love you for what you are, and I will love you for what you have done."

As she spoke she made no move to leave, and Dupont could see that she was determined to stay with him until the end.

He lifted the glass in his hand.

"Farewell, my love," he whispered softly, kissing her gently first on one eye, then on the other.

And then, with a sudden quick movement, he pushed the tiny but deadly plants into his mouth, washing them down to the depths of his stomach with the water in the glass.

KNOYDART, SCOTLAND, OCTOBER 2046

The old woman sat alone on the first floor balcony of her solitary home and gazed across the loch towards the heather-clad mountains on the far shore. When she had been a young girl she had often climbed those mountains, springing lightly from one tuft of heather to another, but the fact that she was now only able to gaze upon their slopes did not disturb her greatly. For she had reached the time in her life when reflection was easier than action, and a whole lifetime of memories provided her with a more than ample supply of material on which to ponder.

She looked down the slope of the low hill on which her house was built towards the cottage where she had spent her childhood years. It was a ramshackle affair today just as it had always been, a traditional whitewashed crofter's cottage surrounded by the usual chaotic collection of impromptu outbuildings. Sometimes, when she was in the mood for reminiscing, she would slowly make her way down the hill from the computer-controlled comfort of her present palatial home to the cottage. Then she would sit a while in the old living room, listening to the insistent bleating of the sheep on the surrounding moors. It was a kind of comfort, a way of spanning the yawning gap between the tranquility of her early years and the tranquility of old age.

Her eye rose once again towards the highest of the mountains opposite. It was particularly clear in the crisp autumnal light, its outline stark against the soft blue tone of the sky. And as she looked at it she realised that her own long life had been rather like a day on a mountain: a long slow ascent followed by an equally long slow descent as evening fell. Neither the ascent nor the descent had been particularly painful experiences, for each stage of the adventure had been rich and fulfilling, but there could be no mistake about the pinnacle of her life, the moment when she had finally reached the summit and gazed upon the view of the promised land beyond.

It had been the night of François Dupont's death nearly forty years before. She closed her eyes and remembered the terror and the ecstasy of that night, as Dupont had writhed and squirmed in agony while the poison gradually drove the life from his body. It had been several hours before he had finally found peace, and throughout that time she had held him in her arms, trying to comfort him as best she could. But with every passing minute of that terrible ordeal, she had grown in wisdom several years, and when he had finally fallen still she had realised she would never be the same woman again.

From far away in the east, beyond the end of the loch, a small white car appeared around a corner, gradually growing larger as it approached. She reached for her stick and rose to her feet, wondering now as she had wondered many times before how he would react to his old adversary's final surprise. Slowly and somewhat painfully, she made her way into the living room and started giving the household computers their final instructions to make ready for her guest.

Several minutes later there was a quiet knock on the living room door and a tall upright man entered, a shock of white hair swept casually to one side of his face. To her he still looked young, despite the fact that he was nearly seventy years old.

"Bjorn," she said softly, "it's good to see you again."

The Scandinavian crossed the room and kissed her gently on the cheek.

"It's been too long," he said, and she could see from his face the emotion he felt at their reunion.

"Four years, I think," she said. "Not since the last time I was in Paris for the memorial lecture you gave at the university."

Bjorn sat down opposite her, but for several minutes they did not feel the need to speak. They were content to sit and remember their shared past. But then their reverie was interrupted by a gentle clatter from the corner of the room.

Bjorn looked in the direction of the noise.

"I don't believe it!" he said. "It's ancient!"

Rachel turned and looked at the cause of Bjorn's remark with a smile.

"Don't you remember Johann? I could never bear to part with him. Of course, while Tom was alive he had to sit in the garage, but now I'm alone again I decided to have him repaired. It cost me a small fortune finding the spare parts." She turned to the machine. "Johann," she ordered, "go and get us a cup of tea!"

Johann clattered off and Bjorn's face turned serious.

"It's been nearly six months since Tom died, hasn't it? How are you bearing up?"

Rachel frowned. In truth she was still missing Tom terribly.

"I get by. It was a good marriage, especially since . . ."

Her words trailed away. At the time, before the brief interlude when she had lived with Dupont, she had supposed her marriage with Tom to have been good. But afterwards, when he had returned to her and helped her heal the wounds of that traumatic time in her life, she had found a new tranquility in their relationship, a tranquility that had lasted forty more years until his recent death. But during those forty years he had never once asked her about the time she had lived with Dupont, as if he had known that it was a part of her life he would never really understand.

She remembered her companion and the reason she had asked him to visit.

"Do you think about Dupont much?" she asked abruptly.

Bjorn thought for a while.

"Every day I think about him. I imagine we are both still living under his shadow. He had a quality that set him apart from other men."

She looked at him sharply, surprised by the generous tone of his voice.

"A change of perspective?"

Bjorn thought for a minute and smiled.

"I'm not blind, Rachel. Forty years of history speak for themselves. It would be churlish of me not to accept that the universal prosperity in the world today is in large measure due to the actions of François Dupont."

He fell silent for a moment.

"I'm still not certain he had a right to do it, though," he added softly.

Rachel smiled.

"You always were a thinker, Bjorn. Never a man of action. François would have said you were a ditherer. In some ways it's why I've always had a soft spot for you."

"And Dupont?"

"Ah," she said quietly. "François was something different. Not better, you understand. Not in the human sense, anyway. But different."

Somewhat to Rachel's relief, Johann interrupted their conversation by arriving with the tea things, carefully handing each of them a small china cup.

"There's something I've always wanted to ask you, Rachel," Bjorn asked.

She stirred her tea and looked at him.

"Did François suggest that you put yourself forward for public office after his death?"

Rachel took a sip of her tea and laid the cup gently on a small inlaid table beside her chair.

"No," she replied. "I think he imagined I would return to Tom and continue my life much as before. Perhaps he had supposed it was what I wanted. It was only later, only after I realised the full extent of his popularity, that I decided to stand for election in the first democratic elections after his death."

"A debt?" Bjorn interjected.

"Not a debt, Bjorn. More of a duty. François was unable to finish the work he had started, to organise and inspire the reconstruction phase of his grand design. Sometimes I think he hoped he would be able to, but at the end he came to accept it could not be. But I understood the blueprint of his plan, I understood the central role he intended for Europeans in helping the world to recover from the White Death. I wanted to make sure that his vision survived him, that his terrible experiment had not been in vain."

"In that, at least, you succeeded," Bjorn said.

Rachel accepted the compliment without a word. For twenty long years, through more election campaigns that she cared to remember, she had held on to the Presidency of Greater Europe, determined to persuade European taxpayers it was in their best long term interests to help the rest of the world catch up. At the time it hadn't been easy. But then getting voters to take a long view had never been easy.

She shrugged.

"Enough of me, Bjorn. Let us talk a while of you. Are you not old enough to hang up your white coat and retire?"

He laughed.

"The trouble with being a ditherer is that you can never make up your mind. Every time I try to retire I feel the pull of the laboratory, urging me to go back and discover something really original in my life. And then I go back."

She looked at him sadly.

"You're too hard on yourself, Bjorn. Much too hard."

He smiled.

"You were a President. I was just a fraud. Maybe my role was even harder than yours."

If François Dupont had gone down in history as a European hero, Bjorn Haverstamp had been forced against his wishes to become a global hero. For the corollary of his reluctant decision to agree to Rachel's request and suppress the truth about François Dupont had been having to accept the credit for eradicating the White Death.

She nodded slowly.

"I suppose you could say it's why I asked you to come and see me."

He looked at her sharply.

"Next month is the fortieth anniversary of his death?" she continued. "I am going to speak at the memorial ceremony in New Vienna. I wished to speak to you privately prior to that ceremony."

Bjorn said nothing. She looked at him carefully, trying to judge if he had guessed what she was about to say. But his eyes gave nothing away.

"There is something I have never revealed to you about the night François died. For nearly an hour after he took the poison mushrooms he remained perfectly lucid. During that time, he gave me some final instructions."

She reached out for her stick and rose ponderously to her feet. Even forty years later it was hard to remember that night and remain composed. But she made an effort, and walked slowly over to the bureau in the corner of the room, collecting a small envelope and returning to her chair.

"François knew that public knowledge of his actions would make the reconstruction phase more difficult. The pain was too close, the danger of a violent backlash against all Europeans too great. I told you that at the time and you were generous enough to play your difficult part in keeping his secret. But he was equally adamant that the deceit should only be temporary, that historians should one day have a chance to judge François Dupont on his true merits, and not on the tangled web of lies he had constructed about himself. In his dying moments, he charged me with being the custodian of the truth."

Bjorn was watching her silently.

"For forty years?"

She nodded her head.

"He's lucky I made it, isn't he, although I did write it all down just in case. But if my frail form will permit me to travel as far as New Vienna next month, I am planning to reveal the truth."

Suddenly, unexpectedly, Bjorn started to laugh, tears of emotion flooding down his face. For several minutes he could not contain himself, until eventually he started coughing uncontrollably.

"Johann!" Rachel called. "A glass of water, quick!"

Johann hurriedly fetched a glass of water. Bjorn sipped the drink gratefully and gradually managed to recover his self-control.

"The old bastard. The manipulating old bastard," he said as soon as he could speak.

"I thought you'd like it," Rachel added. "For forty years I've been waiting to see your face when I told you. I'm just glad I've lived to see the day."

"And he told you not to tell me?"

She nodded.

"Made me promise. You see, he didn't think too much of you either," she said with a smile. "He thought you'd rather like the idea of going down in history as the greatest scientific hero of all time. So he made me promise I wouldn't tell you until the forty years was up."

Bjorn's face grew serious.

"How do you think they'll react. The Dupont memorial ceremony is the biggest gathering of world leaders for years."

Rachel smiled.

"François always said that the hardest audience to render speechless was an audience of politicians. But I expect my revelations will do the trick."

"Of that you can be sure. But seriously, what do you think they'll do?"

Rachel stopped smiling.

"I don't know, Bjorn. Really I don't. Maybe they'll lynch us, if lynching a pair of geriatrics like us gives them much fun. But somehow I don't think they will. My judgement is that François made the right choice when he told me to wait forty years. It's all a very long time ago now, and heaven knows, the world's surging prosperity is living evidence he just might have made the right choice."

A thought occurred to Bjorn.

"And Justine? Have you warned Justine?"

Rachel nodded.

"Two days ago I spoke to her. I hadn't seen her for nearly twenty years."

Bjorn looked at her with curiosity.

"Do you really think she miscarried after she went away, like she claimed at the time?" he said.

"I don't know," Rachel murmured. "I don't know and I didn't ask. But I do know she was terrified of the truth coming out about François and the effect it would have on any child of his. I sometimes think she might have given the baby away to an adoption agency in order to give him a more ordinary start in life. But I imagine we'll never know, will we?"

For several moments they sat together in silence, but then Rachel remembered the envelope sitting on her lap. She pulled out the single sheet of paper that lay within.

"At the memorial ceremony, when I have finished my description of the events of that time, I am proposing to read out this document. It was written by François after he had eaten the mushrooms, so I suppose you can say it is his last testament. But before I read it to the world, I would like to read it to my oldest living friend."

She knew within her heart that she might fail herself on the day, that her foolish human sentiment might choke her as she read out the last words of the man whose memory she still loved with an almost unbearable intensity. But now, before the man who had once been his sworn enemy, she would at least have a chance to practise.

"I am writing these words," she began, "to a world I do not know, a world I will never know because it exists forty years after my death. But your world has been shaped by my world, my world has been shaped by my deeds, and I know in my heart that you have a right to stand in judgement over me.

"Some of you, the older amongst you, will remember the terrible time of the White Death from personal experience in your youth. Others, the majority, will only know of it from history books. But I hope, I pray, that you will now know a better world than the world I inherited in my youth. My world was a world heading for disaster, in which the divide between rich and poor was becoming wider by the hour as the resources of the planet were stretched ever more thinly across a population thirsting for plenty. Mine was a world of greed premised on poverty, of hope premised on despair, of wishful thinking premised on fear. It was a world heading for destruction.

"As you now know, I was brazen enough to change my world, to alter the course of events on our planet through a simple yet cataclysmic paroxysm of hurt and suffering. You should know that I took the final decision to launch my plan with a heavy heart, and only when I had convinced myself that it was the best of an unpalatable range of evils facing my species and my planet.

"I do not say this to exonerate myself, for in the normal range of human behaviour my actions can only be described as thoroughly evil. Such destruction, with all the human pain it inevitably brings in its wake, must never be counted a good thing. I am prepared to accept responsibility for that suffering, and you will know from the record that I have administered to myself the rightful personal punishment for the crimes of which I am guilty.

"But I do not wish the truth to be buried alongside my mortal remains for all time. A new and better world, a world with more solid foundations than my world, cannot be built upon a historical lie, and you must at least accept that I am a part of your history. So you must take my truth and do with it as you will, and then, in the fullness of time, form your own views about François Dupont.

"I feel the pains coming upon me. It is time I bid you farewell and prepare myself for the end. All I ask is that you think long and hard, my friends, before you decide whether my dream of your future was really a dream too far."